THE

OF SOPHIE

SCHULTZ

SNP I

By

R. P. TORKINGTON

ISBN-13: 978-1548392789
ISBN-10: 1548392782

CONTENTS

ACKNOWLEDGMENTS

Elena Gamboa.

PREFACE

Two hundred light years away from our Earth, the concerns of two planets regarding the future of our world were being debated by humanoids with little concern about the danger to themselves. They had visited Earth many times over several centuries and watched the growth, mistakes, and the promise that humans had shown. Without their intervention, Earth would have surely perished long ago. Now the protectors of Earth, and even Earth itself were in peril from a race called the Breeche and their less than willing associates the Kai.

Sworn enemies of each other, they had made an uneasy peace in the mutual interests of economics. Their constant warring with each other had kept the Breeche preoccupied and controlled. Invasion was now all that their neighbouring planets could expect as they became aware that a peace treaty had been signed. As expected, the Breeche were now on the move and were poised ready to strike at the heart of the next inhabited world that lay before them.

Touscal and Mylin were two very different planets. Touscal was cool with little difference between the seasons. The Touscal were perfectly adapted to their environment and seldom left the planet. On the other hand, Mylin was not unlike Earth, with continents and a variety of races. Its people had lived amongst humans for many years with minor cosmetic prosthetics and were responsible for several jumps in Earth's technology during the twentieth century. Soon to be on the Breeche agenda would be the Mylin. Their home world, being rich in minerals, precious metals, and technology made them an irresistible target for the Breeche to attack. The Mylin were aware of this due to a network of paid Kai spies. Peace between the Touscal and the Mylin had existed since the Mylin made their first interplanetary flights six hundred years earlier in crude vessels.

Both had shared technology with each other with a mutual trust and had evolved together at the same pace in peace and perfect harmony. Mylin had made Touscal aware that they may well be next in line on the Breeche list. Their greatest fear was that Earth would fall and that human destiny would be halted. On Touscal it was felt that, above all humanity must continue as it was written in stone on their home world, although *who* had written it was a mystery. Some of the Mylin had their suspicions that a secret organisation within the Touscal called the Omicron order had written it themselves for reasons yet unknown. These Mylin mistrusted the Touscal to some degree, as there was no history of the Touscal prior to their first meeting with the Mylin. Many of them had asked the question, "Who are the Touscal really and why are they so interested in Earth?" Touscal and Mylin were worlds in which weapons had never been developed and, to take a life would be unthinkable, even a Breeche life. But the Omicron order knew that Earth wasn't confined by Touscal's own ethics and would most certainly fight if given enough encouragement.

The Breeche had only been able to travel in space for a hundred years but had advanced much more than the Touscal and Mylin had in centuries. Their lust to destroy and conquer for wealth was the engine that had driven their evolution so far in such a short time. They were a handsome race, standing an average five feet ten inches tall with small fangs, long braided hair, and a lifespan of only thirty years. They had little respect for humanoid life and suffered from a psychosis. Their reluctant partners in crime were the Kai, a race that looked similar to the Breeche but had little in common with them. The Kai lived approximately the same life span as humans but had no love of the Breeche nor the treaty that existed between them. Their relationship with the Breeche was at best based on tolerance rather than friendship, and many Kais felt that it was a relationship that had run its course. Before the alliance, there were twenty-two populated planets in that sector of the galaxy, but now only fifteen remained populated, Earth being one of them. Earth was a complex planet, with technology, religion, hatred, and benevolence all living in the same place. With a much slower pace of evolution than the Breeche, Earth would not survive an alien onslaught. The Touscal and Mylin knew this and had started making preparations for some of the humans to survive.

A thousand years earlier, an ancient tablet was found on Touscal prophesising the growth of a race, troubled by war and disharmony, who would grow more than anyone could possibly imagine and would stretch from one side of the universe to the other. Kindling new worlds would be helped and guided by them. The humans were to be the eyes and voice of nature itself.

The Mylin had given credence to this by living amongst the people of Earth, studying the way that humans could love, fight, destroy, build, and show enormous amounts of compassion for their own and other species.

They had shown a greatness to overcome strife and obstacles and had built on the lessons learned. The Mylin believed the prophecy to be true, and both planets felt that the human race could well be the race spoken of in the prophecy. To interfere directly with the fate of humanity could be dangerous in itself. So a solution was found by giving the humans the ability to build an Ark – a vessel that could help them to escape the Breeche and build another Earth, where the prophecy could be fulfilled. It was decided that the Mylin would create an underground complex in Vermont enabling the humans to build their life saving vessel. The Mylin living there would oversee the construction of the machines and program them to bury themselves in a remote area until needed.

There they would vaporise the soil to create a deep cavern. Metals would be shipped in to build the wall linings and a single passive female would receive an enhancement in order to select the best people on the planet to build the Ark. With the guidance of the enhanced individual, it would be a ship large enough for at least two hundred humans. The female would receive a mental enhancement, a painful process of installing huge amounts of information and the ability to upload and download information to and from computers. This would be a mental and physical process, it was decided the physical enhancement would be installed first. This process would change the individual permanently by allowing the muscles to draw a great deal more strength when needed without causing physical damage to the internal structures, thus making them work a great deal more efficient.

It would be easier to give many humans mental enhancements, but the Mylin had observed humankind for some time and knew that too much power could easily corrupt humans at this stage of their evolution. The Mylin had no idea what the effect of the mental enhancement would do to the human brain and this was their reason for choosing a passive female. They hoped that reason would prevail over might and hoped that the result would be a fairly positive one. However, unknown to the Mylin or Touscal, the Omicron order had tampered with the program. They had written an aggressive sub-routine that was contained within the enhancement program itself. This sub-routine would eradicate fear and promote strength of character in the individual female. The order were of the belief that humanity must fight for their planet if they were ever to achieve their real potential and fulfil their destiny amongst the stars.

The Mylin had decided that the complex construction should begin as early as possible, as predicting when the Breeche would start their expansionism was at best uncertain.

As a gifted financial race, they were exceptionally

adept at transferring money and interacting with cash machines and, as this seemed to be beneficial to humankind, could see no wrong in engaging in a little pilfering!

Premises were hired in Detroit, along with human labour for casting, electronics, and assembly of the robot diggers. This wasn't a problem for the Mylin as the appearance of the diggers was not unlike plant equipment scattered around the planet at this time. The fusion reactors were the last pieces of equipment to be installed into the machines and this was done by the Mylin themselves; this avoided awkward questions being asked by inquisitive workers. One hundred were built and shipped to Vermont, three miles from Montpelier. Trucks would leave them at the drop off point where the diggers would disappear into the ground leaving nothing more visible than a little-disturbed soil.

Two months after the decision to help the human race had been agreed, the diggers had completed the work. In record time the cavern had been excavated and measured eight hundred meters by eight hundred meters. They had fabricated thousands of tonnes of steel for the wall linings and, to finish the job, a shipment of Touscal's finest interactive computers: a physical enhancement chamber and a mental enhancement headset were delivered under the cover of darkness by a Mylin freighter. The headset matrix was set to destroy itself as soon as it had been used once as conflict may have arisen between two mentally enhanced humans. The stage was set; the Mylin were on their way home, and an unaware volunteer had been chosen…

CHAPTER 1

William Shakespeare, Twelfth Night Act Two Scene Five: Some are born great, some achieve greatness, and some have greatness thrust upon them. *Never could the Bard of Stratford have imagined that the latter part of this script could apply to a figure so miniscule, so insignificant and so introverted as Sophie Schultz.*

A quiet unassuming female walked along Montpelier High Street on that warm summer morning. She had always thought of herself as an ordinary young woman with the exception of a few minor problems. Arriving at the pharmacy she stood outside whilst plucking up the courage to enter the building. She had been persuaded into running an errand that involved picking up a prescription for an old friend with a chronic heart condition. That was quite a feat for someone who had backed off from life to a point where she was bordering on agoraphobia: her name was Sophie Schultz.

Sophie was a thirty-one-year-old woman who was single, a fashion victim, and a complete stranger to make-up and conversation. Her friend was a thirty-three-year-old electronics engineer called Simon Carter. They had been friends for many years, through college and beyond. Although romance had never been their thing, Sophie had always been there for him, no matter what.

Waiting next to the perfume counter, Sophie sprayed a free sample against her wrist and took in the aroma. Then deciding to move over to the hair care section she helped herself to a handful of free shampoo sachets. There she stood motionless musing over her financial situation as she waited for the drugs to be dispensed. Picking up a bottle of hair shampoo she looked at her last five-dollar bill sitting in the palm of her hand. Feeling ambivalent about whether to wash her hair that evening or buy a pizza she realised that her life had finally hit rock bottom. Looking at the bottle of shampoo she turned it over and read the label. Two lines down and she observed that the print was changing into a swirling motion. As the circular motion started to slow down it seemed to form a face: it was the face of a male with long white hair. His hand was raised and he seemed to be beckoning her towards him. Feeling slightly mesmerised by the situation her eyelids were growing heavy. From behind her, she could hear a voice. "HELLO!" Sophie shook her head and blinked her eyes; looking round and feeling rather foolish she could see the pharmacist waiting impatiently. Apologising, she picked up the prescription and made for the door.

Utmost in her mind at that point was: *Do I get a Hawaiian or spicy beef pizza?* Saying goodbye to the last of her cash she entered a store that was nearby and purchased a Hawaiian pizza.

Walking back towards her old car she consoled herself with the thought: Well at least when you're at the bottom there' not much lower you can go.

Placing the drugs and pizza on the passenger seat, she started the car and made her way to Simon's mobile home. Almost three miles along Main Street the old car jolted violently twice. She thought it strange as it had only been serviced a week earlier. After a few metres further on it happened again – *bang!* Everything on the passenger seat shot onto the floor as the car ground to a halt. All was calm for a few seconds, and then a sudden flash of blindingly bright light hit the windscreen. She could see nothing: the whole area was a complete whiteout with the exception of a hand beckoning her towards it. As the hand faded to nothingness her vision cleared. Startled by what she had seen' she shrieked "What in hell's going on today?" Trying to compose herself, she nervously started the car and cautiously continued her journey. On her arrival at Simon's trailer, she could see that some of the treetops in a nearby forest had turned white, like frosting. Simon was round the other side of the trailer. As she approached him she asked, "Has anything strange happened here in the last five minutes?" He replied, "The radio acted up for a few seconds, but that's all." Placing her handbag on top of the table she pointed towards the treetops, remarking, "It's quite unusual to see frost at this time of the year, even for Vermont." Simon agreed.

He made a living by repairing electrical appliances, from computers to toasters. Sophie handed him his prescription and a broken CD player belonging to her neighbour that needed repairing. She told him, "I've got a pizza for us to share tonight, but I can only stay until about ten o clock as I've got to get up in the morning to alter a dress. It's only fifteen bucks but it helps pay the rent." Looking sympathetic Simon smiled and handed her a DVD case. She could see it was a vampire movie and tried to look enthusiastic, but she wasn't fooling Simon. He took her hand and said, "Cheer up babe." She asked, "Why?" in a depressingly low voice. He laughed and told her, "Well, things can't get any worse can they?" She smiled and said, "I sincerely hope not."

Once the movie was over she took the last slice of pizza and said, "Got to go babe, my bed's calling me." On opening the door she could see a pulsating light and called Simon to take a look. It was where the frosted treetops were about two hundred metres away. She was feeling strangely drawn towards it in a warm welcoming way and felt that it was in some way connected to the happenings earlier that day.

She felt an overwhelming urge to approach the area where the light was emanating from. Simon told her, "Steer clear of it babe; you don't know who or what it is." But his words fell on stony ground as she said, "I have to see this; I don't know why, but I have to." He replied, "It's too far away for me to make it. Here, take this torch and for god's sake be careful." Looking extremely worried he sat in the window and watched her as she climbed the hill towards the light. As Sophie neared the area, she could see a small clearing with a metallic looking disc at the centre. She could see that it was covered by a few fallen leaves; and around its edges was a glowing, pulsating light.

Clearing the leaves away with her foot she timidly stood on the metallic surface as if she was meant to. Instantly there was a whiteout again and an image began to appear.

It was the image of the man with long white hair again, but this time the vision was a little blurry. She could see the disc starting to change at a molecular level; and noticed that it was turning into a state of flux. It was time to panic, but she couldn't lift her feet, it was as if they had become part of the disc itself. Screaming seemed a waste of time at this point, as she began to feel a strange sensation: like heat flowing over her. Within a second, she was standing on a pad in a huge complex with what looked like metal walls and what seemed to be banks of computers, the likes of which she had never seen before. There were also strange looking machines, and what appeared to be robots that seemed to be leaning against them.

The man with the white hair finally appeared before her. This time he was clear; he didn't look totally human to Sophie; as he had a pointed chin and vivid green eyes. He stood about five feet five inches tall and was wearing a white robe with silver beading. She could see that there were five fingers on each hand, but his skin seemed very pale, even translucent. The figure asked her, "Please step from the pad." When he spoke his lips didn't quite seem to match his voice exactly. By tipping his head to one side he seemed to correct the problem and paired his lips and voice in perfect harmony. He told her that she was deep below ground, and that 'he' was an interface, designed to interact with new species. She figured that would explain why its voice was a little out of sync with its lips and thought *Shit, this dude looks like a ghost or something!*

Sophie stepped forward, thinking that she should be terrified, but it was all too intriguing for that. She asked it who it represented, and what had just happened. It replied that she had been teleported half a kilometre below ground level, and that it was a representation of a race of people called the Touscal. It told her, "I have been instructed by a race of people called the Mylin to bring someone here, and you are that person. You have been chosen to build an escape vessel for your people." Sophie was confused. It's face softened and a slight smile emerged. It told her, "Soon the Breeche will come in vessels of immense power; they will enslave your people and destroy your way of life. Come with me and you will know everything."

Sophie closely followed the ghostly image as it floated through the complex to a chamber about one hundred metres on. It was made with thick metal walls and had a small porthole on the front. It asked her to enter for her preparation and assured her that entering the chamber would be an enormous enhancement to her physical being. Hesitantly she moved towards the entrance; she couldn't see any reason why it would wish to harm her, and gingerly entered the chamber. The door hissed and slammed shut, Without warning a pressure wave immediately pushed her against the wall. The interior of the chamber gave off a brilliant white light, along with some vibration and after a couple of seconds the whole thing started to spin, faster and faster. She could feel herself being pulled into the centre of the chamber, she noticed that her feet were no longer touching the floor. Within seconds she was totally suspended within the centre of the chamber as it rotated at a furious rate. She could feel heat from above. Suddenly she felt a massive spasm from every muscle in her body, over and over. It was unbearable; it was as if she was being torn apart from inside. After a few minutes, the chamber started to slow down. As it finally ground to a halt all fell quiet. Looking at her clothing she could see that her tee shirt and jeans had split in certain places and her underwear felt like it was cutting her in half. Her legs were aching but *different*, stronger, in fact she felt as if she was another person altogether; and observed that even her fingernails had grown. Trying to compose herself, though looking like a pile of rags, she moved towards the door. With a short hiss the door opened. There, hanging about like a ghost, was the image. Politely she asked it for something else to wear, as her clothes were extremely uncomfortable. "Well, you should take them off." Suggested the interface. So she did. It assured her that it would find her something to wear later, and off it went again and so did she.

It was turning into a strange day for Sophie Schultz. Off to the chemists at 10.00 am a vampire movie at 8.00 pm, and a long naked walk in a new body with a ghost at 11.00 pm. She pinched herself but still felt that it was all a dream. Some distance away, the ghost stopped by what could only be described as a large chair with an elaborate hairdryer connected to it. The ghost told her, "It's time to enhance your mind." It asked, "By what name would you like to be known?" She looked down and replied,

"Sophie No Pants!" It said, "Well Sophie No Pants - will you sit in the chair please." Sophie thought, *Well last time was quite a positive result, maybe this will be too.* The seat was quite warm and full of static. With a whirring noise, the headpiece started to lower itself onto her head. "Make mine a perm and blue rinse!" she nervously quipped. Slowly everything around her started to change. It was as if she was floating in a large void out of the chair. It was like space. She seemed to be free floating in space with mathematical equations floating all around her. *Well, that's wrong* she thought. It was a formula for a nuclear fusion-powered engine. She quickly realised that the formula was right, just not very efficient. Everything seemed so easy; the effects of thermal dynamics on organic matter - child's play she thought.

Faster and faster it came, more and more, until she was taking the information faster than the machine could give it. She found it was like waiting for a dial-up computer. Soon she found unsolved equations that the Touscal had left; she found the solutions simple and delved even deeper into a treasure trove of information that lay hidden in secret data files. Having learned several languages she found herself fluent in all. Next up were the schematics for a space vessel that was referred to as The Ark. Hearing a voice in the background she found herself back in the chair. With a whirring noise the headset retracted and seemed to collapse in on itself, and within seconds all that was left of it was a small pile of metallic residue. The ghost asked, "How do you feel?" Sophie smiled and said, "I feel really alive like I've been reborn. I feel different, very different." She asked, "Have you found me any clothes yet?" It pointed to a patterned sheet hanging over a machine; Sophie wrapped it around herself like a Roman toga and checked her reflection in a piece of glass. The ghost had no record of anyone drawing such a large enhancement as Sophie's; she had been connected to the machine for five hours. The effect on the human brain was very different to what the ghost had anticipated. It knew that even for short periods most beings felt some pain while being connected to the mental process; whereas Sophie had felt no discomfort whatsoever. She had risen confidently from the chair, a very different person to the shy, retiring one that had sat in it five hours earlier.

Sophie knew all about the Breeche now, and a bad bunch they seemed to be. Accessing more information she found that she could create and store blueprints in her mind for just about anything from computers to fusion powered reactors. In fact, the mental process had proved to be highly beneficial to Sophie in every way imaginable! She was keen to start work the next day, but not work on an escape vessel. Dismissing the idea of building an Ark, she concentrated her energies on something larger. Something harbouring antimatter weapons and shielding systems: something like an Intergalactic Warship. She felt strange like a warrior with a cause to follow. It was as if her life would never be the same again, and maybe that was a good thing. An interface implant behind her right ear served as a reminder that what had happened that night really wasn't a dream.

As it was now six in the morning Sophie was feeling the need to sleep. She told the ghost that she would be back at midday. It affirmed that it would be there and reminded her to buy some larger clothes. Once on the pad and looking a little like Cleopatra, Sophie used her implant to interface with the teleport, relieved she found it was working just fine. It was fine outside too as she ambled down the hill to the trailer. Simon seemed to be wedged up against the window and fast asleep, and that was probably the best way to leave him. Climbing into her old car she headed for home while rabidly chomping on a chocolate bar. Wearing nothing but a patterned sheet and covered in chocolate she wearily opened the front door to her apartment and fell onto the bed.

As soon as her head hit the pillow she was out. Vivid dreams of strange beautiful places entered her head: animals unlike anything on Earth, and then fire in the sky, burning homes and people on fire.

Bang – bang.

"Ugh." She was awake, and had a good idea who was at the door. On opening it she apologised for being late with the alteration to the clothing, and asked the elderly female to enter the apartment. Appeasing the woman with a cup of coffee she set about taking up the hem of the dress. Threading the needle on the first attempt she was all done in ten minutes. Thanking the woman for the fifteen dollars, Sophie squeezed into a dress of her own and escorted the woman onto the street. Standing at the gate was Sophie's neighbour George; he was sixty-seven and alone since his wife had died six months earlier. Sophie asked, "How's it hangin' George?" He replied, "OK Sophie," and laughed as he looked at her dress, commenting, "You know, you really need a thong with that dress." She looked down and saw where he was coming from. Pulling her panties off, she stowed them in her handbag. George nearly burst his sides with laughter as a distracted delivery driver mounted the kerb next to her. She thought, *Well at least I've made someone's day!* It was now eleven thirty and time to go. Bidding George farewell she walked towards the high street. She needed some cash and, on her arrival at the cash point, she was attracting some strange looks as her dress looked as though it had shrunk two sizes. She knew that the twenty dollars in her account along with the fifteen dollars for the dress alterations wouldn't get her much more than a cheap skirt. However, she was quite surprised when the machine popped out a hundred dollars even though her card was still in her bag. After a little more interfacing with the cash point, she realised that she had enough money for a whole new wardrobe!

One quick stop at a trendy clothes shop, and she was set. By now It was one o'clock and she was late, with no time to stop at Simon's. She dumped the car and ran into the woods. All that she could see were leaves. *Where was it? Think! That's it! Think.* With a little concentration, the disc illuminated. Relieved, she stepped onto it; and in less than a second, she was in the complex. Before leaving the pad, a voice could be heard; it was the ghost, "You're late, Sophie No Pants!" Sarcastically she replied, "I'm, sorry I hope you haven't been waiting too long." It said, " I hope your not going to make a habit of it," and told her that she didn't have to travel by car any more as she could use her implant and it was a great deal faster too. After a little explaining, it was clear that the implant was capable of sending and retrieving her from anywhere on the planet, and that if she interfaced with the design computer, she could even build a teleport of her own.

Sophie needed a list of the 'who's who' in the world of rocket people. She had a little job for them. The ghost related to her that she would have to do it herself as it needed to asses her new skills. As she sat at the console the ghost offered to tutor her through the procedure. With a little concentration, a name popped up in her head – Dieter Hans Schreiber. He once worked for NASA and was now lecturing at Oxford. Visualising it in her mind she thought, *Oxford* and the next sound in her ears was that of people talking with an English accent. She found herself sitting on her backside on the floor of an English pub. A young man helped her to her feet and asked if she was all right. She replied, "Oh yes, thank you - I seem to have mislaid my chair somewhere."

Dusting herself off she realised that flitting from one spot on the planet to another was going to take a while to master, but she was in Oxford, England, and that was a good start. Quickly making for the door she thought *It's time to find this Dieter Schreiber.*

Finding another pub popular with students, and eavesdropping on their conversations, it wasn't long before she came across a few students from the engineering department. Asking the group where she might find Dieter Schreiber, it didn't take too long before she had an address!

Arriving at the address, she found it to be an old house quite near to the university. Sophie didn't knock. She just centred her mind onto a narrow field and found herself on the other side of the door. To her surprise, standing in front of her was the ghost. It asked her if she was carrying out a robbery. She said, "No!" and told it, "Clear off will you." Quietly she crept into what looked like a study, with the ghost in tow. A fair-haired man of about thirty was sitting in a chair reading a newspaper. She called out, "Dieter Schreiber, I presume?"

Jumping out of the chair, the man shouted, "Who the hell are you?"

"I don't think she's a burglar," stated the ghost. Sophie looked at it with a stony glare and said, "Oh, will you shut up before you get us both arrested!" She turned her attention towards Dieter and told him that she was recruiting for the ultimate experience, and advised him to ignore the ghost as it probably low on charge.

Dieter asked, "Who are you really? And what's that supposed to be?" Sophie replied, "I just might be your boss for a start, and *this* is a representation of a race called the Touscal, It's a planet two hundred light years from here."

She warned Dieter that Earth was on the brink of invasion and she desperately needed his help. Looking like he was going to have a heart attack, Dieter shouted, "I don't believe you! You're a nut with a clever party trick." *A little demonstration seems necessary to convince him*, thought Sophie. She grabbed his hand and visualised the International Space Station. In a flash they were there floating next to three technicians on the ISS. Dieter noticed that he still had the newspaper in his hand and felt a little stunned as he espied Earth through the window. He handed the newspaper to one of the technicians and said: "It's today's, there's a good piece in there on page four, it's about nightmares!"

He could hear a familiar sounding message. "Control - we have a problem!"

The next moment Dieter was standing on Sydney Harbour Bridge. He asked Sophie, "How are you doing this?" She explained that the teleport rearranges an object's frequency so that it is out of phase with everything else. She also explained how it interfaced with her implant and could send her like an e-mail. If she was to hold onto anything, i.e. his hand, that would go too, and of course the rest of him with it, making him an attachment. She asked, "Are we OK then?"

Dieter was astonished as they arrived back in his study. He went into the kitchen and came out with two Budweiser's. He asked the ghost if he could get him anything. But It just seemed to hang in the air watching Sophie, as if it were doing an appraisal of her conduct. Dieter admitted that he was hooked, and offered to be of help, as he slumped onto the sofa and handed Sophie a beer. She asked the ghost if it was OK to drink having had the implant. It replied, "You'll just talk more baffling garbage if you drink enough, but that's all." Sophie lay back on the sofa, drank a little from the bottle and filled Dieter in. From what she had accessed she understood that they, the human race, had a guardian angel or, rather, two passive planets that believed the human race to be in mortal danger. Looking Dieter square in the face she told him, "They're convinced, above all, that humanity must survive. Their plan was for us to build an Ark and abandon the planet. They've given us the means to make that possible; I've already received a brain enhancement and possess the knowledge to build it."

Sophie also mentioned that the Mylin had left them with banks of advanced computers that she seemed to be able to interact with.

Dieter asked, "You're from the East side, right?" She affirmed, answering, "Yes, Vermont. That's where the freighters to be built; the complex is already complete and ready to serve." Dieter asked, "Freighter I thought we were supposed to be building an Ark?" Sophie answered, "Screw that! We're building a battle cruiser, but we need the freighter for collecting the raw materials. You do want to fight for the planet don't you?" Dieter seemed relieved and said, "Yes, of course I want to fight, when do we start?" With the word "Now." She grabbed his hand, and instantly all three of them arrived at the complex. Dieter was amazed as he approached a computer. He could see that part of it seemed to be made from pure crystal. It was very different from what he was used to. Sophie told him, "Its capacity and speed outstrip anything that you've seen before and prompted him to talk to it. Pushing him towards it she said, "Go on it won't bite you." Stepping forward he said, "Hello." The computer sent out a blue plume of what looked like pure energy and asked him to come closer, as it needed to confirm his identity. After a couple of seconds, it confirmed, "Dr Dieter Hans Schreiber." Sophie explained, "When I first came across the complex I was intrigued and jumped in with both feet. I was weak-bodied, and didn't really have an opinion about anything. When the ghost told me that Earth was going to be attacked by the Breeche, I felt a sense of purpose for the first time in my life. After the enhancement, that sense of purpose increased tenfold. The enhancement was based on Touscal physiology. Human physiology worked in a very different way. The Touscal way was to flee, the human way was to fight. My enhancement was an extremely large one. I've found I can fashion engines, life support systems and anything else concerned with Touscal or Mylin technology. It's all there crammed in my head."

She added, "The Touscal thought that they had given us the ability to build a fusion reactor powered engine, powerful enough for us to escape from the Breeche. But they didn't realise that for humans the information flow was a two-way street. While I was being enhanced mentally, I managed to gain access to the Touscal's unsolved equation files, one being the production of antimatter weapons. As pacifists. hey had never learned how to apply the science beyond antimatter reactor's and vessel propulsion systems. However, now with our world being threatened, I found that I couldn't ignore it. So I made the link in spite of the Touscal's beliefs. I now posses the knowledge required to build such weapons."

She told him that the human intellect wasn't bound by protocol problems, such as fighting an enemy like the Breeche. Clenching a fist she said, "And fight them we shall!" Dieter pondered for a moment. He could see that Sophie's face was taut. He knew a professor who was studying dark matter; her name was Sarah Neilson. He knew for a fact that she would be ecstatic at the thought of producing an antimatter engine.

Sophie stressed, "We need manual workers, electronics engineers, forward thinkers that would double up as a crew." Dieter asked, "What about the fuselage fabrication for the cruiser?" She answered "I know the Mylin use extremely tough alloys for vessel construction. They source the ore and metals locally from an asteroid about fifty light years from their home world and I believe there's a source of antimatter in the vicinity too." Sophie could see Dieter becoming evermore excited about the prospect of space travel and smiled as he said, " I have a great many contacts, some in high places. All I need from you is a phone."

Over the next two weeks, the banks took a pounding as Sophie committed a white-collar crime wave of immense proportions across most of the financial centres of the world. The FBI and Interpol had been close to catching her, but she always managed to elude them! Iron ore for the freighters fuselage and raw materials were just teleported out from their storage silos. Workers had been vetted and recruited, experts in every field of engineering were drawn in via a resourceful friend of Dieter. Her name was Holly Farley, a recruitment expert from New York.

Holly had promised the greatest move forward in the history of mankind. She worked at the top end of the recruitment business and knew exactly who could be trusted and who couldn't. Qualified people had joined together from all over the globe and were drawn to the complex like moths drawn to a flame. Doctors in science, medicine, and every other technical field were willing to help with the undertaking and agreed to be locked in, under strict security for the duration of the project. Before long they were living, eating, and breathing at the complex.

The Mylin had designed and built a huge universal construction jig and left it in the middle of the complex. With everything in place, Sophie announced that work on the freighter could now commence. Though foremost in Sophie's mind was the cruiser. She knew that if they were to succeed in their mission to save the Earth from the Breeche onslaught, the cruiser would have to excel in build quality, firepower, and strength.

Dieter noticed that there was a report on the Mylin database that antimatter could be found close to the asteroid suspended within a cloud of unique properties. This interested Sophie more than anything as she knew that if they were to stand the slightest chance of winning the war, it would be heavily dependent on the use of antimatter. Locking herself away in an office Sophie started to draw the plans for the freighter; the build time was set at three months. Dieter felt that three months was a little optimistic, considering what was involved. However, Sophie did her best to convince him otherwise, by making the plans for the freighter as concise as possible. But within the first two weeks, things had already starting to go dreadfully wrong as the project started to fall behind schedule and finally ground to a halt by the fourth week.

The build was now well into it's first month and was starting to run out of balance. Problems with the construction side of the project had caused a component backlog the size of a small mountain. The components were logged and numbered but were randomly piled into a massive heap. Dieter's men had spent the best part of a morning looking for one part among the pile. Sophie had expressed her concerns to Dieter about the time factor and, after a blazing row with him about sorting the components into the order that they were required, she stormed into the corner of the building and vanished from sight.

Teleporting to the quiet of her apartment she smashed a cup against the wall and screamed. Trying to calm herself down she sat on the sofa and closed her eyes. Moments later there was a knock at the door. On opening it, she could see that it was George, her neighbour. He could see that she was in a desperate state; quietly he disappeared into the kitchen and emerged two minutes later with a cup of coffee. Sophie called him a life saver and asked him to sit with her for a while. After chatting about his wife she found that a large part of his life was now missing. But one thing that interested her more than anything was to know what line of work he was in when he was employed. She listened very closely as he went into detail about his life as an agricultural machine parts operative that involved detailing, cataloguing and sorting parts into accessible order. Putting her hand on his, she asked him "How would you like a job". He shrugged his shoulders and said, "Why not?"

The next morning Sophie knocked on George's door and said, "Ready?" He asked, "Where's your car?" She laughed and said, "Who needs a car?" Taking his arm she teleported the pair of them straight into the heart of the complex. George couldn't believe his eyes as they fell upon the half- built freighter. He asked, "What the hell do you think I'm gonna do in a place like this? And how the hell did we get here anyway?" Sophie smiled and pointed to a massive pile of heavy panels and components that were all mixed up, and said: "All you've got to do is sort that lot out." She introduced Dieter to George and told him, "Right at this moment you're the most critical part in an extremely complex piece of engineering." After putting Dieter in the picture, he thanked her and took George over to the pile of components while Sophie returned to the drawing office.

At 6.00 pm she strolled over to see how George was coping. To her surprise, he had taken to it like a duck to water and, with a little help from Dieter and his engineers, the project was back on track as the parts started appearing from nowhere and, thanks to George, many of them were now logged and in the right order.

As the project advanced it became clear to Sophie that the inner and outer fuselage panels were far too large and heavy for normal manipulation. She walked over to the jig containing the bare bones of the freighter and searched for Holly. She had temporarily abandoned her career in New York and was feeding optic cables into place on the freighter. Sophie grabbed the end of the cables and helped to pull them through into the bridge area. Handing Holly a cup of coffee Sophie asked: "Do you know any steel riggers?" Holly told her, "I know a team of steel erectors that are led by a man called Big Tom. Why do you ask?" Sophie made it clear to her that the panels for the outer skin were now being processed and were building up at the far end of the complex. What she really needed was an overhead crane system for dropping them into place on the freighters jig.

After making a few calls, Holly tracked down Big Tom's team, who were about to finish a contract on the lower east side of New York. Teleporting to the site on Norfolk Street, Sophie could see a group of men that were welding a steel girder in place five floors up. Materialising at the other end of the floor to Tom's men, she approached via a steel girder. Noticing her, Tom shouted, "STOP! What the hell are you doing up here?" Sophie continued approaching him then, stopped and did a perfect cartwheel across the girder. She stopped and placed her foot down directly in front of him. Grimacing he said, "What are you? Some kind of nut or something? You shouldn't even be in here without my permission. And where's your safety gear?" Sophie pointed to her head and said: "In here!" Calming himself down, Tom said, "You know that's a pretty good trick of yours. I don't know many women who can cartwheel along a girder five floors up!" Sophie answered, "Neither do I, but now to business. I need some heavy-duty steel work done by a professional team as soon as possible. Are you available or should I go somewhere else?" Climbing onto a ladder Tom said, "Listen lady my team and I are going for a drink, as we're finished here today, so why don't you come back some other time? Like never!" As one of Tom's men passed the welding gear down to the next level, Sophie asked him, "Where are you going for a drink?" The man replied, "Mulberry St," and gave her the name of the bar in little Italy. "It's where we always go. I thought you'd know that, being one of Tom's friends."

Waiting at ground level was Big Tom ready to escort Sophie off the premises. He told her, "Don't come back here ever, do you hear that?" Sophie replied, "I hear you," and whispered "*Asshole*" under her breath. Once their gear was packed into the van Tom and his men headed for Mulberry St, leaving Sophie standing on the sidewalk. Looking in the vans rear view mirror he watched as Sophie grew smaller as the van reached the end of the street and couldn't help but feel a little guilty about the cruel way he had spoken to her. Ten minutes later after struggling through busy traffic he parked the van and entered the bar. To his surprise, he was greeted by Sophie, who had four beers waiting on a table.

Without saying a word, Tom downed one of the beers while warily looking at Sophie as he passed her on his way to the bar; where he ordered another four beers. With four full glasses on the bar, Tom went to pay for them but was surprised when the barman said, "Its OK Tom, the lady's got an open tab. She's left two hundred dollars behind the bar." Looking frustrated by now Tom asked the barman, "How long has she been in here?" The barman said, "Hmm around ten minutes give or take a few." All Tom could do was scratch his head and say under his breath, "How the hell did she get here so fast?" Taking a sip from his glass, he turned round and said, "Ok, lady I'm intrigued. What can I do for you?" Sophie took a sip from her glass of Southern Comfort and called his three co-workers to gather round. With their undivided attention, she started to speak. "Maybe some of you will have doubts about what I'm about to tell you, but it's a task of the utmost importance that I require from you. If you choose to accept you will be sworn to secrecy under pain of death. You will be paid handsomely for your efforts or shot if you disclose a word, and that gentlemen I promise you."

Tom could see that the docile cart wheeling woman had left the bar and been replaced by a stern looking female who seemed to believe in every word that she said. Tom pulled a face that told Sophie that he still had doubts. Taking a chair, Sophie placed her elbow on the table and told all four of them to pull up a chair. With an open hand, she invited Tom to arm wrestle. Curious he took her up on her invitation. Pushing with all of his might, he stopped when he realised that he hadn't even moved her arm a centimetre and was starting to think *I'm dealing with someone very strange here!* Sophie called on the other three to join him and just sat there smiling as all four together struggled to move her arm. With a sudden push back from her they all went flying across the bar room floor. Standing up she said, "9.00 am Monday morning, Montpelier, three miles out along Main Street. Look for the trailer." Walking into the corner of the room, Sophie turned to face all four of them and de-materialised. Big Tom and his men just stared at each other in silence.

At 9.00 am Monday morning a van pulled off Main Street Montpelier and parked up. Climbing out of it were four burly men who were still questioning themselves about their own sanity. That was until a figure emerged from the woods. As they approached her, Tom could see that it was Sophie.

Welcoming them she held her hands out and asked them to touch her palms. In a flash, Tom found himself and his men facing a huge jig that seemed to be supporting the super structure of an immense aircraft of some kind. Tom asked, "Is this something to do with Boeing or Lockheed?" Sophie pointed to her right and said, "It's more to do with Mylin; that's two hundred light years in that direction." Big Tom's No 2 said, "God's own truth man; we're building rocket ships now!"

Sophie took the men around the complex to the panel store, where she explained the problem that involved the stresses of carrying such weights and how to manoeuvre them into place. At that point, Sophie knew that she had the right man for the job, as Tom created a 3D picture in his mind that listed every component necessary in order to complete the task. Taking Tom and his group into the drawing office, Sophie displayed a map of the complex, pointing out where they could eat, sleep and drink over the course of the project. With the morning turning into afternoon, Tom had already drawn up the plans for the crane and its supporting infrastructure. Having given Sophie a list of necessary components, she went in search of the raw materials. With tons of steel girders being simply teleported into the complex and robotic welders on hand, the work commenced at an incredible rate.

Four days had passed and the crane hoisted the first of the panels into the air. Knowing the urgency of the project had forced Tom and his men to work continuously around the clock while grabbing sleep where they could. When Holly saw Tom, it was like an old friends reunion. He asked her, "Why didn't Sophie just tell me you were a friend?" Holly replied,

"She judges people using her instincts. If you'd refused to join us she would have respected your decision. I can always tell when she likes someone, and I'm pretty sure she trusts you too." Holly's words made him feel like his group were provisional members of a very exclusive club. He knew that his first meeting with Sophie hadn't ended well, but since then he had grown to respect her and what she was trying to do. Feeling a sense of belonging he hoped that she would eventually consider his group as fully fledged members of that club.

*

It was day five and the last of the steel runners had been bolted into place above the freighter's jig. Activating the crane, Tom ran the hanging panel down to the freighter and lowered it carefully into place. Sophie gave a sigh of relief as she realised that they now had the means of finishing the fuselage. Two days later and the build was now forging ahead as Dieter and his engineers installed the nuclear fusion reactors into the fully enclosed engine room.

Big Tom had just finished welding the panels together and offered him a sandwich. Dieter took the sandwich and sat on the floor with him and talked about the freighters engines. He was totally surprised at Tom's interest in the fusion-powered engine, as the usual response to the subject always ended up with people making their excuses and walking away. But he saw Tom as a kindred spirit who seemed to absorb the information like a sponge.

It was one of those all-absorbing talks with Dieter that had drawn Sophie's attention to Tom as someone more than just a steel erector. An incident involving

George had shown her that within her sights was a brave man who would put himself at risk in order to save others. The incident involved George making a delivery of parts to the bridge of the freighter. As Tom left Engineering, he could hear a crack from above; it was a noise that he'd heard before. Looking up he saw the pulley mechanism snap. While pushing George out of the way, he was hit by part of the mechanism and thrown into a pile of insulation. Running to their assistance, Sophie and a team of medics arrived just in time to see Tom picking George up from the floor. One of the medics could see blood pouring from Tom's leg and went to his assistance. Though only a superficial wound, Sophie had witnessed Tom's true courage and decided there and then that she wanted him and his group as permanent crewmembers when the freighter was finally finished.

Taking George to and from work by teleport for the next two months had pushed the project back on track. Sophie told him his work at the complex was now done as the freighter was almost finished. She thanked him for his help and paid him for his time. In turn, he thanked her for helping him to find life again and added that the friendships he'd made at the complex had made him feel as if he was ready to join the real world again. He looked at Sophie and told her, "My lips are sealed. Do you think you'll succeed?" All that Sophie could say was, "I sincerely hope so, for all of our sakes."

Now that the freighter was nearing completion, the diggers had been re-commissioned to create a launch tunnel. Tom and his group were now working with some of Dieters engineers and together had created blast doors to the complex that were extremely tough. Once the doors were in place, Tom and his team disassembled the freighters construction jig along with the crane and packed them both into crates. The jig itself had been manufactured on Earth under the guidance of the Mylin, it was fully adjustable and extendable in length. Sophie felt that with a few adjustments and modifications it could be used again for the cruiser. She knew that this would be a huge saving on the one commodity that she was in most in need of.... time.

It was payday for Tom and his group and Sophie knew that this was her one chance to get them on her side. Coming straight out with it she said, "Why don't you all stay, I need people like you." Waiting for an answer she pushed her head forward and gave them a nervous smile. After a couple of seconds, Tom scratched his head and said: "I thought you'd never ask." Welcoming them to the project Sophie could feel a weight lift from her shoulders.

It was now time for her to address all three hundred members of the project. Many of the technicians had worked on tokomaks and didn't really believe that the system that had been drawn out for them by Sophie could ever really work. She knew this and thought a demonstration was needed to renew their enthusiasm.

The ship was now sitting on two large pads and was ready to be powered up, this would be the crowning part of the presentation. The members were all gathered at the far end of the complex. The ghost had become a regular sight around the place and announced Sophie as 'The Captain'. Feeling quite happy about her new title. She thanked the personnel for their efforts and hoped they could maintain some order in their corner of the galaxy.

She told them, "Although It's not the vessel we need to fight the Breeche and might only be seen as a cargo ship, it's pivotal to the mission's success." She knew that a great deal of the work had been carried out by the robots and thanked the programmers for their hard work at applying their skills to their full extent. She praised them for their commitment to the task in hand as without them none of it would have been possible. Turning around to face the freighter, she signalled Dieter, and a colleague to power up the reactor.

With a deep whine, it droned on for a second, and then, after a little fine tuning from Dieter it burst into life. Sophie shouted over the noise from the engine, "Well done everyone," then they all listened to the sound of the engine: the engine that they had built.

CHAPTER 2

Two weeks had passed and all of the avionics, navigation, and life support systems were functioning. The freighter was now sitting on its pads astride a conveyor. It was inside the complex facing the doors to the tunnel and was ready to go. Sophie made the decision that it would launch at 1.00 am. The destination was an asteroid called 'Perness.` It was an asteroid swathed by a blue gas of unique properties that held the antimatter within its grasp. The antimatter itself was a remnant left over after the big bang. Named by the Touscal, Perness meant *Great Power*. Sophie had been interacting with one of the computers for hours, studying antiproton and positron behaviour. NASA had been experimenting for many years trying to create a moderate amount of antimatter, It had been an expensive business with mixed results. Sophie knew that the secret lay in the gas surrounding the asteroid. Its properties seemed to hold the antimatter at bay, separating it from ordinary matter. The gas seemed to be charged with an unknown element that seemed to have an arresting effect between matter and antimatter. A system of harvesting it was needed, together with force field technology and a containment chamber. Sophie just hoped it would be possible to control the flow of antimatter without an explosion. This work would have to be undertaken during the voyage.

At 9.35 pm the proximity monitor picked up an intruder in the launch tunnel. Holly was the first at the console; using the close circuit cameras she could see that it was Cameron Porter, who was to be the first officer on the mission. Arriving seconds later Sophie looked at the console and agreed that it was definitely Cameron. Holly suggested killing him and warned Sophie that If he told anyone about the complex they would be finished, and so would any hopes of saving the planet. Looking at Sophie she waited for a decision. Questions were going through Sophie's mind. *What could Cameron do? Who would believe him?*

Feeling that the complex was fairly secure. She told Holly, "Once Cameron's out of sight we can change the holographic camouflage over the entrance of the tunnel." With Cameron Porter gone Sophie changed the hologram from a cliff face to a grass covered hill with trees and plants. She told Holly, "I doubt that that he'll ever find this place again." Now Sophie had no first officer and felt that it was a mystery why he'd deserted them at such a crucial time as this.

With her confidence waning, she summoned the ghost, who could see that Sophie was a woman with a problem. She told it, "I know that I'm not going to have any more insight about the mission than anyone else on board once we're out of range of the complex. I'm not even sure that I should be the Captain with no first officer to act as a buffer." The ghost came closer to her, its voice lowered, and it told her, "Sophie, you were chosen. Last year when you visited a clinic for a free medical, Dr Halse; the clinical lead hadn't made you aware that he had been doing a great deal more than just checking your blood pressure. He had been analysing your character by means of the strange questions he asked you. The device he placed against your temple was an extremely sensitive scanner that tested brain waves, thought patterns and a great deal more. The results of those tests had astounded him to a point that he made his decision at that moment to select you. From the readings taken by his equipment, he could see powerful qualities deep inside your mind and was confident the enhancements would bring those very same qualities to the surface." "What qualities?" Sophie asked. The ghost looked into her eyes and said, "Responsibility, bravery, trust and much more. Do you know what that makes you?" She answered, "No not really." It said, "The right choice if Earth is to survive."

The ghost added, "Dr Halse, and many others like him, had been testing likely candidates who might have been suitable to receive the mental enhancement. Dr Halse was from Mylin, and he was the last to leave when they were recalled home. You were his final patient, which is why the complex was built here. It could have been built anywhere, but it was built here because you were here; as you were the chosen one." The ghost told her, "Go and see Holly; I think she's feeling very sorry about the poor choice she had made for the appointment of the first officer. And don't be too hard on her as the job of recruiting is an extremely vague task at best. You will always have her trust as she respects you, and trust is everything." As Sophie turned to walk away the ghost said, "You know, you were right to choose to fight, I didn't think that Ark business was a very good idea, not even for a second." Thanking the ghost for reassuring her confidence in the project, Sophie went looking for Holly completely oblivious to the fact that the ghost was working under the instruction of the Omicron order.

*

When Sophie found Holly, she put her arms around her and gave her a hug. She told her, "Don't worry. I think I can find a stand-in for the first officer's position."

She hadn't seen Simon for a week. Ambling down the hillside she could see him through the window of his trailer. The only reason she had not put Simon through the physical enhancement before was because she thought that it could kill him. However, she knew that he would make an excellent first officer. She also knew that he had the capacity to absorb fresh ideas, had the ability to instil confidence in others and was unquestionably loyal: he was also her friend: her loyal friend. There was no one else available for that position as all three hundred technicians were already in their various positions. Two hundred and fifty were staying behind to concentrate on fighter construction as the fighters were the mainstay of Earth's defence if the cruiser was destroyed.

Entering Simon's trailer Sophie asked him if he would like to meet someone. He asked Sophie, "What's she like?" She explained that, "She's quite big but carries her weight well and she's pretty fast too." Sophie assured him that he would like her, particularly when he got acquainted with her. He was intrigued and asked, "She's not outside is she?"

*

Although Simon had noticed the changes to Sophie's body and personality, he had avoided asking her directly what had happened in her life to make such a drastic change. He also feared that the question itself may cause a relapse to the woman that he had known and respected for all those years. He was just happy that she was finding her feet again and knew that she would reveal her secret, only when she was ready.

Sophie asked him, "Well do you want to meet her? She's not very far away. C'mon, I'll help you." Placing her shoulder underneath Simon's arm she supported him, and within a second both arrived on the pad at the complex. By this time Simon's heart was pounding. Looking around, he could see that Sophie's secret was finally out, and collapsed in a heap on the floor.

Dr Phull, who was to be the freighter's resident physician, was nearby calibrating a scanner that Sophie had fashioned for him earlier that week. The hand-held scanner told the whole story. He offered to operate there and then, but with Simon's heart in such poor shape, he couldn't guarantee anything. Sophie trusted Dr Phull's judgement but made one of her own. Pulling Simon onto a trolley, she and the Doctor dragged it down to the physical enhancement chamber. On their arrival, Holly joined them and offered to help. Picking Simon up they took him into the machine, then backed out and programmed the chamber for one individual. All three stood watching as the door slid shut and within a second the chamber began to glow. Sophie stood in silence as the machine started to do its job. If he survived she knew he would need some pants.

It was only ninety minutes until the launch of the freighter and most of the crew were at their various stations. Sophie had found a larger size shirt and a pair of pants that had been donated by one of the engineering crew. She felt that they would have to do for now. Dr Phull and Holly were still waiting outside the chamber when Sophie returned; all three watched as it finally ground to a halt. As the door slid open they could see that Simon was alive. Ragged, but alive. Sophie shed a tear as the Doctor monitored his vital signs, anticipating the worst. She asked him, "Will he be OK?" To which the Doctor replied, "He will be when he changes those clothes!"

Simon looked up at Holly and said, "Well, you don't look that big!" Holly looked surprised as Simon eyed her up and down. Sophie put her hand under his chin and pointed at the freighter, then he understood. She looked at her watch; it was only one hour before the launch. Simon was asking questions and when he stood up he noticed the chamber. Now it was clear to him that he had been through the same process as Sophie. His heart condition had gone; he knew that the heart was just another muscle like any other in the human body. Sophie told him she had appointed him as the first officer of a space freighter – that frightened him the most. He had a feeling that he would be in great need of his new friends after Sophie had made him aware that no mental enhancement was available.

Ten minutes to go, and everyone was feeling a little strained, then… relief as Dieter managed to balance the gravity plating, making the crew weigh ten kilos less.

Holly engaged the conveyor, and they had forward movement for the first time. Dieter brought the engine online and handed control to Jamie McTavish, a Scottish test pilot with a flair for handling difficult planes. With the sound of voices repeating *check* over the com system, Jamie psyched himself up for his greatest challenge of his life. A light on Holly's console told Sophie that the blast doors were now closed and the vessel was finally in the launch tunnel. After three months of constant problems, she realised that it was finally time to begin the mission. Sophie took the Captain's chair and paused there for a second, She could now feel the true weight of responsibility bearing down upon her shoulders and could feel an anxiety attack attempting to grow within her, clenching her fists she thought *Not now. Not ever again.* Jamie asked, "Are you, alright Captain?" Finally banishing her demons for the last time, she answered: "Sorry Jamie I was miles away: when your ready, take us out."

Sophie could almost feel the tension on the bridge as she noticed that the com system chatter was gradually being replaced by silence. With a row of green lights facing him, Jamie felt his adrenaline rise and turned to face his Captain, with a wink from Sophie he activated the thrusters. With a massive surge forward he engaged the main engine and the freighter hurtled down the launch rail. Leaving the flaming support pads behind, the freighter blasted out of the tunnel and headed skyward.

Adjusting the angle of ascent Jamie guided the vessel over Montpelier. Holly had navigated a course away from the planet avoiding the busiest flight paths. Having put their faith in Sophie, the crew now felt confident that they were finally on their way. Climbing at five thousand feet per second the freighter rattled and groaned like an angry beast as Jamie made a slight course correction and passed an A380 at 30,000 feet. At sixty thousand feet he watched the curvature of the Earth disappear as he responded to coordinates fed to his console by Holly. Adjusting the power settings, Jamie calmed the beast as the rattles and groans disappeared. They were now accelerating at a constantly quickening rate and approaching the Moon. Soon it would serve as a dockyard, as it was the place where the cruiser was to be built, and where the raw materials were to be processed. Simon curiously monitored it as they passed.

His curiosity regarding the moon landings was soon satisfied as he monitored a great deal of space junk scattered at certain locations. He also noticed a flashing light on the panel and asked Sophie to take a look; curious about what he'd found, she went over to him. She could see that someone was monitoring them too and said: "It could be the Russians or the Chinese; it's something we can look into on the way home."

*

With the Moon far behind them, their speed was now at one hundred and twenty thousand miles per second and, according to the Touscal database, time to enter hyperspace. The engineering crew were now called on to create a hyperspace pocket around the vessel. Once the pocket had been achieved, Dieter gave the go ahead for Jamie to proceed. Jamie responded with the flight adjustments; and like a hand slipping into a glove, the ship entered hyperspace for the first time. Jamie then engaged the hyperdrive and automatic navigation systems and with everything running at one hundred percent and the vessel accelerating at incredible speed, the bridge crew could now take a break for a while. With handshakes and hugs, the crew celebrated the small success they had achieved that day but knew a greater challenge still lay ahead of them. Sophie took Simon's arm and started to walk towards the centre of the vessel. He told her, "You know I'm here for you; just ask me anything and you can consider it done." Sophie smiled and thanked him. He felt like he had been reborn and said to her, "You seem like Einstein with great boobs. How's all this possible?"

Sophie put Simon in the picture while they strolled around the freighter, and started to introduce him to the other members of the crew, the first being Dieter, who was studying the schematics of the proposed antimatter engine together with Professor Sarah Neilson. This was something that interested Simon as his engineering mind went into overdrive. Dieter sensed that Sophie's choice for the first officer was well justified as Simon seemed to grasp everything that he told him about the new engine. On leaving Engineering, Simon could see that the freighter was a long way from being finished; he could see a group of twenty struggling to reinforce the storage areas.

Rolling up his sleeves, he went over to them and lent a hand. Sophie knew that he could soon become popular with the crew, even though he was new to the project, and was confident that his winning ways with people would make him friends in every department.

As the days rolled by Simon became more adept at his responsibilities as the first officer and had taken several watches on the bridge while the crew slept. He was familiar with most of the systems on the vessel and was currently receiving a crash course in deep space navigation, combat and diplomacy from Sophie, although she knew he didn't really need the last one. They were two weeks into the mission. Sleeping in hammocks and eating ration packs was beginning to take its toll.

On the fifteenth day, they had arrived, as the ship dropped out of hyperspace. There it was in the distance: Perness. It had a beautiful blue aura around it. The bridge quickly filled up with most of the crew trying to get a peek at it. Jamie looked up from the console and alerted the Captain, "It seems we're not alone." Leaning over his shoulder Sophie scanned the other vessel and loaded its signature into the system. The Touscal database had listed it as a Breeche scout ship. Quickly altering course, she brought the freighter into the shadow of a small asteroid. Without weapons, defence shielding, and combat experience, Sophie announced that this was to be a stealth mission.

Sarah Neilson, known now simply as, "The Prof", was to be in control of the antimatter harvesting. During the journey, she and Sophie had completed the containment device and both women just hoped that the effect of the gas would keep the antimatter stable until it was within the confines of the containment chamber. The two women would have to collect the antimatter with as much stealth as possible if they were not to be noticed by the Breeche. Simon would remain on board, suited up and on standby.

Jamie edged the freighter forward towards the asteroid, keeping it in the shadows he knew that the last thing they needed now was a confrontation with the Breeche. Sophie and the Prof were fitted out with environment suits that Sophie had fashioned; they were tough with fusion reactor driven motors. On exiting the airlock the Prof tested the motors and got it totally wrong. She had underestimated the strength of the thrusters and was heading straight for the Breeche; Sophie went after her. By this time the Prof was getting the hang of it. She could see two Breeche, and they had seen her. They looked as if they were collecting antimatter too. They drew their weapons. So logically, well, logically to the Prof, she flew straight at them. With an almighty crash, she hit both of them. Their suits seem to fly apart as they were smashed against the hull of the Breeche vessel. A third Breeche looked out of the window. The Prof went for the airlock and Sophie followed entering the airlock the Prof equalised the pressure and the door slid open. A view of the Prof's backside and a blast of the thrusters blew the third Breeche across the room, stunning her.

The vessel seemed to have an oxygen-nitrogen atmosphere. Taking their helmets off, Sophie gave the

Prof last prize for stealth, and said, "You must have been absolutely rubbish at hide and seek." The Prof queried, "Hide and what?" Rolling the third Breeche over, the Prof commented, "She's very good looking for an alien; are those fangs in her mouth?" Sophie lifted her top lip and said, "She's Breeche alright."

The Breeche vessel was a fully armed medium range scout ship. Sophie felt that it might be a valuable asset in the coming conflict, and as there was nothing else to do with the Breeche female, she decided to take her with them. One of the languages that was uploaded into Sophie's head was Breeche and, on closer inspection of the ship's computer, she uncovered a disturbing piece of information stating that the invasion of Mylin would commence within the next five months.

The Prof had stepped back into the airlock with the antimatter container. Leaving the Breeche vessel she closed in on the blue plume surrounding Perness. When she was close enough, she activated the chambers containment field and pushed it towards the plume on a rigid extended leash, carefully she released the door. The head-up display in her helmet notified her when the container was full. Gently she withdrew the leash and headed for the scout ship, which was slowly drifting towards the freighter.

Once on board the freighter, Sophie gave the go-head for the raw materials to be collected from the surface of Perness. The ore lay in the southern hemisphere where there seemed to be an absence of gas and antimatter. As most of the business of the day had been dealt with it was time to have a word with the Breeche female. She was now awake and sitting in the corner of the scout ships bridge. With a sudden lunge forward, she flew at Sophie with a curved blade. Instantly disarming her Sophie grabbed her by the neck. It was the first time that Sophie had ever had to defend herself from anything in her life and was just happy that her reflexes were as sharp as the knife that the Breeche female had been wielding. Pushing the Breeche female backwards she demanded information about the pending attack on Mylin.

By now Simon and Holly had joined the Prof in the hold and could hear Sophie's voice from the scout ship. She was shouting in a strange language. With a crash, the Breeche female came tumbling through the hatch with Sophie right behind her. The Prof told Simon, "Do not interfere." All three stood there as Sophie went head-to-head with the Breeche female. Sophie found her adversary a worthy opponent as she found herself being thrown across the hold floor and quickly realised that her overconfidence was a mistake. The Breeche female grabbed her by one leg and started spinning her round. Sophie closed her eyes until the Breeche released her; taking advantage of the female's dizzy state, she picked herself up and grabbed her around the neck. Struggle as the Breeche female might, Sophie wasn't letting go and tightened her grip on her neck, after a few seconds she patted Sophie's leg: the Breeche female was done.

Locking her up in the freighters brig, Sophie decided to try and question her again later. The hold was now fully loaded with ore and a Breeche scout ship, with the hatches sealed, the freighter was ready to depart. So far out, Jamie was having trouble with locating home as the freighter's star chart database was acting up. Dieter came over the com system asking him, "What's the hold up?" Jamie felt a compulsion to just go, but common sense prevailed, and a NASA technician was summoned to the bridge. Her name was Luma Tyrol, a young curvaceous beauty with a brain to match. She had brought star charts on paper with her. As they studied the charts Jamie's mind kept drifting. Luma tried explaining it to him, but her beauty had left him distracted. Noticing his vacant face she said, "Will you stop ogling my boobs!" and explained it again, very slowly. After a few minutes concentration from Jamie, they were finally off. Luma sat with Jamie for a couple of hours. They talked and laughed; Jamie felt a little less stupid, and Luma had a pretty fair idea about how he felt about her.

In the hold, Dieter and Sophie were going through the manifest. They had collected several different types of ore that were necessary to smelt into alloys needed for the cruiser. Sophie asked Dieter a little about his past. He talked about his early life in Hanover Germany, his university days, and old girlfriends. Sophie felt a little embarrassed about her humble beginnings as they all seemed a little lacklustre compared to his life. She made her excuses and left leaving Dieter a little confused about her unwillingness to talk about her past.

Dr Phull was using the sick bay to its full extent, not because there was an epidemic, but because two weeks of staring out of a window into blackness had made him a little stir crazy. Everyone was in peak physical condition, basically because he was performing medical scans on all of the crew and running a zero gravity gym class twice a day in the aft section of the freighter. It was a relief for everyone on board when Jamie announced that they were about to leave hyperspace.

The Breeche captive was still not talking, despite Sophie's regular visits. Sophie wanted to know what they were up against. She had tried compassion, terror, and intimidation, but all that she had found out was that her name was Triez and she was born on Kai, captured by the Breeche, and conscripted into the armed forces. She had no special place in her heart for the Breeche as they had slaughtered her family. Sophie had a pretty good idea that there was no love lost between her and the Breeche, and knew that this may work to her advantage. With a sudden jerk, the freighter jumped out of hyperspace. Holly tried to contact the complex, but with no success. She advised Simon of the situation. Sophie was just entering the bridge as they came within range. She asked Simon to take the Captain's chair and told him to back the ship away from the planet. Now being out of range to use her implant, she made her way to the teleport room, where she asked the technician to send her to the complex. As she materialised, she could see soldiers and they had seen her too. Quickly, she flitted to the other side of the complex. Hiding behind a wooden crate, she observed that the army was starting to move some of the equipment out of the complex via the launch tunnel.

The blast doors had been smashed, as well as vital equipment. She could only think that it was the same old story of *ignorance and greed*. She now believed that the human race had sealed their own fate. Pure anger overwhelmed Sophie. She stepped out from behind the crate and asked loudly, "Which one of you assholes is responsible for this outrage?" A row of guns pointed towards her. Scanning the group, she soon found the four-star target.

She tried to interact with the ghost; nothing for a second, and then it appeared, greeting her as "Ms No Pants". She explained the situation and made a request, "Distract the soldiers and stop calling me Ms No Pants." The ghost asked, "How do I distract them?" She suggested singing or dancing. The ghost answered, "I've got no feet for dancing!" She replied, "Well, sing then!"

The ghost manifested itself in front of the main group of soldiers. It was monitoring a local radio station and gave its rendition of 'Tutti frutti'. Sophie thought the ghost's version sounded truly awful, but it did distract the soldiers long enough for her to get to the General. She grabbed his arm and called Simon asking him to approach Earth and teleport two persons directly into the captive Kai's cell. Two minutes later Simon teleported them both to the captive Kai's holding cell on board the freighter. Sophie told the General that the Kai female was really pissed off and pushed him against her. With an almighty punch, the General flew across the cell and landed in the opposite corner. In the Kai' s own language Sophie told her this is your executioner. The General just sat there confused, as the Kai approached him. Sophie warned him of the impending danger he was facing, and asked, "Who betrayed us?" Grim-faced, he said nothing. Sophie backed off and the Kai resumed. Picking him up by the scruff of his neck, her hand went around his throat and the Kai said in her own language, "Execute me, this maggot." Laughing she lifted him off the floor. Her gums receded to expose two small white fangs. At this point, the General waved his arms about furiously. Sophie gently touched the Kai female's arm and she put him down. The Kai stood back away from Sophie and rolled her shoulders, she seemed to relax a little and sat on the bed without uttering a word. Sophie told her in her own language, "If you behave I'll let you out off here" Standing there with raised eyebrows she waited for an answer... "Well?" The Kai gave a weak smile and said, "OK." She could see an understanding between them was starting to take place, Sophie opened the door and all three stepped out of the cell.

It was late afternoon and time to take the freighter down onto the Moon's surface. Sophie took the helm this time, with Jamie as co-pilot. The low gravity of the Moon was something he'd not experienced before and he watched Sophie like a hawk. However, she felt as if it was something she had done a thousand times before and, with the slightest bump the freighter landed.

With an hour of freedom behind her, the Kai, Triez offered to help in some way and made it known to Sophie that she had some experience of logistics and offered to help unload the ship. Agreeing to Triez's request she gave her a translator and within a couple of hours, she was conversing with some of the crew. At this point, Triez was starting to understand that humanity was a great deal more fun to be around than the Breeche.

Still angry with the General, Sophie made her way to the surgery, where he was receiving treatment for minor injuries. She told the him that he would need something far more substantial than a plaster when the Breeche arrived. Regarding Sophie's question as to who had betrayed them, he said without reservation, "Cameron Porter: he told us about your group." Sophie wasn't surprised that it was him and asked the General what his reasons were. The General said he agreed with Cameron: that the technology, the massive leap forward, and the fate of the planet, should be the concern of everyone, not just a handful of do-gooders. Sophie congratulated him for letting the shit hit the fan as her plan had been considerably compromised. She explained, "I don't even know if we can defend ourselves, let alone the Mylin and Touscal."

A call came over the com system in sickbay for Sophie. It was Simon on the bridge; he told her, "We're being monitored again." Sophie wondered who could be up there besides themselves. She told Holly and Simon to get suited up as they were going for a ride. Sophie activated one of the diggers from the hold; climbing aboard it, all three-homed in on the signal. After eight miles it stopped; Sophie programmed the digger to locate the source of the signal. Dismounting the machine, it disappeared into the ground. It churned out moon dust everywhere until it detected metal and stopped. Using the remote X-ray on the digger they could see that it was a tunnel of sorts and prepared to enter it. All three held hands and Sophie teleported them inside.

There was plenty of air in the tunnel, with no dangerous pathogens present. Removing their helmets, Simon took the lead. After a few metres, he noticed that there was a room with equipment that could be computers or possibly scanners. There were no dials, switches or levers of any kind. Moving on down the tunnel Sophie said, "I hope they're not too hideous, with six heads or something worse," and just hoped that the occupants might be friendly for a change. Leading off that tunnel was a short tunnel which took them to a larger chamber. As they entered it they couldn't believe their eyes. They were looking at a grey disc-shaped object that Sophie assumed was a vessel of sorts. Within a second all three felt a sharp pain in their heads and collapsed in agony. Simon and Holly couldn't move a muscle, but Sophie just about managed to put up a barrier.

Still hurting, she stood up and noticed three brown creatures approaching from the doorway. Grabbing her legs they dragged her through a longer tunnel, and into to a room at the end. At the centre of the room was a large table. They struggled to put her on the table but Sophie decided to fight back; they were pretty strong but no match for her enhanced body.

As she fought back, two of them hit an illuminated wall, smashing some of the filaments. The other stopped as if it had been chastised. Stepping into the room were two grey humanoid-looking hairless beings with large black eyes and white clothing. Telepathically they asked her who she was. She told them why she was there, after a little more telepathic conversation, they released Simon and Holly and had them brought to the chamber.

The grey humanoid-looking beings seemed very interested in what Sophie had to say as she warned them that the Breeche would be a threat to them too. She couldn't help but feel that they knew more than they were letting on and seemed emotionally detached, as they didn't seem to react to anything that she had to say. However, they did have knowledge of the Breeche, the Touscal, the Mylin, and much farther distant civilisations across the galaxy.

She felt they were hiding something or there was something that they didn't want her to know. She asked them about the brown creatures that had tried to attack her. They called them *trained dogs* and apologized to her. She thought *I haven't seen dogs like that before, at least not in this millennium.* She asked them about their home world and civilization but they just seemed to clam up as if there was a dark secret that humanity was better off not knowing. She was beginning to have her suspicions about who they really were, but felt that she should keep it under her hat until she had more information.

CHAPTER 3

By this time Sophie had worked out that the grey beings were the same ones that had been abducting people for years, thus making the conspiracy theorists correct. She asked them why they had been abducting people. They replied that it was because they had become sterile, and as a race, they were dying. They needed to test humans in order to find a solution for their own problem. But Sophie felt that they were still holding something back and thought *Why test humans, there has to be some kind of link between them and us. But what is it?* At her request, they agreed to another meeting to discuss the Breeche problem, and all three returned to the freighter.

The General was now getting impatient. The Prof had been boring him to death with chit chat about sub-nuclear particles, antimatter reactor theory, and the price of beer in England! Entering the freighter's makeshift lounge, Sophie sat down opposite the General and asked for the complex to be given back. He apologised but said it was out of his hands, as there were greater powers than him in control. However, he said he had a few questions for her. Frustrated, she grabbed him by the arm and teleported them both back to the complex. Holding the General as a shield against his own soldiers, she summoned the ghost and asked it whether it was possible to teleport everything at the complex to the moon. It advised her that it was possible, except for the teleport itself. She ordered it to do just that. Thousands of tonnes of machinery and computers started to vanish from the complex. As the last item disappeared, so did the ghost. Sophie backed up to the teleport and released the General. Switching the teleport to overload, she shouted at the soldiers, "You've got thirty seconds to get out of here!" The teleport had one last job – to take her back to the freighter.

The next morning Sophie rallied the troops. Triez, the ghost and the Prof joined her in Engineering. She announced that they would have to build a new teleport system. Triez suggested, "We should build it based on Breeche technology as they used an out-of-phase system too, but with one difference, anyone can use it." Sophie liked that idea and started drawing the plans. The ghost offered to help her with the changes but told her that there was a more serious problem. It told her that the equipment from the complex was still sitting on the surface of the moon and with the extreme temperature changes on the surface, some of the components may be compromised.

It said, "Asking the Greys for storage space seems to be the best idea, but without a working teleport there's was no way of accessing their facility." Taking matters into their own hands, Luma and the ghost searched through the equipment on the surface for the parts necessary to fabricate the teleport. With a flash, the ghost disappeared! Luma reported to Sophie that the ghost had just vanished.

The Prof was monitoring the temperature on their part of the moon when Luma called in. It was far too hot for the ghost's control unit to function properly. Jamie was quick off the mark at offering to help Luma and understanding the gravity of the situation she willingly accepted. Once they had found the ghost's main control unit, they loaded it onto the back of a digger and transported it to the loading bay of the freighter. Placing a fan next to it they waited for a few moments as the ghost slowly came back online. At that moment Simon arrived at the loading bay. He asked the ghost if it could access the Greys' computer system without being detected. The ghost responded by suppressing its imaging system and assured Simon that its electrical system was shielded too, making it undetectable to the Greys. Simon told the ghost that Sophie suspected that the Greys were hiding something and she was eager to know what it was. With no way of entering the grey's facility, the ghost told him that it would have to wait until a working teleport was back online.

On the surface of the moon, it had only taken a short time for Big Tom and his clan to master their thruster suits. They had unpacked the construction jig and resized it to accommodate the cruiser, and this was all done within two days. Tom knew that it was the moon's low gravity that had made light work of the task and pushed them so far ahead of schedule. But it wasn't just easier it was also a great deal more fun and it wasn't long before the jig was sitting on the surface along with a pair of Moon-ball goal posts.

Over a period of three days, Sophie and Triez had made good progress with the teleport. After finishing the arrival pad, Triez offered to test it and confidently stood on it. Sophie set the destination and engaged the system. Triez arrived on the bridge of her own vessel and could see that the hold door was wide open.

After a few minutes, she asked Sophie to take her back; Sophie was relieved. Triez asked, "Why my ship? And why was the hold door open?" Sophie replied, "I want to know where your loyalties lie." Triez sat down and asked Sophie to join her. She explained that she had no wish to see another world fall to the Breeche. She was Kai and had no love for their kind whatsoever, She made Sophie aware that she wouldn't rest until she had freed her people from servitude and destroyed the Breeche killing machine that had taken so many lives.

She thanked Sophie for being civil, patient, and having shown her friendship: qualities that had been lost on her home world since the Breeche arrived. She knew of the prophecy from Touscal, and so did many of her own people. Sophie stopped her there and asked, "What prophecy?" Triez said, "The Touscal are under the impression that humans are a race of people mentioned on a tablet on their home-world. The tablet tells of a race of people that are destined to end all strife in the Galaxy and beyond." She also knew that if Sophie made a stand against the Breeche, many of her own people would join her. This was what Sophie wanted to hear and asked Triez if she would be willing to help. Triez swore that when it was time, she would be there for her, and added: "I'm beginning to think that the tablet on Touscal may be a guide for all of us to follow."

At the next meeting with the Greys, Sophie found them very obliging and gave her the space she needed, but made a slight wheezing noise at the sight of Triez. Sophie assured them that they were absolutely safe as she was now a friend. Sophie was surprised when she heard that the Greys had teleported all of the equipment to its new location. It seemed to her that they were a little too eager for the work to begin on the cruiser. On entering the new facility she found it was fully operational with fusion generators on standby for every machine, computer, and robot.

Within a day the smart tool-design computer that Sophie had designed as well as the advanced software, was excelling at configuring the bulkhead structures. The new stronger alloys that had been harvested from Perness were ideal for the cruiser's sub-assembly. But one problem remained, the project had lost two hundred and fifty technicians, some of them highly specialised and irreplaceable; this was a serious problem.

Taking a break Sophie went to see Dr Phull in the medical centre, nervously approaching him she said, "I want you to take Triez shopping. He protested that he was a Quack, not a personal shopper. She explained that wearing all that combat gear made Triez look like a real psycho and was frightening the crap out of the Greys. The Doctor asked, "Do they have names like us?" She replied that they did, but people would have trouble pronouncing them, and explained that she just called them Charlie One, Charlie Two, etcetera. She told him, "We need food too for the crew, and as you know more about nutrition than anyone else on board you're the man for the job." Sophie had some tags for them. She told the Doctor, "Place them on the food and I'll teleport the goods to the Moon on your return journey via a relay on Triez's ship." The Doctor protested again about being a shoplifter too. Sophie explained, "We need money for certain components as we've lost a fortune, thanks to Cameron Porter."

An hour later the Doctor met Triez at the entrance to the hold, he was carrying an overcoat and a hair brush. He hadn't had any experience with aliens whatsoever and walked towards her warily. Triez stood there looking rather bold and asked him, "What's the overcoat for, do you think I look menacing?" He looked her up and down and saw that her leather trousers came with accessories, a particle weapon in a holster, a nine-inch dagger and something that looked equally lethal on her right-hand breast. He poised there for a second as if in a trance. She said, "Like what you see, doc?" He replied, "Yes! Great breasts and an arsenal full of weapons - the perfect date if you're a couple on a killing spree." Triez laughed and said, "I like you, your funny." Breathing again the Doctor was relieved; at least she had a sense of humour.

Triez was a fairly good pilot, but also did an excellent job of alerting every radar station on the Eastern seaboard. The F18s were everywhere, and if one got close enough, she would make what the Doctor figured out to be hand gestures with some sort of sexual connotation. Activating the airbrake thrusters she went from supersonic speed to 200 mph. Skipping over several treetops she activated the landing thrusters and the vessel descended straight down onto the flat roof of a square building. The Doctor, trying to get his breath back, thought that they had landed somewhere in New Jersey. After disarming her he gave her the overcoat, and de-braided her hair until she looked almost human! Disembarking from the vessel they both made for a door at the corner of the roof. Two flights down, and they were at street level.

Noticing a street sign the Doctor could see they were on Monmouth Street New Jersey. Like an excited child, Triez stopped outside a bar. Pulling at the Doctors arm she said: "I want a beer...now!" Luckily he had about a hundred dollars on his person and accompanied her inside. Two hours later, and she had won a hundred dollars on a drinking contest and had two phone numbers, though she didn't really know what to do with them! On seeing a dentist's on the other corner the Doctor said, "I know you're totally shit-faced but don't bare your fangs at any of the shop assistants or we'll both be in trouble." She agreed, but he knew that in her present condition, her word meant nothing.

On finding a supermarket the Doctor spent the first ten minutes trying to stop Triez from sampling most of the red wines and being generally abusive towards the staff. He handed her some tags and reminded her that they had a job to do. Agreeing to finally help him, they spent an hour tagging what was required and decided to head back to the vessel.

On the way out of the store, there was a TV mounted on a platform showing footage of a vessel travelling at extraordinary speed at treetop level, shrugging her shoulders Triez placed a tag on the TV and headed for Monmouth Street.

On their arrival, they became aware that there were police officers outside the building and a helicopter hovering above. Triez calmly walked towards the building but two officers stood in her way. They told her that she couldn't go in there. She slurred "Why not?" One officer answered, "I'm not allowed to disclose that information, madam." She replied, "I'm the only thing that's saving your mothers from being disembowelled by a bunch of alien psychotic bastards, you assholes!" Baring her fangs she picked the female officer up by the neck and held her out in front. Pulling out his gun the male officer told Triez to drop her; totally ignoring him she held the female tight whilst being careful not to choke her. Backing her way to the stairs, she turned the officer round and slowly ascended them. Looking more than a little concerned by now the Doctor followed.

There were two more officers next to the vessel and, as expected, both pulled out their guns. The Doctor quickly entered the vessel, while Triez held the officer as a shield and backed into the ship behind him. The Doctor could only apologise to the young female officer and told her that she would have to go with them. The young woman asked him where to. He answered, "Shopping in New York, of course." He asked what her name was she replied, "Sally Mason." The Doctor introduced himself as Dr Robert Phull from England and said that Triez was a drunken nutcase alien from Kai. Sally asked whether the Earth was in trouble. He informed her that it would be if they didn't do something to stop an alien invasion. Sally offered to help. She said, "I'm a crack shot with a pistol, but I'm not sure about a ray gun." Leaving the helicopter far behind, they arrived at Fifth Avenue. Triez had found a perfect spot that looked like a disused loading bay. After a shaky landing, all three left the vessel and went into a very expensive-looking store. The Doctor had explained the situation to Sally and trusted her not to shout for help, he had also relieved her of her gun and tucked it into the waistband of his jeans.

*

Once inside the first store he Handed out some tags to Sally, and gave the rest to Triez. With Sally in uniform, the three of them raised little suspicion and wandered around the stores at will. Not too happy about the fact that he'd robbed three stores and two extremely expensive shops, the Doctor decided that it was time to return to the vessel. This time there was no police presence, and they made a clean exit. Sally was glued to the window as the small ship left the stratosphere, she had often felt that space travel was just the stuff of dreams but now realised that she was actually living the dream. Triez slowed the ship down after seeing the International Space Station in the distance and sidled in for a closer look. She saw a face at the window and out came her breasts and the sexy hand gestures again! With a quick spin and a wave, the stoned Kai female laid in a course for the Moon. The relay on Triez's ship was buzzing away all the way back to the Moon causing the Doctor to feel as guilty as sin as he wondered just how much gear they'd stolen.

There to welcome them home in the hold was Sophie, she was looking a little astonished to see one of New Jersey's finest in uniform. The Doctor apologised and said, "Triez was totally shit-faced and just picked up anything that wasn't nailed down, including police officers." With a little explaining, Sally was welcomed to the group. On entering the main body of the freighter Sophie stopped next to the teleport room and peered around the door.

When Dr Phull noticed the amount of food and designer clothing on the pads, he tried to close the door to stop Sally from seeing it. However, Sophie had already seen it and opened the door wide. Sally agreed that supplies were necessary, but drew the line at a fifty-inch TV, six men's wrist watches, a designer wedding hat, and a six-foot pile of mixed designer clothing! Triez's excuse was that it was important not to frighten the Greys. Sophie laughed and offered to build a catwalk so that she could put a proper show on for them.

The construction of the cruiser was well underway by this time, with robots working around the clock, and the crew putting in a fourteen-hour day. In the sickbay the Doctor was trying to get to grips with the new medical equipment; the Touscal database illustrated that it was possible to replace skin almost instantly through rapid cloning. Sophie had upgraded many of the procedures for treating particle weapon damage and had added several pages of her own. Dr Phull felt a little insignificant by the experience but promised himself that he would be up to speed and oversee the installation of the new equipment into the cruiser himself. Simon was busy designing the bridge layout. Sophie had written a program which allowed very quick response times to react to incoming weapons fire, which incorporated several layouts of the bridge. Simon was doing mix and match after dry-run scenarios. There were programs and databases for everyone to work with, but one problem remained – the work was taking too long and they didn't have enough technicians.

Once the life support had been commissioned, a few cabins with doors were available. Some of the women shared, while Big Tom and his group shared a communal area with Triez and a few others near the engineering section, where it was a little warmer.

It was time for a second visit to Earth. With many of the crew living aboard the cruiser, the freighter was free to be used as a transport vehicle. It was time to coax some of the technicians back from the first complex, that's if they could find them.

Sophie picked out the people for recruiting; Holly was the first choice as she could have talked Rasputin into a vow of celibacy. She was joined by Jamie, Luma, Sally, and Triez. Triez was not an obvious choice, but with her lust for adventure and an attraction for Earth men, she might just sway a few. With her new clothes she was quite a picture; in fact, everyone involved looked like a model from a fashion magazine. Sophie gave Triez a few tags and told her to get some good material for uniforms.

Dieter and the Prof were ready to test the engine and Sophie had asked Charlie Two to join them. Although they hadn't offered them any new technology, Sophie felt that if she involved the Greys as much as possible they might let her know what they were hiding. The containment field was a work of art and Sophie was quite proud of it. The antimatter reaction chamber generated the field so, in theory, the faster they went, the stronger the containment. The Prof had mastered the intermix and injection system, and Dieter had pulled the whole thing together. There were three external pods that would carry the crew faster than any humans had travelled before. A system of fusion-controlled thrusters would take care of precise and instant manoeuvrability. Dieter powered up the system and all three pods illuminated. A powerful sounding whine told them that the reactors were efficiently transferring power to the engines. Feeling confident, the Prof activated the primary drive and thrusters and the whole vessel lurched forward on its landing gear like a giant leviathan, then shut down. As the engine died down Sophie felt that it was time to name the ship.

Charlie Two looked at Sophie – she could swear he was smiling! *He!* she thought. *He might be a she!* However – *it* – complimented her on building a fine vessel. They had avoided helping her technically, but they had supplied the complex and she was happy that they were on her side, or so she believed. In her mind, Sophie believed the Greys had met the Breeche previously and felt that it was important to them that humanity met the Breeche an equal footing.

Upon its return from the Greys' base, the ghost had little to tell Sophie about the Greys other than most of their computer network was encoded. What seemed strange to her was, of all the planets to choose from, they chose Earth to restore their DNA and, rather than approach humanity, they chose to hide away on the Moon.

CHAPTER 4

The next morning while Sophie was completing a lighting circuit in the teleport room, her attention was drawn to the noise of the cruiser's teleport activating. Materialising on the first pad stood a full-sized tobacco store Indian. Tied to its hand was a machine pistol and at its feet were men's socks and underpants. Moments later on the second pad appeared hair shampoo, deodorant and some fishing rods. As the third pad activated Sophie burst out laughing as she saw Triez with a Tag on her ear, wearing a bikini, a cowboy hat, and rigger boots whilst licking an ice cream! A name for the ship presented itself – *Crazy Horse*.

Thirty minutes later the freighter touched down next to the cruiser. Holly had managed to re- recruit eighty-five of the original freighter technicians. Sophie knew most of them as friends and was overjoyed to see them again. Now she was feeling a great deal more positive about their chances of stopping the Breeche.

The technicians soon settled into life aboard the *Crazy Horse* and, for the first time since work had commenced on the ship, a family atmosphere could be felt again. There were sixty cabins that had been partially completed; the robots had constructed the walls, but none had working doors. With an early start the next morning, the technicians set about correcting the problems, including weapon systems and environmental controls. Simon had worked out the optimum layout for the bridge and, with Sophie's agreement, the work pushed ahead at an accelerated rate. The *Crazy Horse* was now an imposing sight on the surface of the moon; it measured five hundred feet long and thirty feet wide. The engine pods glowed permanently as they provided heat and power to all of the on-board systems.

A daily flight to Earth was now established, with a permanent relay positioned mid-way between the moon and the Earth. A teleport had been installed onto the freighter, as well as heavy shielding, up-rated engines and photon weapons. Sally was now spending most of her time down on Earth tagging anything that she felt would be necessary for the mission, such as mattresses, medical supplies, and a host of other essentials.

Four and a half months had passed since Sophie had discovered the plans regarding the assault on Mylin. And, with the *Crazy Horse* having been finished for over a week, it wouldn't be long before the vessel entered the theatre of war. It was now fully armed, fully stocked, and had a competent fully trained crew.

Hand-to-hand combat training had been the order of the day, and many of the crew, who were expected to see physical combat had been physically enhanced. Jamie and Luma were now an item, and with a war with the Breeche now on the horizon, there was uncertainty about how long they would have together before they had to face the possibility that one of them may be lost to that war. Like many of the crew they felt the need to explore their relationship while there was still time and spent as much time together as they possibly could.

After the uniforms were dispatched, the crew acknowledged the call to arms and knew they would be leaving soon. It was 10.00 am Tuesday 16th September when Simon made the announcement to detach all umbilical connections with the surface as it was time for space trials.

Sitting at the pilot's station, Jamie adjusted his seat and engaged the thrusters. From the Captain's chair, Sophie felt the true strength of the vessel, as an enormous blast of power thrust the *Crazy Horse* upward. With the vessel accelerating and rapidly turning, it was just possible to see the launch dock disappear below a huge cloud of moon dust. Levelling the ship out, Jamie increased the speed while Holly forwarded the flight plan to him: it was Perness.

For Jamie, it was a disturbing reminder of where they had first met the Breeche. Reclining his seat a little he relaxed in the knowledge that this would be a much shorter journey than the last time he had travelled there. Leaning forward, he increased speed and allowed the ship to glide into hyperspace.

One hour had passed and, exactly on time, the ship dropped out of hyperspace. There before them was Perness, as beautiful as ever and still adorning its blue haze. At that moment Triez entered the bridge. Sophie reminded her that this was where they'd first met and asked her if she missed home. She said, "I miss the bars, Brooklyn Bridge, and the chilli dogs. Looking confused, Sophie said, "I meant Kai." Triez told her, "Not much, compared to Brooklyn, and I'm pretty sure I wouldn't have made lieutenant there either." She thanked Sophie for her trust and friendship and told her, "Yes... Brooklyn every time." Sophie thought, *Well, the uniform seems to suit her, and apparently, so does the lifestyle.*

Not one to waste an opportunity, the Prof volunteered to collect some antimatter in a containment chamber. She had also found rare metals mixed with the last batch of ore from Perness that she believed if smelted together would make excellent alloys for particle weapons. The Prof felt fairly confident that she could increase the yield of their existing side arms by at least fifty percent if she was given time.

While on the moon the Prof had re-designed the thruster suits to give ten minutes of phase shifting. This was linked to the teleport, and she hoped would help prevent triggering an antimatter explosion. Sally, excited but in a terrifyingly fun sort of way, offered to go to Perness with the Prof.

Operating the teleport Simon placed the Prof and Sally right in the middle of an area where the blue plume seemed even more beautiful than before. The Prof felt relieved as the phase shifter seemed to be working extremely well and was shifting them both in and out of phase and halving the risk of a huge explosion.

Back on the *Crazy Horse* Simon was carefully monitoring the system and doing a balancing act with the teleport. He estimated that they had eight minutes left before they automatically returned to normal.

Out of the blue, a warning siren sounded; the shielding activated, and a sudden shockwave travelled through the ship. Jamie tracked the attacking vessel as it travelled in an arc. Leaning over his shoulder Triez told Sophie, "It's a Breeche cruiser, Captain. If you want to test the *Crazy Horse's* metal, then this is the ship to do it." Holly kept trying to contact the cruiser but it was a dead channel. Triez told her, "These bastards don't talk, they just fight."

Completing the arc, the cruiser closed in again and fired a shot. This time it made a direct hit to midships as it passed. Simon called the bridge informing the Captain that two relays had just blown out and that if they lost another, they would lose the Prof and Sally too. Sophie gave the order to retrieve them as soon as the phase shifter stopped running, and gave the command "Bring the photon cannons on-line and target that ship."

Luma was sitting in for Sally at the weapons console. She had done virtually no combat training beforehand and was shaking like a leaf. Sophie could see this but knew that, just like everyone else on board, it was now time for Luma to face her own personal demons. Jamie manoeuvred the *Crazy Horse* towards the Breeche vessel and made a pass. Luma fired the cannons but completely missed the cruiser. Jamie activated the rear thrusters at full power and brought the ship about. Luckily the Breeche return shot was wide of the *Crazy horse*, narrowly missing them. They were now directly behind the Breeche ship. Sophie said nothing as this was Luma's time.

Tensed to the limit, Luma targeted all forward weapons on the cruiser as Jamie accelerated the vessel to combat speed. With renewed enthusiasm and a stern look on her face, Luma hit the fire buttons screaming, "TAKE **THAT**, YOU BASTARDS!" Triez detected an orange flash and a mass of debris spraying out from the aft section of the Breeche cruiser as Jamie pulled the vessel hard to port. She was pretty confident that Luma had done a thorough job on the Breeche and gave her a pat on the back.

Now the Prof and Sally were back on board, the atmosphere was jubilant. Luma was the toast of the vessel and received a round of applause from the bridge crew as Jamie took the ship out of the battle zone.

Sophie was pleased that she had said nothing, and was proud that Luma had found her inner strength and vindicated herself. Triez informed Sophie that since the colour of the flash was orange, the main drive was out and therefore they would not have been able to continue the engagement.

As the *Crazy Horse* approached the Moon the Prof was in the hold checking the quality of the ore that had been teleported aboard. It was everywhere including much of the shuttle bay. Simon and Triez joined her asking if they could be of any help. While Simon was filling a sample bag for the Prof, Triez started sweeping the ore from her scout ship, which was half buried. Looking a little guilty, the Prof promised to help her clean it off once they were back on the Moon. Triez asked, "How far will the ore go?" The Prof told her "There's enough ore to build a small squadron of fighters and an ample amount for the construction of side arms once smelted." Triez pointed out, "I think we're going to need them after today's skirmish."

*

By 8.30 pm there was a party atmosphere on the moon that evening. With Triez acting as host, it was like a bootleggers' convention, with champagne, wine, beer, and spirits aplenty. Sally's halo had slipped somewhat recently as she had been robbing liquor stores in a serious way!

Dancing with Dieter, Triez was getting dirty and was all over him like a blanket. She had a liking for Earth music, and the more grungy the better. On her home world, the Breeche had almost eradicated music, so now she was making up for lost time. Sophie gave Triez a hand up after Dieter had escaped her advances and left her in a pile on the floor. Sophie poured herself a drink and asked Triez if she was happy about how the day had gone. Triez had learned quite a lot of English and made an attempt to speak without the translator. "Yes, we stuck it to their ass, no?" To which Sophie replied, "Yes we certainly did!" and turned on her translator again.

Now that Triez could be understood again, she gave a warning to Sophie. She told her, "After today's confrontation with the Breeche they'll come to Earth sooner. We should go to Touscal and Mylin as soon as possible to drum up support, but we daren't leave Earth undefended." Her warning had given Sophie something to think about.

The next day Sophie called a meeting with the Prof, Simon, Holly, and Dr Phull. She made it clear that the Breeche threat would soon be upon them. The meeting lasted for two hours, and what was resolved changed the order of things: Simon was no longer the first officer aboard the *Crazy Horse*. His role would now be to take charge of the base on the moon, oversee the construction of defence fighters, and protect the Earth at all costs. The Prof would be at his side setting up a defence network. Sally had learned quickly and was now an accomplished pilot, but she would now have a new challenge. Although the freighter was well armed and protected by an efficient shield system, it was too slow for a quick response. Sally would now have to train as a fighter pilot together with Simon and be responsible for training a full squadron made up of twenty-five technicians.

Triez was to become the first officer on the *Crazy Horse*; her knowledge would be crucial in the fight against the Breeche. As Luma Tyrol was the first crew member to engage an enemy in battle and win, she was a natural choice for weapons officer. Dieter Schreiber would remain chief engineer with a staff of fifteen. Dr Phull would help with a medical training program, both on the ship and with the Earth defence crews via a hyperlink, and would have a staff of five. Finally, Holly Farley had shown so much talent for navigation that she would share a post with Jamie – they would work as a team, both having pilot and navigation skills.

Two weeks later and the fighters were already under construction. The hold on the *Crazy Horse* was full of fuselages, engines and spare parts. The five fighters to be built specifically for the *Crazy Horse* would have to be assembled en route. Triez had been setting up a serious weapon that was so powerful and unstable that, once primed, it would probably destroy the host vessel as well as the enemy. Sophie questioned its usefulness, Triez said: "If necessary it will serve as a doomsday weapon." Scratching her head, Sophie said, "Okay!"

It was launch day, and everyone that had been reappointed was now in their respected positions. Sophie kissed Simon goodbye and said she hoped that she'd see him again soon. He comforted her by saying "Given the choice, I wouldn't change a thing, and I've got a feeling the best is yet to come." With a wave, Dieter's polished engines burst into life: next stop Touscal!

Two hours into the journey, Sophie walked across the bridge to Triez who was with the ghost. They were speaking in English, with the ghost standing in as a tutor. It was using everyday phrases such as "How are you? Do you come here often?" to which Triez replied with a finger. "You hitting on me? You dumb mother." The ghost told Sophie that apparently, Triez had been teaching herself English by watching the fifty-inch TV and gangster DVDs.

Switching on Triez's translator, Sophie expressed how reliant she would be on her over the coming period. Triez responded by telling her that she would support her Captain even if it meant losing her own life. Sophie felt that the time and effort that she had spent to befriend this strange alien was well spent and told her.

"Well, let's hope it doesn't come to that!"

It was the second day in hyperspace and Holly was standing in for Jamie at the pilot's station. She was familiarising herself with some of the bridge controls when a distress call came in. On the short distance scanner was a vessel about one light year ahead of them. Pressing the general alarm she brought the bridge to alert status. She could see that the vessel she was tracking was small and slow, reducing the power to the engines she took the *Crazy Horse* in for a closer look. With the ship now standing off the port side, Holly tried to contact the small vessel; over the com system came a distressed voice requesting help with casualties and system failures.

Holly alerted the Doctor to the teleport room as well as an engineering crew. Jamie returned to relieve her, thanking him she made her way to the teleport room also. Once aboard, she opened a visual link to Sophie. They were humanoid, with slight differences to the ears and nose; Holly said: "I think they're from Mylin Captain." Sophie asked her to stabilise the situation, bring them aboard, and dock their vessel in the hold.

The Mylin skipper was escorted to the Captain's chamber where Sophie, Triez, and Holly were waiting. On entering, he sat down and thanked Sophie for her help. She offered her condolences for the loss of some of his crew members. He stated, "You're human. Sophie acknowledged that she was human, and told him they were en route to Touscal.

She added that her name was Captain Sophie Schultz and asked what had happened to his vessel. He told her it had been attacked by the Breeche, for no apparent reason. Triez assured him that it had nothing to do with her own people. He had seen a small tattoo behind her right ear when he entered the room and was aware that she was Kai. He told her, "I have many friends on Kai and know of your plight, but why are you travelling with the humans, aren't they supposed to be building an Ark?"

Sophie summoned the ghost who said, "You're wasting your time." The Mylin Captain angrily stated, "You were supposed to arrange the human exodus. What went wrong?" to which the ghost repeated, "You're wasting your time."

Sophie enlightened the Mylin Captain that the effects of brain enhancements on humans had the opposite effect that the ghost had expected and added: "You must understand that humanity would always choose to fight." He replied, "It's not that I agreed with what your doing one hundred percent, but, I did live among humans for five years in Amsterdam," and added, "I was extremely happy living there, and I can understand why you feel that Earth is worth fighting for, but what do you propose to do about the Breeche threat?" She offered to protect Mylin if they were not too late and free Triez's people from servitude. The Mylin Captain warned that the Touscal wouldn't thank her for interfering, as they were pacifists. Sophie asked where the Mylin stood on the matter. He stated that they were more flexible than the Touscal, as living on Earth had made them that way.

Sophie headed for the bridge and ordered a course change from Touscal to Mylin. Jamie engaged the main engine and fed the coordinates into the navigation computer. Powering up the engines the

Crazy Horse accelerated and shot into hyperspace at maximum speed.

Dr Phull had been keeping in touch with Simon's group over the hyperlink and was making sure that the medical staff were up to speed. He was now feeling confident that they were almost ready for anything. Contacting the Prof he found that she had detected a scout-sized vessel that had disappeared in the vicinity of Mars. She informed him that it hadn't been seen since, and could only assume that it was a prelude to invasion. She added that Simon had ensured that the fighters were ready to go and the freighter was fully armed. As a footnote, she mentioned that some of the ex-NASA team had adapted Triez's idea of a doomsday weapon and had rigged up a tether that could be trailed behind the freighter allowing it to be taken to the target under tow. They only hoped that the tether would be long enough to allow the freighter to escape in time.

On board the *Crazy Horse*, Jamie and Luma were having quality time together, making lots of noise before the big game. One of the technicians, Peter Hazelwood, was covering for Jamie. He was keen to get involved with the piloting side of the ship and was welcomed by Holly who knew that if Jamie was killed, everything would fall onto her shoulders and felt that another helping hand might be useful if Jamie was lost at the height of the battle.

On his way back to the bridge Jamie joined Sophie as she left her quarters. She took one look at him and said: "You look as if you've just run a marathon." He replied, "Aye, Captain, I like to keep fit." But blushed as Sophie remarked, "I didn't know Luma had a gym in her quarters." Arriving at the bridge she took the Captain's chair as the *Crazy Horse* closed in on Mylin, and watched a very tired Peter hand over control to Jamie who took the pilot's chair. Looking rather flushed, Luma arrived shortly afterwards and manned the weapons console. Sophie noticed that for a change Triez was sober at her station, and asked, "Signed the pledge, have we?" Triez answered, "The way you talk anyone would think I had a drinking problem." Sophie smiled and sat back in the chair.

With a slowing surge, the ship dropped out of hyperspace one hundred thousand kilometres from Mylin. As they approached, they could see something glowing on the surface. It was as if some of the cities in the Northern Hemisphere had been attacked. Holly detected a large cruiser emerging from behind Mylin's moon.

As battle stations sounded throughout the ship, Sophie commanded Jamie to spin the ship around and head for the moon. Jamie showed off his combat skills and lined the ship up at an optimum position for a first strike; that was if the Breeche vessel was exactly where Sophie had hoped it would be. Time was passing and, with no sign of the enemy, Sophie knew that they must have been seen by the Breeche on their approach. Trying to understand the Breeche Captain's game she told Jamie to take them from pole to pole. Turning the vessel Jamie winked at Luma and took the vessel up to attack speed.

As the *Crazy Horse* approached from the south, Luma could see that Sophie had been startled by something in the distance. Telling Luma to bring forward weapons to bear at thirty degrees on a wide angle , Sophie just hoped that the flicker in her eye moments earlier really was the Breeche cruiser. Taking a calculated risk, she told Luma to fire on the vessel immediately. Luma fired the photon cannons into empty space and, sure enough, hit the Breeche vessel's bridge as it came into view.

Sophie's instincts were right and, with a nod from her, Luma fired again and hit the engine, but not before the Breeche vessel had returned fire, hitting the *Crazy Horse*. With a heavy crash, the vessel had taken a shot to the bridge causing some of the systems to go off-line; smoke was billowing everywhere. As the *Crazy Horse* rolled to the left, Luma saw an opportunity and fired a shot while they were listing at forty degrees. The cannon hit the Breeche vessel directly in the belly and, with a white plume of plasma, she had taken out a section of the aft quarter of the ship.

Triez, during her combat training, had become part of a group that had sworn an allegiance to defend one another no matter what. Feeling that it was time to test the loyalty between them, Sophie asked Triez to take her group and board the Breeche vessel. Meeting at the teleport room, Triez instigated a group hug and with a nod to the technician, all five disappeared. Arriving in a corridor aboard the Breeche cruiser with her four shipmates, Triez silently pointed her hand towards the aft of the ship. Triez's group had been part of a construction team that had worked on the first complex. They were hard as nails, physically enhanced and very fond of Triez. Her favourite was Big Tom. Nobody quite knew what the relationship was, but he could drink her under the table, and that was something she could respect.

As the damage on the Breeche vessel was quite extensive, Sophie asked Triez to offer assistance to the Captain, but this was a Breeche vessel and she had other ideas.

From the doorway of the engineering department came three Breeche warriors. Taking cover behind some of the fallen wreckage they started firing particle weapons at Triez's group. One was an officer that Triez instantly recognised: he had beaten her senseless while she was serving on a Breeche cruiser. *Payback*, she thought and, in a split second, she grabbed a large piece of alloy and threw it at him, knocking him over. With a sudden charge, she grabbed him by his braids and dragged him towards what was left of the engine room.

Taking a grenade from her pocket, Triez pulled his tunic open, pulled the pin and tucked it into his trousers; then she threw him over the barrier into the fusion intermix chamber. Her crewmates had done an equally efficient job by stunning the two Breeche crewmen and locking them in a closet. On seeing Triez standing by the door with a smile on her face, Tom ordered instant transit. Immediately all five arrived back on the *Crazy Horse*.

The Breeche vessel exploded with such ferocity that it created a massive shockwave that rocked the *Crazy Horse*. Sophie arrived at the teleport room moments later and asked Triez "I can only assume that the Breeche vessel was unsalvageable?" With a nod from her, Triez said: "You're absolutely right, it was unsalvageable; we only just got away with our lives." Looking a little sheepish Tom agreed. Triez's face was awash with guilt too as she was fairly sure that Sophie knew what she and Tom had been up to. With a nod, Sophie made her way back to the bridge and smiled to herself feeling safe in the knowledge that there was indeed loyalty between the group, even if it was just Tom covering up for Triez's gung-ho approach to life.

In the distance, Holly had detected two smaller vessels heading away from the carnage. She informed Sophie on her arrival at the bridge about the situation saying, "I really don't think their crews have the stomach for a fight Captain." Sophie asked Jamie not to pursue them, which was just as well as the *Crazy Horse* needed some serious repairs. But Dieter, with all his German efficiency, had a team on the job straight away. Once power had been restored, Jamie took the ship into a high orbit around Mylin.

Sophie joined the Mylin Captain and crew in the teleport room, and together they travelled to the surface. Arriving outside the chancellery building they found it to be a hive of activity since the Breeche attack the night before. Leading the way to the chancellor's office, the Mylin Captain warned Sophie that the chancellor was a very physical man. She said, "Do you mean touchy-feely?" The Mylin Captain answered, "Yes - very!"

Finally reaching the chancellor's office Sophie knocked on the door and on hearing the chancellor's voice both of them entered. She was quite surprised as the chancellor himself gave her a hug and patted her on her backside and asked: "Who do I have the pleasure of meeting?" She told him, "Oh, let's just say I'm Sophie from Earth." He answered, "Ah thank you for assisting our vessel, I'm quite impressed, aren't you Captain?" The Mylin Captain gave an awkward smile and said: "We all are Mr chancellor." Looking a little confused the chancellor asked: "Why haven't you taken me up on my offer of building an Ark ?" Feeling frustrated at having to keep repeating herself, Sophie spoke in an assertive manner, "We've chosen to fight, and we have a powerful cruiser with us. Are you with us or not?" Again he gave her a hug, and patted her on the backside saying, "You really should have built the Ark, then at least then some of your people would be safe from the Breeche." By this time she thought he was really getting off on fondling her ass and made her excuses. With her feathers feeling slightly ruffled, Sophie left the chancellor's office with the Mylin Captain. She asked him, "Has the chancellor always been a pervert?" The Captain laughed and said, "Oh yes!"

Outside of chancellery building, Sophie looked out over the ocean and noticed that Mylin had a great deal in common with Earth. And like her own planet, it had some beautiful resorts. She was in the southern hemisphere and could feel its warm comfortable climate against her skin. Closing her eyes and looking skyward she thought *Oh my word it feels so good to have the sun on my face again.* She pondered on that thought for a moment and thought, *time to give the crew a break.* She knew this would be a fine place for some shore leave before the journey to Touscal, and remembered what the ghost had told her about Touscal's weather. It had informed her that the temperature on Touscal's surface seldom rose above zero degrees. So, it would be woollies and thick socks from then on. Opening her eyes again, she thought *but first, some sun.*

The Mylin Captain was extremely courteous as he had booked rooms for many of the crew in hotels along the beach front and was excelling at being the perfect host. Sophie asked him, "Why haven't you stood for the chancellorship position yourself? as you would have made a far superior leader than him." He answered by telling her "I know he's shallow, thoughtless and wrong about most things, but he does have one redeeming quality." Sophie asked, "Oh really what would that be?" He answered, "He's not dangerous, he keeps us safe from war. What more could a world like this want?" Sophie looked him square in the face and told him, "That kind of thinking is going to get everyone on this planet killed? It's time to wake up and smell the coffee: the Breeche are at your doorstep with a switchblade and you're waving daisies at them." Her words were harsh, and she could see from the expression on his face, that his outgoing persona had turned from a happy go lucky chap to a man with a serious problem. Sophie placed her hands on a table that separated them and leant towards him. Frowning she said, "There's an extremely large elephant in the room, and it's an elephant that you adamantly refuse to talk about." His reply was, "What's an elephant?" She answered, "It's an animal with braided hair and fangs. You know very well what I mean."

Sophie could see his concern manifest itself on his face, it was like a grey veil of depression that seemed to sadden him. She was now feeling rather guilty about ruining his day. Trying to appease him, she made a promise that three fighters would stay behind on standby while the *Crazy Horse* was at Touscal. Looking across at the sun-drenched bay, she knew there wouldn't be any shortage of volunteer's from the crew to stay behind. The Mylin Captain had grown to admire Sophie's honesty and told her, "Be careful on Touscal, some of them are not exactly who you think they are. Many of my people believe that some of them might be dangerous." Sophie kissed him on the cheek and said, "Thanks, but I already have a few suspicions of my own about who they really are and what they want from humanity."

The next day Sophie caught a rapid transit tube to the northern hemisphere with the Mylin Captain, Triez and Dieter. After a terrifying one hour journey down a steel tube at mach 3 they had arrived. Walking to the site of the attack, they could see that there were quite a few burned out buildings. The structures had been badly damaged when the Breeche had attacked two nights earlier. The buildings were mainly sited around the commercial district of the city. Triez warned the Mylin Captain that the Breeche would soon return and made him aware "They'll come in strength next time and finish the job!" As the weather was closing in, Sophie decided to return to the warmth of the south. Arriving at the southern hemisphere transit station one hour later, Triez told Sophie, "These people don't really deserve our help. They won't even acknowledge that the Breeche are a threat. They've chosen to sleep while the Breeche ready themselves for war." Sophie told her, "Watch the Mylin Captain as I think he's about to finally wake up." Needing a drink, Triez told Sophie, "After that potentially fatal trip down that tube thing we deserve a couple of very large cocktails." Sophie agreed, and they went looking for a bar.

On the beach later that afternoon Sophie asked Dieter if he was sleeping alright as he looked awful. He told her that it was mainly due to the noisy bastards next door. Triez protested that she was in the next room to him. He asked, " What have you got in there with you a gorilla?" With a grin, Sophie said, "No just Big Tom being Big Tom." Triez stated that Tom had beaten her and subjected her to all sorts of perversions for hours. She bowed her head and wept. Dieter put his arm around her, at which she burst out laughing, expressing that she had enjoyed every second of it. Reluctantly Dieter cracked a smile.

CHAPTER 5

Three days had passed and it was time to pack their bags and visit Touscal because Sophie thought it only polite to thank the people who had given them so much technology. She also needed their help against the Breeche, although after what the Mylin Captain had told her, she wasn't holding out much hope of that.

Once everyone was aboard, Holly fed in the coordinates for Touscal and Jamie took the *Crazy Horse* into hyperspace. Dr Phull was busy giving the crew inoculations based on Triez's physiology when the call came in from Simon. He reported that there was a great deal more activity on Mars at that time. As ships were arriving every day he was convinced that it would only be a matter of time before the Breeche launched their attack on Earth. Relaying the message to the Captain, Sophie felt that their mission had just gone up a notch and asked the Doctor to try and reassure Simon that they were working on a method of drawing some of the Breeche ships away from Earth.

On arrival at Touscal, they were met by a shuttle. On observing Sophie over the com system, its occupants gave her a direct instruction to follow it. Sophie asked Jamie to follow the shuttle until he was directed by the Touscal shuttle to do otherwise.

With the *Crazy Horse* in orbit, coordinates were given to the Captain and first officer to teleport to the surface. Moments after their arrival, they were greeted by a being that looked very much like the ghost. He introduced himself as Ruman and then set about accusing Sophie of jeopardising her race's future. He also accused Triez of corrupting her, referring to her as a Kai puppet of the Breeche. Sophie didn't think much of Ruman at that point and explained that she had met the Greys and didn't fancy her future much. Ruman asked her what she meant.

Staring at him with accusing eyes she told him, "You know what I mean. That's us, isn't it? Admit it. That's our future, that's what we have to look forward to, having to adapt ourselves and change our appearance to live on planets that were never meant for us." Looking sheepish, Ruman asked her, "How long have you known?" She answered, "Soon after the first meeting with the Greys – *shit* - even the dogs looked different!" She demanded, "Show me the stone tablet, its no good denying it, I know all about it from Triez, I want to see it for myself." Ruman knew he had no option but to agree to her demands and offered to take them there.

It was a pretty cold day on Touscal for venturing into the wilderness, particularly in the form of transport favoured by the Touscal. It was like a small bus without a roof and was capable of hovering on an electromagnetic field. As Ruman accelerated the vehicle, it displayed a very fast turn of speed, causing the wind chill factor to increase considerably. With the wind cutting into Sophie's face she huddled together with Triez for warmth. After twenty minutes of freezing conditions, they had arrived at a cliff face and found themselves standing on a frozen ocean. Ruman walked ahead and waved his hand indicating the way forward. Trudging through the snow they followed him for about eight hundred metres where he stopped and turned to face a stone tablet, Sophie could see that it was adorned with hieroglyphics.

Interacting with a handheld computer she made a rough translation of the stone. It read:

'Of all the species born to the blackness of space, one shall prevail: they shall become the eyes and ears of the universe, and shall serve as saviours through benevolence and understanding. Their influence will stretch far and wide in every quarter until the end of time.'

Engraved at the bottom of the stone, were the coordinates of Earth.

"What bullshit is this? It couldn't possibly refer to us as we're destined to become very grey and very sterile," Ruman told Sophie that the stone was based on her success at defeating the Breeche. Sophie asked, "And if we fail?" Ruman told her, "The greys are living proof that you've already failed as far as history's concerned." Confused, she asked him, "Then how is it possible to change history?" Ruman pointed to the stone and told her, "This object stands outside of time. It depicts the future as it finally plays out, and pointed out that there are always opportunities for changing history, as time itself is fluid and ever expanding." Sophie questioned,

"And?" He told her, "Like the stone, we stand apart from time also and, although it is against our better judgment, I have been chosen as your guide." Sophie told him, "My head's starting to hurt it's time to get back to the ship!"

On the return journey, Ruman stopped at a beautiful ice formation. He explained that it could only be seen in winter as it was formed by a regular wind that blew that way every year and always looked the same. He pulled a flask from inside his thick robe and handed it to Sophie and told her, "This will warm you." It tasted a little like very smooth brandy; she passed it on to Triez who, with her head tipped back, finished it off. As they walked beneath the ice sculpture, Ruman asked Sophie what she meant by "Bullshit" back at the tablet. She told him, "The human race isn't special. Yes, we need help and, with any luck, the Breeche attention will be more focused on Earth now. This could be advantageous to us as we won't have to defend you or the Mylin anymore." Even though being an omnipotent person and miles above Sophie on an evolutionary scale, her words had the effect of making him feel quite inadequate as a man.

Arriving back at the central government building, Sophie put it to a group of Touscal scientists that if they didn't help her combat the threat from the Breeche, Earth might be lost, and that they would be next. They flatly refused, stating, "We have given you a guide, and that's all we're prepared to do. Any hostility would have to lie in the domain of the Earth's defences." She decided that enough time had been spent there and left the building with mixed feelings about Ruman and the Touscal in general. Running after the two women Ruman stopped them and said, "I'm sorry about the reception you and Triez received in there, but there's much you don't know about my people." Triez said, "Oh you mean the Omicron order." Ruman looked startled for a moment and said, "There is a secret organisation called the Omicron order that are living amongst us. They're active on every level in our society and you're living proof of their existence, as you were supposed to deliver some of your people to safety, not fight a war at insurmountable odds. It's now obvious that your enhancement was tampered with in some way. I can only apologise and swear an oath to both of you that I will be there when you need me most." Sophie's enhanced mind told her that Ruman was only speaking in half truths and had the feeling that he was holding something back. Thanking Ruman for his concern Sophie told him, "I'll be in touch."

As they walked back to the teleport pickup site, Triez said, "So that's why your such a hard nosed kick- ass bitch!" Sophie laughed and said, "I guess so, that makes two of us." Triez said, "As one psycho speaking to another, I think we should travel to Kai as it's a far better place for recruiting help. There's a strong hatred there amongst many of my people towards our overlords on Breeche Prime."

Once they were back on board the *Crazy Horse* Sophie told Jamie, "Kai! As fast as you like." En route to Kai, Dr Phull was trying out some prosthetics on Sophie to make her look a little more like Triez. He had modelled a nose with small faint ridges at the top. Triez entered the surgery to see how it was going.

Placing a hand on Sophie's prosthetic nose she pulled it until she looked like Pinocchio. She looked at Dr Phull and said: "I'm not having Sophie with a cuter nose than me!" Grabbing a lump of prosthetic material, Sophie pushed it onto Triez's brow, calling her, "Dickhead!" Feeling that he was wasting his time, the Doctor made for the door. With a lump of rubber hanging out of her mouth, Triez mumbled, "Where are you going?" to which he replied, "For a long cold beer and some intelligent conversation."

Arriving some distance from Kai Triez told Sophie that establishing orbit around the planet was out of the question as Breeche scout ships were in evidence. Jamie had followed instructions from Triez and had stopped the ship at coordinates given to him by her. Having friends in high places was Triez's greatest asset, as she had arranged for a scout-sized vessel to rendezvous with the *Crazy Horse*. Along with Sophie, Triez was to travel to an underground meeting on Kai. If things went pear-shaped, it would be Jamie's job to get them out of there.

When the scout-sized vessel arrived at the *Crazy Horse*, it seemed similar to the one Triez was piloting when Sophie captured her. Sophie enquired whether Triez harboured any ill feeling towards her for killing the Breeche that day. She said that she didn't as they were Breeche, and said she would have killed them herself given half a chance. Triez told her, "You'll have to toughen up as it gets dangerous from here on." She suggested that if Sophie had killed Cameron Porter when she was supposed to they wouldn't be in the mess they were in that day. Sophie felt as though she had been scolded, but understood that Triez's words held some truth. However, deep down inside she knew that killing wouldn't come easily to her, no matter who they were.

Triez reminded Sophie to stand upright and not to slouch, or the game would be up before it started. She also made her aware that there would be plenty of Kai that were loyal to the Prime and would turn her in for gain. She then commented, "That nose the Doctor gave you, it's quite cute."

At first sight, Sophie thought that Kai looked a little like nineteenth-century London. She had expected a space-bearing society with spaceports and huge cities, but the scout ship had landed in a small field next to what looked like a tarmac road. Standing next to a fence at the road's edge both watched as an old rusty car approached. Stopping next to them the door opened and a voice from inside told them to get in. Very much like a car from Earth, she was surprised that as advanced as they were, they still relied on wheels. Passing through several small ramshackle villages the vehicle pulled into a car park and, with the screech of tyres, the car stopped. Without ceremony, they were escorted to a house like something out of a Charles Dickens novel. Sophie enquired why her home world was so out of date. Triez blamed the war with the Breeche as it had wasted most of their best minds and resources. Sophie asked how they had survived; Triez explained: "The Kai are braver than the Breeche and, although we love peace, we fight like demons." She accused the Breeche of being cowards that hid behind their technology and added: "We had to agree to a truce before it was too late, but we didn't really want it."

The escort took Triez's arm and led her into a large cellar where there were about twenty Kais, mainly male. A large Kai passed Sophie a drink, wary about the contents of the glass she asked Triez "What's in it?" She hinted that it was quite potent and that if she drank three of them, she'd be anybody's for the taking! Heeding Triez's advice Sophie sipped it very slowly. A Kai female approached her who had been briefed by Triez over a com-link before the meeting, and therefore knew a little about Earth. She suggested that it would be beneficial to both of their worlds if Breeche Prime disappeared off the celestial charts altogether, and confirmed that it was true that the Breeche were building up an invasion fleet on a world close to Earth. The Kai female then moved to one end of the cellar and clapped her hands. Sophie assumed that she had been talking to a big player in the game as she seemed able to command the attention of everyone there.

The Kai present at the meeting represented several different countries of the Kai home world, they were renegades and totally illegal in Breeche eyes. She spoke of betrayal by the Kai government, and an alliance with certain worlds would be desirable. She knew from Triez that the Earth Defence Directive would side with them and expressed it to the room. She spoke of rebuilding the planet and regeneration of all that was lost in wasted years of conflict.

As she came to the end of her speech, there was a crashing sound as the door flew off its hinges. The Kai speaker just stood there wide-eyed and motionless as an explosive device was thrown amongst the people at the front. It exploded with great force, killing all those that were standing near to it, including the speaker herself. Both Sophie and Triez were blown off their feet and covered with debris at the back of the room. As they struggled to climb from underneath the rubble, Sophie could see a Breeche soldier with a club; hitting her with it once he knocked her senseless.

The next thing she knew, she was lying on a stone floor in a cell; she could see Triez sitting on a bench, and felt the swelling on the side of her head. She asked, "What the hell happened?" Triez told her that they had been betrayed by the driver and that the best they could hope for now would be torture for information and then execution. Sophie asked Triez if she had any ideas about how to get out of there, but all she could come up with was, "Your nose is hanging off you know!" Pulling it off completely, Triez tried it on for size. Sophie had an idea. She suggested that she should pretend to be ill and attack the guard as he entered the cell. Triez pulled off the nose and said: "They'll probably scan you, and know that your play-acting."

Sophie assumed that Triez's fangs weren't deadly, which gave her an idea for another plan. Looking confident she asked Triez to bite her. Looking confused at Sophie's request she wrinkled her nose and said, "Okay." Like a badly acted vampire movie, Triez leant over, exposed her fangs and bit her on the neck. Feeling only the slightest twinge Sophie asked, "Is that it?" Triez informed her that she only ever used the tips, like needles. She explained that similar to baboons on Earth, they were mainly just for show.

She then asked Sophie how she was feeling. She replied, "I don't feel ill, just extremely horny." With a smile, Triez said, "I'm not surprised." Sophie asked, "Exactly what sort of poison do you have in those fangs of yours?" Triez pointed out "It's not poison, they're pheromones, and extremely strong ones. We use them for mating," laughing she asked, "You are going to screw the guard aren't you?" Feeling her hormones exploding Sophie groaned, "Oh shit....No, well…er... I don't know." Breaking into a sweat she began to pace the cell like a wild animal. Mumbling under her breath *Bloody Baboons.* Looking at Triez, she thought *There's a big one sitting on that bench over there.* Trying not to look amused, Triez put her hand over her mouth, but couldn't stop herself from laughing as she found it totally hilarious.

Sophie hammered on the door and after some choice language, a young Kai answered; by now she was completely overcome by the pheromones and threw her arms around his neck, reeling him in! She tore at his clothing, and, after a loud cheer from Triez, she threw him against the wall, and all hell broke out. He was no match for her enhanced body, as she used it as a tool to satisfy a burning that she had never felt before. Ten minutes later and the effects of the pheromones were wearing off. Sophie struggled to pull herself away from the young Kai and tried to hide the look of shame on her face. Triez picked up Sophie's clothes and gave them to her. She then proceeded in clapping her hands as a sign of appreciation for the floor show. Seeing the funny side of it Sophie smiled and took a long naked bow.

Once she had dressed, the young Kai promised to

get them away from the holding cell and protect them with his life. Triez said, "He'll be like that for days. I can't see him refusing you anything." Sophie said, "It's probably my fault as humans produce pheromones too when we're sexually aroused." Triez asked, "Where are your fangs?" Sophie answered, "We don't have fangs we just secrete them." Triez pulled a face and said, "Yuk that sounds disgusting." Looking at the lust that still lingered on the young Kai's face as he hasn't been introduced yet she admitted, "They must be very potent as far as Kais are concerned, as I've never seen a Kai male that passionate before." Sophie asked, "Where's my underwear gone?" Triez told her that the young Kai had it and that she wouldn't get it back as he was so besotted with her.

Back on board the *Crazy Horse*, Jamie had taken the ship out of the range of the Kai patrol vessels. Whether they would fire on them or not was a choice he didn't feel qualified to make without more intel on the Kai situation.

The Doctors daily hyperlink call came in late that morning. A vessel had left Mars; it was believed to be small in size, possibly a fighter headed for Earth. Simon and a squadron of six were shadowing the vessel just out of range. It didn't seem to be in attack mode and seemed to be more like a reconnaissance vessel. The message ended there.

On the Bridge, Jamie was receiving a signal from Triez's transponder. He felt It was time to go in; moving closer to Kai he encountered two small combat vessels. Holly hailed one of them. It responded instantly by asking them not to fire and told them that they were friends of Triez. Jamie asked what had become of her. They assured him that both Triez and Sophie were fine, and asked him to come aboard. After a few personal questions about Triez, Jamie was quite happy to listen to them. They told him that Sophie and Triez were on their way to Breeche Prime via a Kai transport vessel. Sophie's prosthetics had been fixed and a com-set had been issued to both of them.

They explained that the first plan was dead in the water as it was hoped that enough Kai could be convinced to gather a strike force together, but the explosion had killed most of the key figures. It was now expected that a more direct approach was necessary, such as a major strike at Breeche Prime itself.

The Kai further explained, "With most of the Breeche combat vessels on Mars, Triez hopes that a strike on Breeche Prime would mean a recall of some of those ships to defend the home world. Only then would an attack on two fronts be possible." They hoped that if enough of an impact was made on Breeche Prime, many of the Kai serving with the prime fleet would change their loyalties. They advised that no further action should be taken until contact with Sophie was made.

The young Kai was still with Sophie even though he wasn't under the influence of her pheromones anymore. His name was Diel, which meant truth in Kai. Sophie knew he was to be trusted, as Triez had promised to tear his neck out of its socket if he betrayed them. Trusting her word that she'd do it he kept a low profile throughout the journey. As they had little money between them, Triez had managed to purchase the shuttle from a friend on Kai.

Needing constant attention the vessel was making the journey to Breeche Prime a fairly arduous one. Many of the problems were due to the vessel being very old; and unknown to any of them, it had also been condemned as a death trap two years earlier.

On entering Breeche Prime's upper atmosphere, the thrusters for slowing the ship down had stopped working. They knew nothing of the fact, that the only thing that would be saving them from being turned into charcoal on entry was a fifty-year-old heat shield. As the vessel dived deeper into the upper atmosphere the front of the shuttle starting to glow red. Triez engaged stealth mode and activated the heat shield. Instantly a white hue covered the front of the vessel. As the shield flickered from white to red, Diel asked Sophie whether the ship was functioning properly. She told him, "Relax! It's fine." With staring eyes, she looked to Triez for reassurance, but all that she did was shrug her shoulders and say, "It's OK don't fret." At two thousand degrees, the heat and noise were unbearable as the heat shield constantly flickered intermittently. With smoke rising up through the floor, Sophie shouted: "Where on Kai did you find this pile of crap?" Triez assured her "It was from a good friend." Sophie shouted, "Did she catch you screwing her husband or was it something worse?" Triez replied, "Actually it was from a male friend, an ex-friend, an asshole!"

At fifty thousand feet the vessel was shaking uncontrollably, Triez struggled to level the shuttle out and applied the antiquated braking thrusters again.

This time they seemed to work as she felt the vessel slowing to some degree. Below them lay one of Breeche Prime's major cities. Sophie pointed at a lake ahead of the shuttle and told Triez to ditch it there. Quickly circling and losing height, Triez plunged the wreck into the water. The fact that water was coming up through the floor reminded them of what a very risky atmospheric entry they had just made. Sophie opened the hatch and said, "I'm feeling lucky today!" Lowering herself into the water she was joined by the other two for a very cold morning swim.

Once ashore, they watched the vessel disappear below the surface of the lake and then headed towards the city. As the weather was starting to warm up It was decided that they should stop to wring out their wet clothes. Triez had found a suntrap in the corner of a field and stripped naked. Averting his eyes Diel did the same and was joined by Sophie. Resting there for a couple of hours as naked as the day they were born, Sophie asked Diel, "Can I have my underwear back now? Please." Reluctantly he passed them back to her.

Triez remembered from a previous visit that there was a military base not far from where they were sitting. Facing Sophie she told her, "You know, it might be a good idea to steal a vessel, overload the reactor, and plough it into a fusion reactor station. That would certainly bring some of the Breeche vessels back home!"

Sophie thought it sounded like a plan, although a suicide mission was not what she had in mind. She was in agreement with Triez but felt there should be an amendment to the plan and suggested: "We should all survive and live happily ever after." Triez agreed to say, "We could do that too!"

Putting their damp clothes back on it was decided that they would need some weapons if they were to steal a vessel from the military base. Breeche Prime was nothing like Kai, it had a modern infrastructure, and weapons would not be easy to come by without currency. Entering the city, they seemed to fit right in with the Breeche civilians. There were bars and stores, everything that you would expect from a modern metropolis, but with one exception: there didn't seem to be any people over the age of thirty and most of the bars and stores were just derelict remnants of a once thriving city.

Across the street, were what looked like two police officers, who were beating a man with clubs. One drew a pistol and shot him in through the head. Very quickly a floating truck arrived; two men picked up the body and threw it in the back. Sophie asked Diel, "Why did they do that?" He replied that the victim was probably just drunk and jaywalking and that the police officer would probably end up killing his partner over the cost of a drink.

Sophie noticed the smell of death and the blood-stained pavement where she was standing. Triez informed her that divorce was quickly sorted out there, one spouse kills the other, and that was fine. Sophie asked if that was OK with her. Triez explained that it hadn't always been that way. When the Breeche first landed on Kai they gave them technology and introduced them to intergalactic travel. The Kai were a simple people, many went to live on Prime. But it was soon discovered that the only reason that they had visited them in the first place was to exploit their planetary resources. War beckoned, and the rest was history. With the smell of death still haunting her, it made Sophie's flesh creep just standing there.

CHAPTER 6

Triez had noticed a great change in the Breeche over recent years and told Sophie, "The police here used to keep order to some degree, but now they just seem to be either paid assassins or Psychopaths. It's probably the cloning effect that's affected the whole race giving them some kind of psychotic fever that has left them with an inability to interact with each other or anyone else for that matter. If they could conceive naturally it might end this madness." Sophie asked, "Then they're born sterile?" Triez answered, "Yes they're cloned in a laboratory from genes that have been over used and manipulated over the years. The purpose was to give them some sort of individuality, but it all went wrong somewhere along the line leaving them with a life span of only thirty years and psychotic tendencies."

It was agreed between Sophie, Triez, and Diel that this was a culture in decline, with very few morals and possibly no way back from the pit of fire that it was about to descend into. All three were united in thinking that, above all, everything should be done to prevent this dreadful contamination of humanoid life from spreading onto other worlds.

Triez suggested that the best place to get weapons would be from a gunsmith and set about locating a local manufacturer of photon rifles and pistols from a list of businesses on an electronic public information screen. Triez picked up a piece of waste paper, dipped it in a puddle and wiped the blood from the screen. Listed under firearms was a factory four kilometres to the north of their present position. As they had no money and, as dangerous as it was, it seemed the only way to get there would be on foot. Sophie was appalled at the smell of rotting corpses and blood-spattered walls along the way.

*

Within an hour they had arrived at the factory. It was in an isolated area outside the city. It seemed to be closed for the day but was guarded by two males of large stature. Triez walked over to one of the guards and started flirting with him. As he touched her backside she punched him in the stomach. Then, as he bent over, she broke his neck with a single blow. Picking up his rifle, she rolled across the concrete and targeted the second guard; with a single shot to the head, he toppled backwards. Sophie now saw the true strength that had been given to Triez after her enhancement and understood how she used it with as much precision as a surgeon with a scalpel.

Triez boasted, "If you thought that was good, you should see me open beer bottles with my yin yang!" Sophie assumed she was talking about her groin and remarked: "So that's why the beer on the *Crazy Horse* has tasted a bit strange lately!" Diel was already at the door and impatiently waiting for the banter to finish.

Sophie picked up the other photon rifle and blasted the door off its hinges. An alarm bell rang, and weapons fire sprayed the opening. Pointing the gun into the air she blew the bell box off the wall, and the gunfire ceased. Diel threw the dead guard's helmet through the doorway. All was quiet. However, they decided to proceed carefully.

While the defence mechanism was resetting itself, Sophie trashed the control unit inside with a gun butt and took the system down. Looking through a window she could see that there was a vehicle behind the building and what looked like a start-up fob on the desk. Sophie couldn't believe her luck and picked up the fob. Searching through a locker Triez found a grenade launcher and some ammunition. She handed them to Diel who loaded them into the trunk of the vehicle. Sophie had been searching the upstairs of the building for hand-held weapons and came downstairs carrying several different types of photon pistols and a mobile satnav. Taking leave of the building, all three climbed into the vehicle. Sophie made herself comfortable in the driver's seat and could see that it was a very different vehicle to what she was used to. It had no wheels and just sat on jacks. She was quite sure that it would handle something like a hovercraft and prepared herself for some awkward manoeuvring. Inserting the fob into the ignition, the dashboard lit up and the jacks retracted, leaning out of the door she looked underneath the car and could see that it was being supported by a powerful electromagnetic field that glowed with a blue hue. Closing the door and pulling away, she assumed that the steering mechanism was some kind of multi-linear beam system that encircled the underside of the car. After a couple of hundred metres she found the vehicle to be very precise as it hugged the road with great adhesion, and quickly realised that it was also quite fast.

Travelling back towards the city, Sophie asked Diel why they didn't have these vehicles on Kai. He told her, "After the war, some of the more wealthy Breeche had them on Kai, but abandoned them after returning to Breeche Prime. On finding a few of the vehicles abandoned, some of the Kai started to use them for a while but, when they ran out of spare parts, they just abandoned them again and reverted back to the old transport methods."

Noticing a car very close behind in the door mirror, Diel warned Sophie that a vehicle was following them. Triez leant over the seat and smashed the back window with a gun butt. She told them "It's not the police so it's probably carjackers. Sophie opened the throttle wide while Triez fired at the vehicle behind. With her enhanced eyesight, she managed to hit the driver, which sent the vehicle crashing through a store window. As Sophie accelerated the vehicle to its maximum speed, Triez could see a police car pull out from the side of the road and start to give chase. Taking the grenade launcher in her hands she fired it at the police car while Sophie drove through the city High Street at over a hundred and twenty miles per hour. In the mirror she watched the car explode and break into several pieces. Leaning forward over the seat Triez said: "My God - I'm hot today!"

The next stop was a military base. Using the satnav Sophie stopped the car twenty metres from the perimeter fence. Climbing out of the car and unloading the trunk of weapons, all three approached the fence. Sophie asked for stealth, but knew she wouldn't get it from Triez. On reaching the fence Triez grabbed it and tore a section down, Sophie thought, *Well no change there.* Sirens went off everywhere. Out came the photon grenade launcher and, with an enormous blast, the barracks were blown into a thousand pieces. Drawing her pistol, she casually walked towards the sentry post. Shocked at the sight of Triez on the rampage, Sophie and Diel drew their weapons and followed her. As three guards appeared before her, Triez opened fire on the sentry post. Once the guards had been taken down, she entered a storeroom next to the post and came out with what Sophie assumed were three jet packs.

A medium-sized ship was sitting on the tarmac with the cargo door open. Triez ran straight for it, while Sophie laid down suppression fire towards six soldiers that were approaching from the main gate. Triez and Diel climbed aboard as Sophie Slammed the cargo hatch shut. Avoiding the weapons fire she quickly scrambled aboard and joined them. After completing the fastest pre-flight check ever, Triez powered up the engine and blasted the vessel through a hailstorm of weapons fire into the blackness of the night.

The attack on the base, and having relieved the Breeche of one of their ships was so unexpected, and so rapid, that its effect had made a pursuit by the Breeche out of the question. Entering orbit around the planet, Triez hid the vessel behind a large satellite. Over a drink of Breeche bourbon they had come to a decision regarding which target to hit. It was a nuclear fusion generating plant six hundred kilometres north of the planet's equator. Triez assured Sophie that with the ship's reactor on overload, it would make a very large hole in the ground indeed. Their escape would be made using the jetpacks strapped to their backs, two pistols a piece, one rifle each and, of course, Triez's grenade launcher. Sophie accepted Triez's gung-ho approach this time and squeezed her shoulder asking, "Are you OK?" Triez replied, "Fine, but its not over yet; the real trouble starts when we hit the ground."

It was busy below them as Breeche patrol vessels searched high and low with intensity. The com channels were overlapping each other and sounded like a garbled mess. Sophie knew that they had created a perfect situation as there was nothing better than a confused enemy.

They had achieved the desired effect and caused mayhem. Helping each other fit into the jetpacks, they prepared for the assault. Sophie knew that if it worked, the Breeche would have to recall some of their fleet and relieve Simon.

Triez engaged the engines and like the wild cat she was, she accelerated the Breeche vessel towards the planet at great speed. As the vessel dived through the atmosphere. Sophie rigged the intermix to overload at one hundred feet and opened the escape hatch below the vessel. She just hoped it would be the exit route from the flying coffin they were presently occupying.

At six thousand feet Triez climbed out of the pilot's chair and came crashing backwards towards the rear of the vessel. Sophie took hold of Triez and Diel and dragged them both through the hatch with her. Seconds later they engaged the jetpacks and put as much distance between themselves and the vessel as possible. As Sophie looked over her shoulder she watched as the vessel exploded only a few feet above the power station. Within a second the shockwaves hit them at tremendous speed, spinning all three of them out of control and gambolling towards the ground.

Triez collided with Diel, smashing the pack from his back. He slumped over and fell helplessly. Sophie could see what had happened and went after him. With only feet to spare, she grabbed his arm and tried to pull him up, but her efforts were of little or no avail. Sophie held her breath as they both ploughed into a row of bushes.

After rolling several feet they both managed to stop. Triez landed nearby and noticed that part of her jetpack was missing; she quickly recognised it when she saw it poking out of Diel's chest! Holding a cloth around the wound, Sophie and Triez carried him towards an abandoned two storey house. Setting him down and opening his tunic they could see that he was bleeding in a serious way and wouldn't last long without treatment. Sophie tried to use her com-set, but the pulse from the explosion had fried the circuits.

Triez could hear an approaching ship and, looking over the window sill, she could see that it was a Breeche troop transport vessel. She took Diel's weapons and pulled out her grenade launcher. As the Breeche disembarked from the ship, another landed behind it. Aiming the grenade launcher at the second vessel, Triez pulled the trigger. The troops on the ground turned around in astonishment as it heaved backwards and exploded.

Sophie fired continuously at the first ship using suppressing fire, while Triez picked them off one by one. But the game was up when three more ships arrived. This time the troops were wearing jetpacks and were throwing grenades as they flew around the house. Dragging Diel from room to room was taking its toll, and Sophie feared for his life.

Triez was fresh out of grenades and most of the photon pistols had overheated. With an enormous blast, the front of the house fell away. Sophie tried to console Diel by telling him that there were only three rooms left and therefore fewer rooms to drag him around! Although in pain, he laughed and told Sophie he loved her and was happy that his last moments would be with her. She answered, "Screw that! We're getting out of here." As another grenade struck, Sophie heard a familiar sound. It was the teleport activating. They had been found, but with only seconds to spare.

Dr Phull was waiting in the teleport room, and Diel was quickly whisked off to surgery. Sophie walked over to Jamie and thanked him. He had detected weapons fire not far from the power station blast and assumed that the pulse had fried the com-sets. So he had isolated their three separate signatures and tracked them accordingly. Sophie told him that he was a sight for sore eyes as she thought they were done for. With a smile, he put his hand on her arm, and said: "Welcome home, Captain."

Triez joined Sophie in the observation room overlooking the operating theatre. She put an arm around her shoulder comfortingly; she could see a tear on Sophie's cheek and said: "I know - I'm worried about Diel too." An hour and a half later, Diel was out of surgery. Dr Phull entered the observation room and told Sophie, "Hopefully he'll make a full recovery as there was no major organ damage." With a sigh of relief Sophie headed for her quarters; it had been a very long day.

Big Tom was ecstatic at the sight of Triez. Picking her up, he gave her a great big hug. She felt so wanted, so loved. It was something more than just sex between them now. He was a friend, her special friend and she knew that nothing besides death could ever separate them.

After falling asleep, Sophie awoke to the sight of the ghost looking down over her. She asked it, "Shouldn't you be out haunting an old house or something?" It seemed to have a problem and told her, "Although my program tells me to do no harm, my logic circuits are telling me otherwise; they keep telling me that I should be assisting you in harming the Breeche." Sophie told it, "Well, at least one of the Touscal's got a pair of balls." Rolling over she closed her eyes and went back to sleep.

Later that morning, after checking how Diel was doing, she paid a visit to Dieter in Engineering. Happy that his repair crews were up to speed, Sophie headed for the bridge. Wishing a good morning to Jamie, Luma, and Holly, she noticed that Triez was absent. Holly told her, "She's still asleep in her quarters and, after all the racket in the night, I doubt that she'll arrive much before the night shift." Sophie queried, "I thought your cabin was a deck below hers!" Holly agreed that it was, but said: "If they carry on like that for much longer they'll end up blowing out the bulkheads before the Breeche get a chance to!" Sophie promised to have a word with Triez. She asked Jamie if there was anything else. He just added, "The ghost self-activated and drifted in here this morning telling me he'd got balls!" Sophie answered, "Hmm, maybe that was my fault!"

∗

Later that afternoon a Kia vessel hailed from a distance with an offer of assistance against the Breeche. It was one of Kai's more powerful vessels. It wasn't really a match for a Breeche cruiser but Sophie felt that it could play an important role in keeping the Breeche frigate vessels at bay.

Within an hour the Kai vessel was off the starboard bow and its Captain asked to be teleported aboard. He arrived to a warm welcome from Triez, as he was an old friend of hers. He had always been a bit rebellious and taken risks, and that's why she had so much respect for him. She greeted him with a hug, calling him a reckless old fart. He responded by telling her that the sight of her filled his trousers! With a big laugh and an even bigger hug, she introduced him to Sophie.

The Kai Captain told her that word had got out about a new faction in the quadrant, and that it had gained a great deal of interest from the Kai. He suggested that together they could eradicate the threat by wiping the Breeche from the history books, thus making it as if they had never existed. He said a great many people would have had better lives if they had never existed. She knew what he was talking about and thought, *God knows the Breeche deserve it*. But felt uneasy about what he was suggesting, as it amounted to nothing short of genocide.

Later that evening over drinks, Sophie took the Kai Captain to one side. She asked him if he was aware of something temporal. He said he was aware that she had seen the tablet on Touscal and assumed that she had suspicions of her own. He told her to trust her own instincts, and that she was on the right path. He hinted, "The future's already happened, and it's grim, maybe together we can do something about that."

He told her that their future depended on the destruction of Breeche Prime and he didn't need to be a fortune teller to advise her of that. He assured her that it wasn't genocide; it was their very survival at stake. She now saw what Triez saw in him and felt that this was a man with a great deal of insight into what was needed for the best result all round. Nevertheless, Sophie thought that was all very good, but they still had to face the returning Breeche vessels, and this had a great bearing on the way Sophie was thinking. If she were to overestimate the amount of help from the Kai resistance, then they would lose. If too many Breeche vessels returned, they would also lose.

The next morning the Doctor received a message over the hyperlink. Simon had monitored and decoded the Breeche communications. Over fifty ships were returning to defend Breeche Prime, that was half of the Breeche fleet. Sophie knew that it would relieve Simon to some degree, but was well aware that she would have to drum up some support from Kai if they were to fight that many vessels.

And then came the really bad news! One cruiser and two medium-sized ships had entered the Earth's atmosphere and Sally, with her squadron, were about to engage them. The Prof was sending encoded hourly news updates from the Earth networks over the hyperlink.

The U.S. Navy had closed in on one of the Breeche vessels. The result was one naval aircraft down and four others rescued by mysterious advanced fighters that came from nowhere. This had the effect of clearing up who the enemy really was.

Simon met Sally at his old trailer in Vermont. They hid their two fighters behind a group of trees and, after a jump start from a mobile power booster, they took Sophie's old beaten up car. Sally asked him where they were going. Simon told her that they had an appointment with General Walters and that he was a lot more interested in talking now.

On arrival at the base, an escort took them straight to the General's office. The General acted very differently. Greeting Simon as he entered the office, he ordered three coffees and asked them to sit down. He was glad to see Simon and greeted Sally equally. He asked Simon what they were dealing with, why they were so hostile, and how he could be of help. Simon gave him a set of schematics for photon cannons and a set of fighter plans, that Sophie had drawn while on their first jaunt to Perness. Simon asked for the best Air Force pilots they could spare, in order to train them to fly the proposed fighter.

The General now had the power to grant this and did so without hesitation. Simon warned the General that the new technologies would push the Earth forward into a new era where the people of this planet would have to take the responsibility for all their actions towards themselves and other worlds. He told the General, "The future starts here, today, and you'd better behave in it, or else!" On that note, Simon and Sally left the base. The Prof had tracked three Breeche vessels to a quiet place in the Great Rift Valley in Africa. She also detected three defence shields had been put in place around those vessels. She found it a strange coincidence that they had landed where all of modern humanity had evolved from thousands of years earlier.

The following day the *Crazy Horse* arrived at Mylin to rendezvous with the three fighters on loan. Jamie had been scanning deep space all morning and had now picked up the fifty Breeche vessels on the long range scanners. He informed Sophie that they had taken the bait and would be there in two days. The odds were 50-2.

Sophie asked Jamie how he felt about those odds. He replied, "Getting a drink out of Holly carried worse odds than that!" Sophie laughed but felt that if they didn't get more support there wouldn't be much to laugh about in two days' time. Triez didn't seem to be contemplating any odds as she had a plan of her own. She had been calculating what impact would be inflicted on Kai if Breeche Prime was destroyed, by taking into account how far and how fast the debris would travel. Using a computer she felt that the odds were favourable, bearing in mind the gravity of a huge neighbouring planet with an extremely strong gravity field. She knew that the effect would be similar to that of a huge vacuum cleaner.

Later that afternoon a couple of Kai vessels arrived, followed by another two an hour later. Jamie alerted Sophie stating, "It's like a gathering of the clans, Captain; things are looking up." Throughout the night they came, some small, some old. It didn't really matter about size or age to Sophie as long as they kept coming.

An exodus from Breeche Prime was taking place by the Kai, with some travelling to defend the home-world and others travelling in stolen ships, arriving at Mylin to join the *Crazy Horse*. The Mylin Captain had put together two vessels that had been adapted for combat, which was no surprise to Sophie. However, the greatest surprise of all was the sight of a vessel with the Touscal insignia on the side. Holly hailed the people on board. It was Ruman with a crew, and they were offering their services as a communications hub between vessels.

After a night's sleep, and twenty-six hours before contact with the enemy, many of the Kai, and almost all the crew of the *Crazy Horse*, had gone down to the surface of Mylin to get some sunshine. Many of them hoped that it wouldn't be the last time, in the knowledge that their task force was neither fast nor strong.

Sophie arrived on Mylin with Diel who had made a good recovery, thanks to the Doctor, who was making last minute preparations for the battle ahead.

Triez was sitting in the sea up to her neck with her

eyes closed when Sophie arrived. She appeared to be in deep in meditation. Laying out a towel for Diel, the pair of them watched her for an hour with a little intermittent sniggering in between.

Eventually, Triez came out of her reverie and sounded as though she had received a revelation. Sophie asked her what was going through her head. Triez told her that they would have to draw the Breeche vessels away from Mylin and towards Breeche Prime, using the *Crazy Horse* as bait. She asked Sophie to trust her, telling her that they had to get them into an orbit around Breeche Prime, or as close to it as possible. Sophie trusted Triez, and as she had offered no explanation, Sophie didn't request one.

That evening, in a restaurant close to the beach, Triez was dancing closely with Tom, nibbling his ear with her fangs she could feel passion within her starting to increase in intensity. With a yelp from Tom, she injected him with her essence. She wanted it to be a special evening for them. He thought that it was just the jitters about what the next day might bring, but she had another plan, one that would probably separate them permanently. Waking the next morning, Tom realised he had seen another side to Triez, a very feminine side. There was none of the aggressive, rough sex that he'd been accustomed to; it had been more like gentle lovemaking, with caressing and stroking, and quiet whispers in an alien tongue. This was a side of her that he loved. Even in the shower, she was subdued – he wondered if something was wrong. As the water cascaded down between her breasts, he could see her shiver. In English, she asked him to hold her. Now he knew that something was wrong.

*

With everyone back on board the *Crazy Horse*, Dieter powered up the engines and Holly fed in the coordinates to the exit point of the Breeche vessels from hyperspace.

Luma was now ready to do battle with the new upgraded weapons system that Dieter's crew had installed earlier that week. She now had three target nodes on her console, that allowed for more accurate targeting, it also allowed for multi-strike targeting. Sophie took the Captain's chair and asked Holly to contact the Kai Captain with a message. It read, ...*Task force to stay put on Mylin until advised otherwise... Will advise on the battle in due course....*

Sophie contacted Dieter, she asked him whether he had completed a phase capture modification to the teleport system. He assured her that he had done it himself, but couldn't guarantee that it would hold up in the heat of battle. She thanked him for his efforts and wished him luck.

Big Tom had gathered his clan together. They had made their way to the teleport room and contacted Sophie with the words, "We're ready Captain." She responded by saying, "I'm on my way Tom, I'll be there soon." Jamie had aligned the ship parallel to where the Breeche would exit hyperspace. He alerted the Captain that the Breeche should have detected them by now. Sophie ordered quarter speed ahead and engage the shielding.

As the Breeche vessels left hyperspace they split into two groups. Thirty of the vessels pursued the *Crazy Horse* as it accelerated away from them. Sophie smiled to herself as she knew they'd taken the bait hook line and sinker: the chase was on. Looking at the Tactical display she could see that the twenty remaining Breeche vessels had slowed down considerably and were heading towards Mylin. Sophie asked Jamie to take control of the bridge and keep on the heading towards Breeche prime. She told Luma to target the cannons at the leading Breeche vessels forward shield and stand by for her signal. Not wishing to delay Tom and his group any longer, Sophie made her way to the teleport room.

Once there, she handed out the weapons: two photon rifles, two pistols and a Navy Seal combat knife each. Sophie contacted Luma and instructed her to punch a hole in the leading vessel's forward shield. All five climbed onto the pad. Sophie instructed the teleport technician to teleport them directly to the bridge of the leading Breeche vessel as soon as he detected a hole appear in the forward shielding. She added, "The hole will only be open for a second and you have that much time to get us through in one piece." With a gulp, the technician said, "Aye Captain."

Luma opened fire on Sophie's signal, and within seconds the shielding was disrupted to some degree. Detecting a hole appear the technician activated the teleport, taking Sophie and the clan directly to the centre of the Breeche vessels bridge.

Having being noticed on their arrival all five ducked down behind any cover they could find. Tom rolled a grenade across the floor and shouted: "TAKE COVER." After the blast, he sprayed the entire bridge with suppressing fire. Taking the initiative Sophie rolled into a corner to draw fire and took out one of the Breeche as he attempted to raise the alert. Tom's Number One hit a second Breeche with a knife between the eyes – it wasn't a pretty sight. There were three left. Tom's Number Three had sneaked up behind the Breeche Captain, grabbed him around his throat, and held him face down against the decking. Now there were just two Breeche left.

Tom charged at the remaining two, he hit one with a pistol shot, but the second one took Tom down with a shot to the waist. As he went down, Tom's Number Four hit the last one with a photon rifle shot to the back.

Sophie rolled Tom over and could see that he was bleeding, but luckily the shot had only grazed his side. Relieved, she called him a big tart and told him to get up. Pulling out a field dressing she covered the wound and asked him whether it hurt. He said, "Not as much as being called a big tart!" Sophie laughed and said, "God forbid Triez would never have forgiven me if your balls had been blown off."

The Breeche Captain was a really nasty piece of work. Sophie had found out that he had executed the chef for cooking a less than adequate meal. She asked him who had been doing the cooking since. He said nobody, we're all on ration packs. She laughed and realised just how dumb he really was.

At that point the ghost arrived. It told Sophie, "I'm here to do bad stuff." As Sophie had a pretty good idea what Triez was planning, she asked the ghost if a space suit had been placed in Triez's scout ship. It confirmed that it had been laid on the pilot's seat, with a note telling her to trust Sophie, wear the suit and signal before she did it. Sophie then told the ghost that its next job was to get into the Breeche ship's systems, and lock the vessel into a continuous orbit around Breeche Prime.

Big Tom's Number Four had welded the bridge doors shut with his rifle, holding the rest of the Breeche crew at bay. They were nearing Breeche Prime when the ghost reappeared. It told Sophie that her instructions had been carried out. Deactivating the shield, Tom called the *Crazy Horse* to get them out of there. Leaving the Breeche Captain behind, they slowly disappeared.

Back on board, Jamie reported to the teleport room that Triez's ship had left the hold and was travelling at high speed towards Breeche Prime. Sophie made her way to the bridge and told Holly to send a coded signal to Ruman's vessel to coordinate an attack on the twenty Breeche vessels that were heading for Mylin. Squeezing next to Jamie on the pilot's chair, Sophie veered the ship hard to port and slowed to half speed.

Two Breeche vessels followed the *Crazy Horse*, with the rest of them following the leading Breeche ship towards Breeche Prime. Luma looked over to the Captain for orders. Sophie told her to fire the rear cannons at will. Contacted the teleport room Sophie ordered the technician to standby for a phase capture procedure.

Triez had squeezed her ship next to the lead Breeche vessel as it approached Breeche Prime. The so-called doomsday device was ready, it was jammed into the airlock with the door open. She knew that when it was dispatched it would destroy everything around it, as well as everything in front of it; and she was physically shaking with fear. She had never faced death at such close range. All she had to do was push the button when she was close enough.

The two vessels following the *Crazy Horse* were firing everything they had, and Jamie's piloting skills were being tested to the limit. Even with Luma firing the rear cannons, the *Crazy Horse* stern shielding was beginning to weaken.

Dieter had recently been clearing out some of the equipment in engineering that was unstable. One item had come to mind. It was a damaged antimatter containment device. With the help of the engineering crew, he filled it to capacity and strapped a time lapse grenade to it and ejected it through the carbon dioxide extraction vent. As the two Breeche vessels closed in for the kill, the antimatter exploded with such ferocity that the shockwave sent the *Crazy Horse* into an uncontrollable spin. In unison, Triez decompressed her vessel, pushing the bomb out of the doorway towards the planet. Closing her eyes, she sent a signal to the *Crazy Horse* and hit the button.

Chaos hit the *Crazy Horse* as her signal arrived as another huge shockwave hit them from the side. The bridge gravity plating had gone offline and Jamie found himself floating. Through the smoke, Sophie pushed herself towards the door. As she left the bridge she fell onto the deck plating; picking herself up, she ran for the teleport room. When she arrived, she could see that the technician was on the floor. It looked as though he had a broken leg. He had activated the teleport, and there was something there, but if Triez didn't have a suit on; she was dead for sure. Sophie boosted the signal and something started to appear on the pad; it looked like Triez, but she was out of phase. Switching to another pad, she was beginning to have substance. Triez had the suit on, *Thank heaven!* she thought Thirty seconds later and Triez was whole. She slumped to her knees on the pad; the phase capture system had worked perfectly. Sophie helped her up and with a smile from her: Sophie knew she was OK.

CHAPTER 7

As the *Crazy Horse* helplessly drifted through space, Sophie joined Triez at the teleport window, from what she could see they were in the middle of a boulder field. With the shield working on reduced power she could see a huge amount of debris impacting against it. It was coming from the direction of Breeche Prime. Sophie recognised a Breeche engine floating past and just hoped that was the last of the pursuing Breeche vessels. Triez smiled in a broken sort of way, as anyone would after committing genocide. She quietly said, "The doomsday device worked well: they're all dead now and that's down to me! No one else - just me."

From the window, all that could be seen was a cluster of broken pieces of rock. Sophie realised that it was all that was left of Breeche Prime!

Triez's face was wet. Sophie asked whether she was weeping for Breeche Prime. Triez replied, "I weep for my family, that they were not here to see it and that Kai is now finally free of the Breeche." Sophie knew that they had to return to Earth as soon as possible, but realised they were going nowhere.

They had a broken ship, two dead and twenty people in sickbay. Sophie told Triez, "We were lucky this time; it could have been a lot worse."

Within one hour Dieter had restored gravity to the bridge and restored some power to the engines. He and his crew had never failed to impressed Sophie and to show her appreciation she made her way to engineering with a large bottle of Jack Daniels. Jamie laid in a course for Mylin at minimum power while the engines were being repaired.

Two hours later and the *Crazy Horse's* engines were back on line. Dieter and his crew had excelled with their expertise once again. Sophie picked up the engineering com- set and called Jamie, "Mylin! Full speed!"

As they approached, Sophie was relieved to see that Mylin was untouched. Teleporting down to the government building, she asked the Mylin Chancellor where the task force had gone. Excitedly he described how the battle was waged, filling her in on details such as how the Touscal hub had put every ship where it needed to be, causing maximum impact on the Breeche vessels. He smiled and said they're out there now chasing the Breeche. "Chasing them where?" Sophie asked.

The Chancellor presumed that as the news of Breeche Prime's destruction had reached the remaining Breeche, they had probably redirected their vessels back towards Earth.

Sophie returned to the ship and contacted Simon immediately on a secure channel. She warned him not to use their doomsday device, as it had proved to have an uncontrollable element. When he asked what it was she replied: "It's just too powerful - you'll end up destroying Earth as well as the Breeche." She also warned him of the Breeche ships heading his way. He asked her if there was any good news; she replied that she was coming home and she was looking forward to seeing him again. She added that he should be careful not to fire on the task-force as they were in pursuit of the Breeche vessels.

In return, he updated Sophie on the lack of activity by the Breeche there. It seemed to him as though they were waiting for something: they both knew that it wouldn't be long before it was a battle for the control of Earth!

As Sophie assisted Triez repairing a module, she asked: "Why do you seem a bit distant today?" Triez replied that she really missed her little ship, as it was the first thing that she had really owned. Sophie said, "Well you shouldn't have used it to blow up a planet, should you? You make it sound like a little red corvette, but it was more like a planet killer in *your* hands." Patting her on the shoulder she said: "I'll see what I can do about getting you a new one."

They were now closing the gap between themselves and the task force. Luma detected weapons fire not far ahead and activated the shielding. They were now passing the stragglers. Jamie weaved in and out between the smaller slower vessels, finally arriving next to the Kai cruiser. Holly hailed the Kai Captain who asked her where they had been. He boasted that he had saved a few for her and especially for his lovely Triez and asked: "Is she still alive?" Holly told him, "Yes, Sophie was a little worried that she may be having psychological problems." The Captain asked, "And what do you think?" She answered, "Me. Oh, I've always known she's a psycho!" The Captain laughed and said, "Praise indeed."

There were sixteen Breeche vessels left. Jamie pushed the *Crazy Horse* forward towards the Kai ships. From nowhere came a mass of rear cannon fire. Zooming in on the tactical display, Jamie could see the Breeche vessels. Jamie's instincts were well ahead of them as he placed the *Crazy Horse* above their maximum target angle. Luma then targeted six ships at the front of the group and slammed the firing buttons into the console. The leading ship twisted to forty-five degrees as the shots impacted against its shielding, causing the second and third ships to collide with it. Holly signalled the Kai Captain to take the task force out of hyperspace immediately as a mass of debris would be ahead of him shortly. The Kai Captain complied.

With the task force safely out of hyperspace, it took thirty minutes for the small vessels to gather at one point. As the *Crazy Horse* joined them, Sophie realised that sixty percent of the task force vessels were missing. Many had been destroyed defending Mylin, one being one of the Mylin ships. Holly contacted the Mylin Captain and offered her condolences, the rest of the destroyed fleet were from Kai.

After a short break to navigate the journey home, the remainder of the task force re-entered hyperspace. Not far in, they monitored Breeche wreckage that had dropped out of hyperspace; it was scattered over a large area. Holly estimated that the wreckage amounted to around eight ships, and realised that there were still eight left and free to re-join the Breeche already on Earth and Mars.

Later that day Simon came over the hyperlink on the emergency channel. The Breeche had started the attack on Earth. He told Sophie to forget about Mars, as it was devoid of Breeche targets as they were either on, or approaching Earth. At this point, Sophie knew that the Breeche were homeless and would see Earth as a place to resettle. She felt it unthinkable that these murderous animals might be amongst them for some time to come, and she deepened her resolve to stop the Breeche at all costs.

Jamie took the *Crazy Horse* out of hyperspace and headed for Earth, followed by the task force. They were monitoring distress calls from all over the planet. Sophie agonised over where to start. Triez suggested that she should advise the Earth-bound forces not to engage the Breeche, as they wouldn't be a match for their firepower, and would be destroyed within minutes.

Contacting General Walters, Sophie told him to leave it to Simon. He surprised her by agreeing, but said that he might lend a hand later, and added that he was working on something himself. The communication was lost at that moment as the *Crazy Horse* was hit by a hail of photon cannon fire. Immediately Sophie ordered the launch of the fighters.

Peter Hazelwood, one of the technicians who had trained as a backup pilot on the *crazy Horse* with Holly, was about to get his chance. Cruising around Mylin for days on end in a fighter had bored him senseless. This had the effect of leaving him with no fear whatsoever, just excitement.

As two Breeche cruisers appeared from nowhere, Jamie kept the launch bay doors as guarded as he could; rolling the ship from port to starboard and back again.

Standing in the launch bay, Triez opened the bay doors while Peter, with a squadron of five, shot out with all weapons blazing This had the effect of taking the Breeche completely by surprise. Jamie increased power to the engines by adjusting the throttle controls and steered hard to starboard taking the *Crazy Horse* back towards the Moon.

Triez had watched Peter in his first real battle and thought he was impressive, saying, "I don't think he's scared of anything, you know. Did you see him?" Sophie answered, "Yes," and agreed with her that he was turning out to be a fine pilot. She suggested that they should now pay Simon a visit for the latest intel and see what he had in mind concerning stopping the Breeche. As they set course for the Moon, Sophie watched Peter link up with Sally's squadron and vanish from sight. The vision of them together left her with a feeling that Earth might just be that little bit safer from then on. Simon was waiting at the docking port. As soon as Sophie stepped off the *Crazy Horse* he picked her up and gave her a big hug.

The reunion of friends didn't last long though and, after a short chat, both agreed there was a war to win. Triez and Sophie sat down with Simon and the Prof. After a short debate on how to proceed, it was agreed that a ground battle was the best option as the latest intel had provided information about the Breeche adopting a new strategy of attacking in small groups using jetpacks and powerful particle weapons. Sophie told the group, "I think they're keeping their cruisers safe and inflicting as much damage as possible before a final assault by air." At the end of the meeting, all were in agreement that the next stage of the battle would be fought on the ground.

Sophie's reasoning was based on the fact that the General's associates didn't have enough viable aircraft to wage total war in the skies. However, she was aware that they would have an important support role to play somewhere along that road. General Walters was now in total control of the air and ground forces and, together with Simon, they were now classed as an allied assault force. Their ability to work together, problem-solving and working out battle strategies, was a match made in heaven. Most of the General's troops were now armed with photon weapons, but as they were dealing with flying armed marauders with no other ambition in life but to kill humans presented a challenge to morale.

It was the second day of the ground battle. Sophie, Jamie, Triez, Holly, and Luma had joined forces with one of General Walter's divisions in Brooklyn.

They had been tracking a group of Breeche that had been using heavy weapons on civilian targets. With over two hundred thousand humans dead in one day, Sophie knew that this was a good place to start. There were half-cremated bodies strewn all over the place. Most of New York and Brooklyn had been deserted. With a great many of the buildings being destroyed, accommodation was becoming a problem for those that had stayed, and keeping a low profile wasn't an option.

Sophie thought, *If the Breeche could kill two hundred thousand people without losing a single man, then we're in serious trouble.*

A middle-aged man was talking to the soldiers when Jamie eavesdropped on the conversation. Apparently, a group of Breeche were heading towards Manhattan. Jamie believed that there were about six of them, all wearing jetpacks, and heavily armed.

On hearing Jamie's news Triez and Holly went in search of some transport. A Dodge Viper was Triez's choice; the fact that it only had two seats didn't really matter, as she thought it was cool. However, before Sophie could criticise her choice, Holly came back with a convertible Corvette. Luma climbed in with Holly, while Sophie joined Triez in the Dodge and, with Jamie sitting on the trunk lid, they set off.

It didn't take long before the competitive spirit between Holly and Triez became apparent. The speed had gradually increased since leaving Brooklyn Bridge, but as soon as they reached Park Avenue, Holly challenged Triez by shouting, "First to the Waldorf!"

Hanging on for his life, Sophie grabbed Jamie's legs. The front of the cars rose as they both raced down Park Avenue, one red light after another until the Waldorf came into sight. Slamming on the brakes at one hundred and forty miles per hour, both cars came to a screeching halt – Triez had won and didn't they know it!

Lifting Jamie out of her lap, Triez climbed onto the bonnet and, with both arms in the air, she started whooping it up while Sophie and Jamie climbed out. Hiding about two hundred metres on, the Breeche lay in wait.

Triez's enhanced eyesight was serving her well. Still shouting, she dropped back into the driver's seat. Spinning the car's wheels, she raced as far as the traffic lights, rolled out of the car, and fired a grenade launcher at the tunnel below the Helmsley building. As it struck, the blast threw a Breeche into the road. His damaged jetpack exploded, with the heat instantly killing him.

Triez ran at an incredible speed towards the remainder of the Breeche hiding in the tunnel. Avoiding the photon fire, she stood with her back to the wall and edged her way towards the tunnel's opening. In front of her, the Dodge exploded from a direct hit. Like giant hornets, the other five Breeche flew out of the tunnel.

Running after them and jumping twenty feet in the air she grabbed the leg of one of the Breeche. Trying to avoid the hot gases from the jetpack, Triez grabbed his belt and started climbing his body. Pulling her knife from its sheath she plunged it into the pilot's chest; the jetpack spiralled out of control, propelling them both into the side of a building.

Letting go of him she found herself falling, and knew that she was too high to survive. An open window broke her fall, sending her outwards causing her to land on the roof of a parked car. Thirty feet away the Breeche hit the road, and his jetpack exploded.

Running through the smoke, Sophie found Triez but was worried that her first officer might be dead. She frantically looked for a pulse as she lay there lifeless. While she held Triez's wrist the others arrived, looking sullen. Sophie started breathing again as Triez opened one eye. Carrying her over to a hotel, they laid her on a couch, while a receptionist came over with a glass of water. Triez commented that unless it had gin in it, she could stick it up her ass – that was when they knew she was OK.

Back on her feet and covered with Band-Aids, Triez thanked the staff and all five headed for the door. Simon came over the radio with news that the army had run into the four surviving Breeche from the tunnel. Using the new photon rifles they had taken three of the Breeche marauders down but had lost two hundred and fifty men doing so.

Simon's group, together with four Navy Seals, had found nothing on the east side. Simon arranged to meet up with Sophie's group at Times Square.

Triez had found a taxi but Sophie suggested that Jamie should drive. Triez reluctantly climbed onto the passenger seat and they left for Times Square.

Passing the Empire State Building, Triez looked up in amazement and asked what the building was for. Holly told her that a giant ape used to hang out there. Triez looked up again and answered, "Naa." Reassuring her, "Holly said !Yeah!"

Times Square had never looked so empty; out of date newspapers littered the streets and the police department building looked like an army base, with a manned photon cannon pointed at the sky.

Jamie stopped the taxi at the Hard Rock; there waiting with Simon were the Prof, Sally, and the Doc. They were in agreement that the battle on the ground wasn't really working.

While relaxing over a cup of coffee in one of only two restaurants open, the com channel came alive. It was General Walters with news that they had captured the sixth Breeche, and without a fight. This was the breakthrough that they needed – with the area code at hand, they made their way through New York. To their surprise, they arrived at the Bronx Zoo. There to greet them was a soldier. As he led the way through the enclosures, Triez was fascinated by the bears, and said: "Oh they're so cuddly and sweet - I want one!" Holly told her that they stank, were extremely dangerous, and shit everywhere, especially in the woods. With an "Eew" she seemed to lose interest.

The soldier stopped at the lion enclosure and handed responsibility to the Captain. He then left, saying "Good luck with that!" The jetpack was intact, but in the corner was what looked like the remains of the pilot, minus the head – that was in the other corner!

There was a large male lion lying in the middle of the compound looking quite contented and well fed. Holly looked at Triez and suggested that she jump over the fence and get it. With a single bound she was over the fence. Looking back from the other side, and feeling a little confused, she could see everyone shouting at her. Holly was calling to her, "Get out of there!" Picking up the jetpack, Triez looked at the lion, jumped against the wall and bounded back over the fence. She asked, "What's all the fuss about?" Feeling a little stupid, Holly realised that she would have to curb her sense of humour and answered:

"Oh, it was nothing."

It seemed to them that the jetpack had stopped working mid-flight, and had crashed to the ground. Holly said, "It's not the best place to make a crash landing." Triez responded: "It could've been worse – if it was the bear enclosure, he'd be covered in shit too!"

The Prof located what she thought might be a transponder of sorts; this was the key to finding the hidden Breeche cruisers. Back on the *Crazy Horse*, Dieter connected the transponder to a computer. The Prof analysed where the information was being sent to and found it to be a very small Portuguese island in the Atlantic called Corvo.

Simon contacted General Walters and gave him the coordinates – he was keen to help and linked the *Crazy Horse* computer to the spy satellite network. If they could give him a time he, in turn, would give them a surprise, which intrigued Simon.

The Prof had the island onscreen and started to zoom in, closer and closer until they could see the Breeche vessel in real time. It was in a large extinct volcanic crater. The vessel had a perimeter shield around it. The Prof explained to Sophie that to get access to the other vessels thereabouts they would need to take the shield down with the ship intact.

Triez contacted the Kai Captain asking him how much firepower it would take to bring a Breeche perimeter shield down without destroying the vessel. This was an easy one for him. He told Triez to hit the shield with medium cannon fire at forty-five degrees and told her that it would take time, but eventually, it would collapse.

Sally's squadron were prepared as well as Peter and his group. They would attempt to get the shield down the next day. Simon contacted the General and filled him in with all the information and a time, which was to be the following day at 07.00 am.

Sophie turned the TV on. It was bad news: the Breeche had attacked the United Kingdom on all fronts, leaving a huge amount of damage across the country, mainly to most of the major cities. The casualties were in the millions and matched that of central Europe, which had also suffered. She knew that the only way to stop them was on that ship.

The *Crazy Horse* arrived at Corvo during the night. It had been a rough journey, with Jamie skimming over the ocean at just twenty feet whilst crashing through a great many waves.

For the last five miles, they had drifted towards the shore using the ships thrusters to guide them in. Once they were in position, Jamie anchored the ship to the seabed with grappling tethers. So far the Breeche had not detected their approach. The sea was fairly rough for the small dinghies they were using and Sophie was glad to get ashore as she made a poor sailor.

Triez was the first one ashore. She had swum the distance with ease and harpooned an inquisitive guard on the cliff top on her arrival. Climbing the rope she removed it from the body and tied it to a tree.

The ascent of the cliff was a difficult one as it was dark, with loose gravel at their feet. Simon was the second to reach the top. Dropping extra ropes down, it wasn't long before the rest were on top of the cliff face. Feeling a little fatigued, he decided it was time for a rest. Five minutes later they were off again. It was a long trek to the edge of the crater and dawn was breaking. A second guard could be seen about five hundred meters further along the rim of the crater. Something had to be done about him. Simon offered to go but, on closer inspection, Sophie could see someone creeping up behind him. Looking around, she could see Triez was missing. In complete silence the guard fell slowly backwards, supported by her hand which was holding a large combat knife. With a twist of the knife, the guard stopped breathing.

As Triez returned to the others, Sophie could hear her talking Breeche in a deep voice. Triez had two com-sets and was checking in with a few added crackles, which seemed to convince the Breeche that all was well.

It was 7.00 am and General Walters was on the tarmac. At the air base, the engineers were giving Sally's fighter a once over. Looking worried she asked the General whether he had any bad news for her. He said he just wanted to see her off and gave her a British police whistle that dated back a hundred years. He told her "It's for luck." She thanked the General, kissed him on the cheek and climbed into the fighter.

Taxiing down the runway, Sally joined Peter and the rest of the squadron while the General crossed his fingers and headed to the canteen to watch the fighters take, off.

On the crater's edge, Simon made a confession to Sophie that he had made an executive decision while she was away. She stopped him there and told him, "It's part of your job to make decisions without me.

137

Transferring you from the *Crazy Horse* wasn't a demotion - it was a promotion! I had to have someone who could be trusted while I was away. If it was your decision, then you should stand by it." Sophie asked him what decision he had made. With the sound of engines in the distance, Simon looked out to sea and pointed at the horizon.

Triez approached them as they looked out to sea and told Sophie, "There's a scout ship inside that cruiser and I'm having it. Any objections?" A little lost for words, Sophie replied, "Fine – you've earned it!" Simon laughed and said, "She's absolutely precious what would we do without her!" As the fighters closed in, Sophie recognised the design. Looking Simon in the eye, she asked him whether he had given the General the design specs for the fighters. He nodded, saying that he had, and had also given him the materials to build them too. Looking Sophie in the face he said: "It's a decision that I stand by one hundred per cent". She patted Simon on the back and said, "Capital thinking! That'll get the shield down."

As the fighters dived down from the edges of the crater, the shield was hit with four cannons from the front and two from behind as the fighters left the area. The combat was heavy as the Breeche returned fire, and it wasn't long before one of the fighters was hit by return fire, causing it to crash into the crater wall.

Sophie knew that they couldn't lift off with the perimeter shield in place, and ordered Jamie to bring the *Crazy Horse* to the crater's edge, just in case they decided to make a run for it.

With the fighters and the *Crazy Horse* ready to fire, Sophie asked Triez why they hadn't surrendered. She replied that they would rather destroy the vessel than give it up. This created a problem as the ship had to be taken in one piece. After a short time-out session, it was decided to get nearer to the action. So, with Big Tom's clan leading, they descended down the inside of the crater.

Sally had just arrived and was making her first run. At forty-five degrees she punched a hole right through the shield. Peter and two of his buddies expanded it large enough for a person to get through. With access to the vessel achieved, Sophie called off the attack for a spell.

Triez ran towards the shield and vaulted through the hole. It was about eight feet off the ground; the rest followed.

The cargo door opened and containers were rolled out. The Breeche came out firing and dived behind the containers. Big Tom threw a smoke grenade to provide cover for Triez. Running sideways with her back to the shield, she avoiding the main firing down the centre. As the smoke cleared she was right on top of them. Firing two photon rifles, one in each hand, she was extremely careful not to hit the scout ship – that was hers.

Moving forward, they were clear of the cargo hold, leaving a trail of dead Breeche behind them. Big Tom's Number Three had taken a shot to the shoulder, but his Number Two had bandaged it up and taped a photon rifle to the sling, telling him that he was now the backup man. Sophie had caught up with Simon, who was right behind Triez. By this time she was doing more clubbing with rifle butts than shooting. Rolling across a corridor, Triez was next to the bridge. Three Breeche guards were protecting it. Switching her rifle to overload she threw it at the guards and dived for cover behind an upturned bed.

The blast took out the wall they had been defending. Triez strolled in and went for the Captain. She ordered the codes from him or she would kill him. He spat at her, bared his fangs and shouted abuse, to which she head butted him to the ground. Taking her by surprise, one of the bridge crew had trained a gun on her. A shot rang out and he was dead. She thanked Simon for intervening.

Sophie interacted with the computer. The codes were complicated and would take some time to decrypt. Summoning the ghost, she asked it to get the codes for her. After a few minutes, it came up with the database. She thanked the ghost, telling it how much she admired its new balls, to which it answered, "Thank you, most kind"

Triez lowered the shield and very carefully delivered her shiny new scout ship to the *Crazy Horse*. Sophie was starting to think that if no incentive was offered, Triez wouldn't get out of bed in the morning.

Tom checked on his Number Three; the wound looked gruesome, but the Doc assured him that he could fix him up, and he would be left with only a small scar.

The result of the battle with the Breeche was zero captives and one damaged Breeche cruiser. The crew had taken their own lives rather than face defeat. Again, Sophie was reminded that fighting a battle against an enemy with no respect for their own lives was bad for morale.

Diel arrived on the *Crazy Horse* after convalescing on the freighter, and nothing could be a sweeter sight to Sophie. He asked "Where are we going to next," Smiling she answered "Europe." With a hug, he bared his fangs, but with a firm, "No," from her, he retracted them. Diel asked, "Maybe later?" To which she answered, "Certainly later." Tweaking his butt, she left for the bridge.

The General requested to Sophie that Sally and Peter, along with the squadron, be reassigned to him. Sophie had judged the last mission a great success. She contacted Sally, asking her if it was what she wanted; she said that it was fine with her. For Sophie it would be a sad parting but if Sally was happy, then she was too.

The Prof had analysed the Breeche codes: there were twenty-eight cruisers scattered all over the globe and thirty smaller vessels. Occasionally a cruiser would go on an attack mission. The Prof had worked out which one was due to go next; it was sitting on an island off Scotland called Soay. According to the database, the target was Oslo, Norway.

Triez told Sophie that they were creating a clearing, made up of the less populated countries. This would give them a foothold that they could defend whilst conquering larger nations. The Prof agreed and stated that as far as they were concerned it was a waiting game. With the satellite cameras angled at Soay, it was time for a rest.

Triez wasn't too impressed with Corvo. Only the

odd cow passed by now and again, and there wasn't even a view, as they were sitting in the crater. At 3.00 am in the morning, she decided to give Tom a visit. Banging on his door she shouted, "Bunny wants her carrot!" Shouting it louder and louder she had awoken half the crew. Eventually, she was drowned out by the crew shouting that they were trying to get some sleep. A blurry-eyed Tom finally opened the door to find her standing there in just a pair of briefs! He could see that she had no translator on her person and complimented her on her English. The door opened wide, and she entered.

*

At six the next morning the battle station siren had gone off. Sophie was first on the bridge. The Breeche vessel was leaving, and she knew this was where they were at their most vulnerable. Blasting off from the crater, Luma brought the weapons online. Hyped up on caffeine, Jamie accelerated fast enough to take them by surprise. By then, Triez had turned up in Tom's shirt. Sophie hinted, "You didn't get much sleep last night." Looking at the bite marks on Sophie's neck she said: "Neither did you, by the look of it!"

The Breeche ship was in sight and didn't seem aware of their presence. Suddenly it banked steeply. The game was afoot. Luma held back as the Breeche swerved; she was having trouble getting a weapons lock. *Think*, she said to herself. *Anticipate*, she thought; closing her eyes she fired into empty space, but that space was soon filled when the Breeche vessel pulled hard to starboard. A full spread of cannon fire hit them midships at point blank range. Triez reinforced the forward shielding and, on Sophie's order to ram those bastards, Jamie accelerated.

With their shielding disrupted, Luma kept firing until she could see daylight through the fuselage. The *Crazy Horse* ploughed through them like a knife through butter. The whole crew fought over the window space just to see the two halves of the Breeche vessel crash into the sea and explode. A loud cheer in unison marked what they hoped would be the beginning of the end.

After a quick circle of the area, no survivors were found.

Sophie went to see the Prof but wasn't happy about not having any survivors again. The Prof reassured her saying, "They wouldn't have it any other way. It's not your fault."

Sitting down at the Prof's desk, Sophie asked her where they were off to next. She replied, "Get your bikini out as the next stop's Greece!"

CHAPTER 8

Travelling across Europe at Mach two, Holly passed the new coordinates to Jamie's console. Climbing to sixty thousand feet Jamie could see Macedonia come into view. The Sithonia peninsula was part of the Halkidiki region of Greece and this was where their next engagement of the Breeche would take place. Zooming in on the scanner he could see that it was a beautiful sunny day down there and told Holly, "You're really going to love this place." It had been several years since Jamie had been there and he was looking forward to swimming in the Aegean's crystal clear water again.

Dieter had adapted the same holographic technology to the Crazy Horse that had been used on the launch tunnel at the complex and was hoping that he could hide the ship as it floated off the coast. The only drawback was that it couldn't be used on a moving object as this distorted the matrix of the projection field. Scratching his head, he trawled through the blueprints of the vessel to find a way to secure the ship against the movement of the tide. He knew that the *Crazy Horse* was equipped with four tethers, one on each corner. On the blueprints, Sophie had given the tolerance figures regarding the tonnage that the tethers could tolerate before breaking. Dieter seemed quite happy about those tolerances, it now depended on the seabed that the tethers were to be secured to. Taking the ship as far as the Turkish border, Jamie turned it around and skimmed at twenty feet across the surface of the water. Using the Breeche transponder signal, he positioned the *Crazy Horse* behind a land mass and gently lowered it into the sea. They were now only a few hundred feet away from the Breeche vessel.

With the ship adrift, Dieter fired the tethers into the seabed and expanded the retainers into the surrounding rocks until the *Crazy Horse* was as rigid as possible. Now, with the vessel fully camouflaged, Sophie opened the upper hatch and found she was standing on thin air. The *Crazy Horse* was now disguised as half sea and half sky. As Dieter emerged to witness his handy work, Sophie congratulated him on a job well done, as the ship was totally invisible to anyone on the beach.

Dieter said in a strong German accent, "Goot! Now zen, we can commandeer all of zee sun beds?" Sophie laughed and realised that he had a sense of humour after all.

It was nearly forty degrees Celsius and felt even too hot for swimwear but, once in the clear water, it seemed like paradise. Triez, Sophie and Dieter swam for the shore and, once there, they just lay on the beach for ten minutes in utter bliss. To their left was a rock formation and they knew that on the other side were the Breeche. Quietly climbing to the top of the outcrop they could see women; more to the point, Kai women lying on the beach and swimming. Sophie asked Triez what they were doing there. Triez told her that the women belonged to a travelling brothel and were taken by vessel to service the Breeche troops. She added that there were probably some Breeche women amongst them too.

She also explained that the vessel was an obsolete model and of no importance whatsoever as it was unarmed with only a handful of crew aboard. Sophie asked about Breeche women in general. Triez told her, "They're not for screwing, well, not until they're past twenty-five, and then they end up down there, with them." Sophie asked her, "What about reproduction?" Triez answered, "As Breeche females can't conceive naturally, the whole of their race are cloned; that's why they're so screwed up!"

Sophie asked her where they would go next. Triez's guess was that they would go into orbit to rendezvous with as many as twelve ships for erotic liaisons. Sophie was now starting to realise that although it was a vessel of no importance, it would join with up with as many as twelve Breeche vessels in orbit. She smiled at Triez and said, "They'll be sitting ducks just ripe for the taking." Looking around her, Sophie asked, "Who's up for being a tart? And Dieter - you put your hand down!"

*

Back on the *Crazy Horse* Sophie accessed the main computer and found that according to the database the vessel was not due to depart for three days. It was to rendezvous with twelve ships that would collect at a specific point in orbit, four hundred and fifty miles above Earth.

Sophie was aiming to be on that transport. She had drawn up a list of names; naturally, Triez would be at the top, followed by herself. The Doc had put two names forward: one was from Dieter's crew in Engineering, and the other from Simon's group. Both were young women who had shown exemplary skills in unarmed combat and, according to Dr Phull's psychological report, they were incredibly stable, with little fear of the unknown.

It was now the second day at Halkidiki and, after observing that no one ever walked to the far end of the beach, Jamie had released the tethers and beached the ship the previous evening. There had been several visits to the beach by locals, but none were aware of the camouflaged *Crazy Horse* at the far end of the beach, or the Breeche vessel that lay behind the outcrop. As there were no cash points for Sophie to interact with, Jamie had printed plenty of Euros and handed them round the ship. With plenty of cash, everyone was looking forward to a night in the local town at a diner called Georgiou's.

After a typical Greek meal consisting of everything connected with aubergines, some of the crew drifted away from Georgiou's bar/grill to the nightclub next door. Georgiou himself was one of the most bombastic and thoroughly offensive men on the planet and, as Jamie had been a regular visitor to Greece, he explained to Luma, "You know, his behaviour's not typical of the Greek people in general; they're usually very friendly." However, Georgiou did have one redeeming quality as far as Jamie was concerned: he accepted his forged Euros, and that was enough.

Luma had just finished her last drink of the evening, while Georgiou was shouting abuse at his staff for not clearing everything away and cleaning up. Walking over to Jamie, she thought that they might just teach him a lesson in manners.

Joining Jamie and Luma, Sophie made it clear to them that she too wasn't enamoured by Georgiou either, and also felt he needed a lesson in etiquette. She suggested giving him a scare by tempting him away from the safety zone of his bar. Jamie was shocked as he watched his Captain outrageously flirt with Georgiou by raising her skirt in front of him and winking. Following her towards the beach, Georgiou's pace quickened; Luma and Jamie followed. In the blackness of the night, Sophie disappeared from sight by entering the camouflaged *Crazy Horse*.

Activating the ghost, she asked if it could change its appearance. It asked her, "What into?" Sophie said, "The demon from the movie, Night of the Demon." The ghost questioned her sanity but, after a short argument, it grudgingly accessed horror films of the 1950s. Georgiou was close to the ship when the ghost appeared.

Twenty feet tall, with long talons and covered in smoke, it made its appearance. Donning a pair of fangs, it made a squeaking sound as it towered over the aggressive Greek. The ghost moved towards Georgiou causing him to run into the sea. Leaving fiery footsteps behind it, the ghost followed. Swimming and screaming, Georgiou clambered out and started running down the coastal road, until he was completely out of sight. Jamie joined Sophie on the beach. Sophie told him that the ghost had taken its form from Night of the Demon, the scariest movie she had ever seen. In a broad Scottish accent, Jamie said, "That's the scariest thing that Georgiou's ever seen too!"

With the ghost still looking like the demon, Triez staggered past, propped up by Tom. She wished Jamie, Luma, Sophie and the ghost, "Goodnight, my friends." Pausing for a second, she looked up at the ghost, and said, "What the hell were you drinking? You look terrible!" Laughing uncontrollably, she fell through the hatch and was dragged away by Tom.

*

It was now the third day and Simon, Dieter and Sophie were going through the plan on the beach; with them were Triez, and the two volunteers, Trudy and Julie. Dieter handed out four small black squares, about three inches by two, to the four women. They were antimatter bombs set in a containment field. The field was set to collapse exactly ten hours after priming. Simon asked the women to calibrate their watches while Dieter pressed the prime button on each device.

Triez explained, "Once all twelve Breeche vessels are gathered around the brothel ship, it's up to us to distribute the bombs as far apart from each other as we can. The explosion will be a huge one and we should make sure that we're well clear of the Breeche vessels when they detonate." Trudy asked, "How do we make our escape?" Triez answered, "In the brothel ship." She looked at Julie and said, "That's your job. Make sure you're aboard at least twenty minutes before the bombs go off, and kill any

Breeche that are hanging about in there." With a nod from Julie, Triez was finished: it was time to go.

All four packed the explosives into the heels of their shoes, and the watches into the hems of their skirts. Sophie and the other two were wearing prosthetics on their noses while Triez had covered the small tattoo on her neck with make-up. Climbing the rock formation to the top they could see that the women were returning to the Breeche vessel. Climbing down the other side, they slipped into the line of women. Keeping their heads down, they entered the vessel. Triez looked around and noticed that most of the women around her were Kai. She asked Sophie what they could do to save the women. Sophie assured her that if it was possible to do so then they would, and laid that duty in Julie's lap.

The accommodation was like an army barracks and, as they didn't have bunks, they stood out like sore thumbs. Pulling Sophie by the arm, a Kai female dragged her down onto her bunk; three other Kai women did the same to Triez and the other two.

The woman asked who they were. Sophie explained who she was and offered to get them out of there. The Kai woman thanked her as tears fell down her face. Over the next hour, she pointed out who was to be trusted and who was not.

The Breeche vessel lifted off twenty minutes later. Looking back at the beach Sophie could see nothing but a few people and smiled to herself, confident in the knowledge that Dieter had done a premier job with the camouflage.

The ship made orbit within the hour. It was

another two hours before the first Breeche cruiser arrived. Meantime, Sophie had learned that her new friend's name was Agil; she was Kai and twenty-six years of age. The Breeche had abducted her at sixteen and since that time it was the only life she'd known.

Three more hours had passed without them being noticed, Sophie was feeling a little more confident, partially thanks to Trudy, who had thrown some water into a conduit and fused much of the lighting aboard.

Two hours later the twelfth Breeche vessel had arrived and, with a loud clunk, the door opened. Agil told Sophie to stay close to her. Walking through the door she could see that it led to a large chamber. There were hordes of male Breeche impatiently pacing about, and a few females too.

Triez pointed out that there were two airlocks, one on either side of the room and figured that there was one vessel attached to each airlock. Sophie observed the airlocks and said, "So there must be six vessels all connected to each other via their airlocks, with only two being connected to either side of this vessel." Triez agreed and told her, "When we make our escape in this vessel the power from the engines should shear off the docking rings leaving all twelve Breeche vessels adrift."

Sophie was a little worried about Trudy and Julie, who didn't have enough room on their persons for translators. Sophie told them, "Mumble a lot and wing it as best as you can."

In a second, Trudy was grabbed by the arm and whisked away by a fairly large Breeche. She was smiling all over her face – now Sophie knew what the Doc meant by no fear of the unknown.

Triez was talking to several of the Breeche males, trying to find out which of them was on which ship. Eventually, she found one that was in the opposite direction that Trudy had taken. To Sophie's surprise, Trudy was back in the room. Sophie asked her, "What happened?" to which she answered, "I didn't much fancy him, and so I planted the bomb and snapped his neck; his body's in the wardrobe." Sophie just hoped that Trudy would have a little more respect for future boyfriends!

Once Triez had gone, Sophie could see a Breeche entering the room from the airlock on the starboard side. Taking his arm she dragged him back the way he'd approached. Once in his quarters, he punched her on the chin and tore at her clothing. She was stunned for a second. This wasn't what she had signed up for. He grabbed her by the hair and dragged her across the room and threw her on the bed.

As he loomed over her she crossed her legs, locking them around his neck and violently twisted him over towards a dressing table. After hearing a loud crack, she knew that his neck had broken. Looking at him sprawled over the smashed dressing table she said, "Bastard!"

There was a knock on the door and she could hear two men talking. She knew the door was unlocked and, with a sudden crash, the door caved in with Julie behind it. Sophie joined her and together they incapacitated the two Breeche permanently. Sophie planted the third bomb in a sock and hid it behind the washbasin. Julie told her, "You really look a state,

Captain, and you're showing your bits too!" Wrapping herself in bed linen, Sophie made the door look passable and together they made their way back to the main room. Triez was back in the room by then and told Sophie, "Time's passing, Captain: we've got to get that fourth bomb planted." Sophie told Agil, "I want you to make sure that you get as many Kai women as possible back to the barrack room within the next hour." Looking excited at the prospect of finding freedom again, her eyes filled up and, placing her hand on Sophie's, she said: "Thank you, Captain, thank you."

It was time to get the last bomb placed. Coming from the port side airlock was a high-ranking officer. Knowing that it was quite normal for them to take two women at a time, Triez grabbed Trudy and said, "He doesn't know it yet, but he's having both of us!" Julie gave Triez the last bomb.

Fondling the officer's arms, they pulled him back through the port side airlock. Travelling along the full length of the ship all three turned right and passed through another two air locks. They were now just where they needed to be, with three ships on either side of them. Turning left into the officer's cabin, Trudy grabbed him round the neck. Locking her hand against her other arm, she clasped the back of his head and pushed. Triez heard him gasping for air as Trudy snapped his neck. Triez accused her of having a real problem with the Breeche, as what she had done was totally unnecessary, but Trudy just smiled, saying it was easy.

Triez helped herself to a drink and placed the bomb behind the wardrobe in the officer's bedroom.

Trudy just stared at her saying, "You really don't like what I do, do you? But you'll thank me one day." Triez stated, "You seem a little too mercenary and a little too detached from the gravity of our situation." Trudy told her, "You've seen nothing yet." Triez could see the madness in her eyes and just hoped that her bloodlust wouldn't be the death of them all.

Making their way back to the main room, Trudy slipped away from Triez by opening the door to an empty cabin; she slipped in and locked the door behind her. Sophie was waiting on the other side of the airlock. She asked, "Where's Trudy?" Triez told that she was probably tearing someone's fingernails out, and enlightened the Captain to the fact that she was a complete psycho. Sophie had her suspicions but just hoped that Trudy was all right.

Just at that moment, the battle station siren sounded. They could hear weapons fire behind the airlock door. Pushing Triez out of the way, a few Breeche troops made their way through the air lock only to face a hailstorm of weapons fire. They were blown backward through the airlock aperture and fell to the floor at Triez's feet, covered in blood.

A second later Trudy came through the door dressed in Breeche trooper clothing and carrying a large photon rifle. She shouted, "Kill them all, Captain, we have to kill them all." Aiming at the incoming troops, she fired indiscriminately, hitting soldiers and sex workers alike. Disappearing through the starboard airlock and down a passageway, Sophie could hear the slam of an airlock door, and Trudy was gone.

Sophie asked Triez and Julie to get the women to the barrack room aboard the brothel vessel and disable the port side airlock. Triez asked her where she was going. Sophie frowned and said, "I have to find Trudy - we can't leave her behind."

Sophie followed the route Trudy had taken and was all too aware that time was ebbing away. Trudy had left Breeche bodies up and down the corridors and had passed from one ship to the next. Reaching what seemed to be the end of the trail, Sophie found herself in an engine room. Stepping over five bodies, she could see Trudy slumped over a rail. Lifting her up, she could see that there was a wound to her chest; she was still alive, but only just. Trudy tried to speak but fell limp. Sophie took her pulse, but there was nothing. She felt hollow inside, and asked herself w*hy didn't I see this coming?*

Triez stood in the doorway, looking solemn. She told Sophie, "You can't possibly know everything. She was a loose cannon and is now a casualty of war." Clasping Sophie's hand, she pulled her up and told her that they had ten minutes until Julie launched the brothel vessel. Luckily, it was a clear run back until they reached the airlock. There were six soldiers trying to force the door on the brothel vessel. Triez quickly stripped naked and stood in the Starboard airlock aperture. At that point, she had the full attention of the soldiers. Diving onto the floor between Triez's legs, Sophie opened fire, spraying the room with fire until the Breeche troops lay dead or dying. Dashing across the floor, Julie opened the door and they scrambled through.

Climbing into the pilot's chair, Sophie powered up the main drive and sheared off the two docking rings causing the vessel to disengage with the other twelve ships. Firing the rear thrusters, the ship made its way from the pack.

With only eight minutes to go until the explosion, Sophie fully engaged the main engine. Shots from the main pack were now hitting the stern of the vessel as Sophie and the others made their escape. With a loud crash, they felt an explosion at the stern of the vessel. Instantly the cockpit warning lights came on, lighting the facia up like a Christmas tree. The main engine had taken a direct hit. Sophie figured the only way to put distance between the Breeche cannons and themselves was to enter Earth's gravity field. Sophie knew that the vessel would have to tolerate searing heat and violent turbulence. She only hoped that the old girl was up to the job and hoped for the best.

The speed of the ship was quickening by the second now as the Earth started to drag them in. Completely naked, Triez joined Sophie and asked her in her native language, "Give me some of that sheet you're wearing." Sophie tore a piece off, two inches square, and gave it to Triez, who said, "Very funny," and, pulling strongly, she ripped the sheet from Sophie's back and tore it in two, handing half of it back to Sophie. Now they were both showing their bits.

By this time the ship was glowing red. Triez sat next to Sophie and used the thrusters to maintain the angle of descent. Sophie struggled with the main engine but was only getting five percent power. Julie came into the cockpit and told them that the sex workers had now changed into firemen, and were trying to put the fire out in the engine room.

As the Earth's atmosphere thickened, the vessel was starting to slow; both women knew it was going to be a hard landing without the main engine. While the thrusters fired at maximum, Triez guided them towards a landmass somewhere in the Pacific. They were now skimming over the water at zero altitude and, as the vessel was about to plunge into the sea, it impacted against something and bounced several times before coming to a sudden stop, throwing everyone on board forward. Looking out of the window, Sophie could see that they were wedged on a sand bank.

She could also see that the vessel had broken its back on the protruding sand. Sophie opened the emergency hatches and checked for any trapped people, but could find none as everyone had managed to disembark. Disabling the antimatter drive, she climbed through the hatch and joined the others on the beach. They looked upwards as an extremely bright light lit up the sky, followed by a sound similar to thunder, then another, followed by two more. Triez crossed her fingers and hoped that the plan had worked.

Looking around her, Sophie had no idea where they were, apart from the fact that they were somewhere in the South Pacific, and it was quite warm. As her survival instincts came into play, Triez made it quite clear that their priority had to be food and water and set about finding some.

Walking along the beach she found a dirt track leading to a wider, rough road. Following it for a short while she came across a clearing that seemed to be a town of sorts.

Strolling along, she did the best she could to cover herself up. A dark-skinned man approached and asked her "Are you lost?" He spoke to her in a language that she couldn't understand and asked, "Does anyone here speak English?" A voice from behind said, "I do." It was an inhabitant of the island who was multilingual, understanding French, German and English but, unfortunately, not Kai. Struggling with Triez's version of English, he listened as she committed a murderous onslaught on the English language for ten minutes. Finally grasping the bare facts, he understood and arranged for a truck to take them to the beach.

A few minutes later they arrived at the beach. After a chat with the man, Sophie found out that they were on an island that was part of French Polynesia. The inhabitants knew little about what had been going on in the outside world, other than it had affected their tourist trade quite seriously.

Sophie asked him if there was a phone nearby, he answered that there was and offered to take her into town but, before they left, another truck arrived with food and drink for the women on the beach. She told him, "That's very generous of you." He replied, "I'm feeling very generous, as I've never met an alien before!" Sophie pulled her prosthetic off and told him, "I'm not an alien. I'm American." He laughed and opened the door for her saying, "It's not a rocket ship, but it's quicker than walking."

As they arrived in town, a woman came out of a house with a beautiful Polynesian dress and handed it to her. Sophie thought to herself, *How nice - she must have seen my butt hanging out!*

Arriving at a bar, Sophie put on the dress and called Simon by phone. He was over the moon at the sound of Sophie's voice again. She asked him, "What impact did we make?" He explained that it was a great success, with only two seriously damaged vessels escaping, which General Walters's group finished off later. Simon offered to come and pick them up then and there but, after feeling the warmth of a tropical island on her skin, she asked him to make it later the next day, to which he agreed.

That evening Sophie's new friend introduced himself. His name was David; he had been born on the island, was well travelled and spoke four languages. Sophie told him, "I love this place. It's like a time capsule in real life, with really nice people who live in an isolated paradise."

Triez was at last decent, with the help of a very kind and beautiful girl who had taken pity on her and found her a dress to wear. She arrived at the lagoon at sunset and sat in silence as she absorbed the beauty of a spectacle she had never seen before. She found it exhilarating and said, "The backdrop of the palms and the beach are stunning." Sophie sat next to her and had to agree.

Arriving back in town, David had arranged for food to be served. Squaring up to Triez, he grabbed her nose and, in turn, she grabbed his testicles. Pulling her nose had been a mistake. Once the screaming had died down, Sophie explained that it wasn't a prosthetic - she was the real deal. David apologised and limped back to the bar.

The next day Sophie walked back to the lagoon. She had been contemplating how she was going to break the news of Trudy's death to her family but decided that it would have to wait as there was a war to win first.

The sea was warm, the sand was white, and as the palms swayed gently, she thought life didn't get any better than this. Walking over to Triez, Julie and David, she sat on the sand next to them, Sophie felt calm and thought, *Its like being in paradise with friends.*

*

Simon was right on time that evening as they watched the *Crazy Horse* land on the beach at sunset. The ship was empty within minutes, and the whole crew sat on the sand enjoying a drink together.

Sitting next to Sophie, the Prof had news about the Breeche. She informed Sophie that they had dealt a worse blow than they thought as the Breeche were now leaving. She had been tracking them through hyperspace, using the Breeche transponder module. It indicated that landings were being made on a planet called Par Kallish. Triez knew of it: she had visited it once and told Sophie, "Its inhabitants are not a space travelling culture anymore as they've seen it all, and are now quite content to stay at home." Sophie asked, "Are they vulnerable to being attacked by the Breeche?" This was something that Triez couldn't tell her. Sophie thanked the islanders for their hospitality, and the crew embarked onto the *Crazy Horse* for the next part of their mission.

CHAPTER 9

After dropping the sex workers off at the General's base, Sophie was listening to the news reports coming in from Indochina and Karachi. They had suffered terribly at the hands of the Breeche, who had left a trail of death and destruction behind them. One consolation was that so far Earth had survived. Sophie knew that she would have to make sure the Breeche could never return; she had them on the ropes and it was time to finish the job.

As the *Crazy Horse* approached the Moon, the base seemed different in some way as there were subtle changes. Sophie couldn't quite put her finger on it, but something was definitely different. Once the ship had landed, Simon opened the airlock and, to his surprise, the humans from the future were packing crates into the holds of their vessels. He looked at Sophie and said, "I feel a little strange, don't you?" She seemed a little vacant too. Both remembered them as historical sightseers from the future that had a base on the Moon. As there was a risk of a paradox occurring since Sophie had discovered them, they had all been recalled home to their own time.

Due to the fall of the Breeche, the Greys had never existed. Time had changed and a certain series of events had been put in place other than what Sophie and her crew remembered. A man came over to where they were standing. Sophie knew him as Michael, alias Charlie One. She shook his hand as he told her that he and his people were leaving; he thanked her for allowing them to watch the demise of the Breeche. But this time there was no telepathy between them as there was before: only words.

Unlike the Greys, the humans from the future had never had to desert the Earth, nor adapt and change their physiology. Sophie and her crew had saved them from being hounded across the cosmos by the Breeche. She asked Michael how far back in time they had come, but he wouldn't answer, in the same way as they wouldn't help with the construction of the *Crazy Horse* – that would have been too much temporal interference, and Sophie understood that.

Michael thanked her for her friendship, and said, "Goodbye Sophie - we have to get going as we have a wormhole waiting and if I'm late I'll miss dinner." Sophie smiled and leant on the handrail to watch their departure. Their vessels swarmed out of the complex and disappeared into deep space within seconds. She was a little sad to see them go, but she was now the proud owner of a huge complex on the Moon. Sophie checked to see if there was any of their technology left behind but found nothing: only her own stuff.

Later that evening General Walters arrived at the complex with a squadron of fighters. He was now Commander in Chief with the directive, although he still preferred to be known as 'The General' – it was a name that he was comfortable with. Simon was pleased to see him and asked, "Are you, Sally and peter coming with us?" He answered, "I wouldn't miss it for the world."

Dieter had a crew taking the engine pods to pieces on the *Crazy Horse* and knew that if they were to finish the Breeche off, it would take every ounce of German efficiency he could deliver.

Triez was teaching the fighter pilots about typical Breeche combat tactics and how to counteract them. Feeling over confident, she was lecturing in English without a translator. Jamie, who had been listening in, thought, *They're all doomed for sure now.*

Sophie was busy taking Diel on a history tour. They had borrowed Triez's ship and had travelled to the Sea of Tranquillity. Leaving the ship, Sophie couldn't wait to touch the landing section of the Eagle: it was like electricity running through her fingers. It was a place that she could never have imagined she would ever visit: almost a shrine to those astronauts that had pioneered the conquest of space. To Diel, it was just space junk, until Sophie explained that men had travelled there from Earth and used part of it to return home with sacks of specimens. Diel asked, "Which part?" Sophie said, "In the upper part that was missing." He was humbled by the fact that people had entrusted their very existence to something so fragile.

Sophie touched the flag and everything else she could find. It all had a special meaning to her. Returning to the ship they took their suits off and had a picnic within sight of the Apollo 11 landing site – it felt like magic!

*

At 11.00 pm that evening the *Crazy Horse* began its journey to Par Kallish. Once the ship was steadily cruising through hyperspace the crew took a break.

The separate crews had gathered together for a few drinks in the recreation area. General Walters was drinking as if the bar was going out of business, and he was only outdone by Triez who felt that getting smashed was a group activity. So, grabbing Big Tom, they joined the General for a game of 'Who can see the black dog in the corner first?' Although Tom was the favourite, Triez knew that the General was the real dark horse.

Above the shouting from Triez's corner, some of the pilots from the General's group were sitting with Sophie. Two of them were family men who were concerned about hyperspace; they had little experience of it, as Sally had only taken them through it for short periods at a time. Their concerns were that, according to Einstein, the closer you get to the speed of light, the more time slows down, meaning that they would be younger than their children on their return! Triez swaggered by on her way to the bar, saying, "I wouldn't worry about it, as you're all dead meat anyway!" Sophie told them to ignore her as she was rat-arsed again, and explained, "Hyperspace is outside of Einstein's theory and is a place where time is contained within the pocket of space that travelled with you." After telling them the facts, she felt fairly confident that she'd settled their concerns.

By the end of the evening, Holly was still sober as well as a little bored. Looking over at Triez and the others, she felt a hunger for mischief that had to be fed. Big Tom was singing, Triez was dozing, and the General was looking a little bemused with everything. Crawling behind the corner sofa, Holly pulled the General over to Triez and, putting her fingers in Triez's mouth, she exposed her fangs. Pushing Triez slightly closer to the General, Holly pushed the fangs into the General's neck. Smiling to herself, she stood back and watched.

Sophie had taken a beer and a sandwich to Dieter in Engineering and, after a chat about the intermix balance, he returned with her to the recreation area. On entering the room, Dieter laughed as he watched the General completely naked, chasing anything female. It could have looked menacing if it hadn't been so funny. Holly and Triez were rolling about with laughter until the General made a beeline for them too!

The next morning the General was on a drip in Doctor Phull's surgery. He was trying to get over a terrible hangover and exhaustion. As Sophie entered, the General asked if he had made a total fool of himself. Sophie assured him that it was no more than anyone else, and welcomed him to the *Crazy Horse*.

Later in the day, as his headache slowly diminished, the General entered the bridge. Looking a little sheepish, he took a seat at the far side. Walking over to him, Holly asked, "Well! Are you going to honour that proposal of marriage?" He just sat there speechless! Holly waited and stared at the General while tapping her foot; with a burst of laughter from her, he knew he had been had, and smiled.

Later that morning Sophie caught up with Triez and asked her what Par Kallish was like. Triez described it as a very spiritual place, with a small humanoid population who were once a space travelling culture. Sophie asked her, "Why did you go there in the first place?" Triez went very quiet and her eyes reddened. Turning to one side she silently walked away. Sophie was curious about what had happened on that last visit which had left her with such a deep scar on her soul. However, being the friend that she was, she respected Triez's privacy far too much to ask.

Jamie was picking up vessels not far behind them on the scanner. A voice came over the com – it was the Kai Captain. He told Jamie, "I'm on my way back to Kai along with four smaller vessels; one of them belongs to Ruman. Can I come aboard?" Jamie told him, "Certainly," and slowed the *Crazy Horse* to half speed while the Kai Captain's group caught up. Teleporting aboard, Triez was there to greet him. He asked her if she would like to travel to Kai with him. She thanked him for his invitation but said that she had to go to Par Kallish. His voice quietened as he told her, "She's with them now, and nothing can change that." Triez answered, "I know that's true, but I'm the first officer of an Earth starship and where it goes, I have to go too." Touching her shoulder in a sympathetic way he asked her, "You will meet me for drinks later, won't you?" Triez answered, "Of course." Placing her hand on his she said, "Thanks for your concern but I'm OK, really."

That night at the bar the Kai Captain asked Sophie to promise him something. She asked him what it was, he replied, "When you arrive on Par Kallish, Triez will feel the need to visit the Temple of Souls. When you see that happen, I want you to accompany her there." He didn't explain why and she didn't ask, but Sophie promised to do so all the same. The Captain liked Sophie and was pleased that Triez had such a good friend that she could always rely on.

Together with the Kai Captain were a handful of his crew; amongst them was a Kai woman that didn't escape the General's roving eye. He estimated that as Kai's had approximately the same lifespan as humans she would be around forty years old. She was slim, extremely attractive and not in uniform. His ogling didn't go unnoticed by Sophie, who took her over to meet him.

As she arrived, he was completely lost for words. Sophie had never asked the General if he was married or even if he had a first name, so she just introduced him as General Walters, and added, "I think he's available too!" The Kai woman asked the General if he had a first name; he told her it was Charles. She slid up next to him and put her hand on his thigh. Seductively she told him her name was Theras. Outrageously flirting with him, she offered to give him a guided tour of her ship, particularly her quarters. "That sounds like fun," he enthusiastically answered. Taking his hand she led him towards the teleport room, the Kai Captain winked at Sophie and asked, "Does the General have plenty of stamina?" Looking surprised she answered, "I do hope so!"

On reaching the teleport room, Triez was just leaving. She said "Hi" to Theras and stated, "You must have screwed every man on your own ship if you're stealing ours now." Theras answered, "I have, what of it?" and smiled at Triez. As he stepped onto the pad, the General wondered what he'd let himself in for. Triez grinned as she operated the teleport, warning the General, "You're in for an out of this world experience. I'll see you in the morning if you're still breathing!"

*

Sure enough, the next morning the General was still breathing and had a spring in his step. Sophie asked him if he had enjoyed himself the night before. He told Sophie that it had been five years since he had experienced a woman as passionate as that and it didn't matter what Triez had said; he totally respected her. Sophie told him that it was Kai culture to slander each other, and likened it to a high five. This brought a smile to his face as he told her, "You know, you have a natural talent for telling people what they want to hear." Sophie said, "Well hear this: the Kai Captain's going with us to Par Kallish and Theras will be around for quite a while." The General clenched his fists and hissed, "YES!" Sophie smiled and squeezed his hand.

It was a parting of the ways as Holly signalled to the remaining Kai vessels, and thanked them for their help against the Breeche invasion. Ruman signalled that he was heading back to Touscal to face the music. Sophie joined Holly at the com station and squinted her eye's as she looked at the view screen. There was something different about Ruman that she couldn't quite put her finger on and was unaware that like the grey's he too had become more human. She thanked him and offered to stand in his corner if it was necessary.

The *Crazy Horse* and the Kai Captain's ship dropped out of hyperspace at a distance from Par

Kallish. Listening in, Holly started to monitor local transmissions and checked to see who was doing what and where on the planet.

Jamie had scanned thirty-six vessels on, or orbiting, Par Kallish: twenty cruisers and sixteen frigate-sized ships. Sophie knew that if they could monitor the Breeche, then they should be able to do the same in return, and ordered a communications blackout. She needed more information about the planet before a strategy for the attack could be formulated.

Triez visited Sophie in her quarters that evening accompanied by Jamie. She had drawn maps from memory and enhanced them with three-dimensional imagery showing vegetation, open areas, and mountainous terrain. Sophie found them extremely useful and spent the night with the pair of them putting a plan together.

It was decided that the fighters would play their most dangerous role yet by keeping the Breeche vessels in orbit occupied, whilst the *Crazy Horse* carried out a strafing mission aimed at the larger Breeche vessels on the ground. While all of this action was taking place, Triez's ship would sneak through unnoticed and find cover in a large cavern on a large landmass, close to the location of the inhabitants of the planet. It was hoped that The *Crazy Horse* would draw some of the Breeche frigates in behind it leaving them vulnerable to fighter attack.

By mid-afternoon, Sally met with General Walters. He informed her that she would be coordinating the attack with the fighters and wished her good luck. He explained that he would be travelling down to the surface with Sophie and the others as guerrilla warfare was what he had cut his teeth on. Arriving in the launch bay the General climbed aboard Triez's ship, it was packed to the limit with weapons and personnel. The General was the last one in; he assured Sophie that this was her show and expressed how much he was looking forward to a good fight.

At 7.00 pm the fighters swarmed out of the holding bay. Once they were away, Jamie took the *Crazy Horse* into a steep dive and opened the launch bay doors.

At five thousand feet Triez left the bay. Her ship shook violently with the turbulence caused by the *Crazy Horse*. Gaining control again, Triez made for the cavern. Sophie watched from the side window as Luma let go of every weapon on the *Crazy Horse* and stared spellbound as it swooped back up into the air; she just hoped that the vessel would draw the frigates behind it.

Triez had located the cavern and was relieved to find that it was easily large enough to accommodate her vessel. Sidling in, she carefully landed the small ship on a flat patch of sand. Their next objective was to meet up with the Kai Captain's men, three kilometres from their present position.

Once out of the cavern, Sophie recognised the sights sounds and the landscape, from the dream that she had after her mental enhancement. She could feel the presence of the strange wildlife and plants of all different varieties.

Simon went ahead of the main group and met up with the Kai soldiers. Sitting on the ground, they shared whatever intel they had managed to gather. The Kais had a more detailed layout of where the Breeche vessels had landed and uploaded it to his pad.

Testing the ghost's portable unit, Sophie told it that she might turn it into a rat or something for gathering intel. This didn't sit well with the ghost as it wasn't happy that it had been used to play a demon and chase an angry Greek into the sea. It was even more disgruntled about playing the part of a rodent or something worse, and made her aware that it was an intricate piece of technology, and not a plaything. Sophie assured it that the work it was doing was vital to the success of the mission.

Triez knew where the settlement of Par Kallish inhabitants was situated, and as she was unsure whether any dangerous predators lived in the area, it seemed a good idea to make amiable contact with them as soon as possible.

Pushing themselves forward through the undergrowth, they came to the settlement. It wasn't what Sophie was expecting. The first thing that she saw was a translucent dome with children sitting on the ground, and what seemed to be a tutor pointing an illuminated baton at a screen that seemed to just hang in the air, completely unsupported.

Lying behind the dome were the remnants of an ancient city with undergrowth growing through every aperture and crevice. Sophie had assumed that the inhabitants were a less complicated people. Triez enlightened her that being a spiritual people didn't necessarily mean a backward people and reminded her that they were once a space bearing race. Sophie stood corrected and apologised to Triez.

As they moved forward into the settlement, Triez was welcomed with open arms by what appeared to be one of the elders of the settlement. He seemed overjoyed to see her and beckoned at the rest of Sophie's group to enter.

Moments later the settlement became alive with people coming to meet them out of thin air. Sophie wondered if they were phantoms of some kind. As they greeted her with a light embrace she was made aware that they were very real and warm-blooded, just like herself, and she was surprised at how similar they were to humans.

Triez took Sophie by the arm and led her over to two rocks with a gap of a metre between them. On top of each rock was a light. Triez pulled at Sophie's arm, dragging her between them. Once she had passed through, everything changed. The dome had gone and the old ruins had disappeared. Before Sophie lay a great city, shadowing anything that the human race had ever built; it left her spellbound.

Back on the *Crazy Horse*, Jamie had lured away four Breeche frigates and they were taking a beating. Dieter was busy trying to balance the power output from the engines as the vessel had not been designed for dogfights, and wasn't faring very well. On the bridge, Holly was helping Jamie with the rapid course changes, while Luma fired a full spread of cannon fire from the rear-facing cannons and disabled a frigate's forward shielding. From nowhere a directive fighter came in and took it out. Hearing "Yahoo!" over the com, she knew it was Peter. Directly ahead of the *Crazy Horse* were two Breeche cruisers that had taken a beating from Sally's fighters. They were alongside each other and full of holes. Scanning them, Jamie could see that their shielding was down and noted that the sub-structure towards midships on one of the vessels was smashed. Not one to miss an opportunity, he increased the power to the forward shield and rammed both ships simultaneously, breaking them both into several pieces. However, the victory was short-lived as four Breeche frigates appeared right behind them. Jamie leant the *Crazy Horse* into a steep bank and managed to out-turn the Breeche weapon fire.

Heading back towards Par Kallish, and now with seven Breeche frigates on their tail, Holly detected four fighters heading their way.

With heavy fire coming from behind, a volley of shots hit one of the *Crazy Horse*'s pods and breached the hull in the engine room. The suction dragged three of Dieter's crew out through the hole before the bulkhead damage shields activated.

Jamie headed for the atmosphere of Par Kallish. Passing the *Crazy Horse* almost head on, the directive fighters fired on the frigates following it. With a severe blast to the second pod, the ship started losing power. Jamie realised that the ship wasn't going to survive this one, and looked for a soft spot to crash. An opportunity presented itself to Luma like a gift from heaven; there ahead lay the same two cruisers on the ground that she had hit on the first run. Passing only a few hundred feet above them, Luma fired again at point blank-range, causing a huge explosion.

The *Crazy Horse* flew through the fireball, trimming off the treetops as it passed. Jamie struggled to keep the nose up as it careered into a forest for five hundred metres before grinding to a halt. Luckily there was no fire. But as the ship had crashed, it had broken into three sections. Most of the middle section had disintegrated on impact. The rear section had spun around onto its side; this had protected most of the personnel in that section. Climbing from the wreckage of the front section, Jamie approached the wreckage of the centre section. He could see that casualties were high and was distressed to see Dr Phull's medical team lying in the undergrowth They'd died as the medical department was destroyed. It was located within the centre section of the vessel. Following Jamie, Luma offered Dr Phull solace by cradling his head, as she had a pretty good idea how he was feeling. He'd been in the engineering section when the vessel struck the ground and had been treating an engineer injured when the hull breached.

As he became aware that the sick bay had bore the brunt of the crash, he started to break down. Holly knew that they were his closest friends and didn't really know how to tell him that all of them had perished. But she eventually found the words. He just stared at her with tears running down his face. Holly put her arms around him saying quietly, "I know, I know."

Back at the city, Sophie asked Triez how this digital world, as sophisticated as it was, could possibly exist. Triez explained that the inhabitants of Par Kallish were far more advanced than Sophie thought and enlightened her to the fact that they had seen it all, done it all, and bought the T-shirt. She told Sophie that where they were wasn't a city at all. It was an ultimate computer, and that it was possible for them to pass from the real world into the digital one by simply walking between the two rocks with lights on them. Sophie asked her how they could change matter into energy so easily. Triez explained that Sophie's body was being held in a stasis chamber, while her mind and digital body were free to wander around the city. She also explained that, unlike the Par Kallish, they would not be able to stay in the virtual world for long periods, whereas they were conditioned to live in a digital world permanently if they so wished. Sophie asked Triez how long they could stay in the city. Triez guessed that it would probably be for a day or so.

The General and Simon joined Sophie as she sat in an arboretum. Simon had spoken to an elder that told him that they would be automatically returned to their bodies if any cell degradation started to take place within twenty-four hours. Sophie noticed Triez approach a transport station and watched her as she pressed a button. Instantly she disappeared. Intrigued, Sophie approached the station. The last destination was a picture of a huge temple. She remembered what the Kai Captain had asked of her; repeating the destination instruction, she followed Triez.

Materialising in a beautiful garden with songbirds and flowers, she could see Triez in the distance as she entered a temple. Sophie followed her as far as the outside pillars where she stood and watched. In the middle of the temple were a group of children playing. One of the children, a girl of about fourteen years of age separated from the others and approached Triez as she knelt down. The girl ran into Triez's awaiting arms, who picked her up, kissed her and stroked her hair. Sophie stayed where she was and sat on a bench, while Triez and the girl talked.

After a while, they walked around the garden. As they approached where Sophie was sitting, Triez stopped for a second and brought the girl over to her. She introduced her as Isalia, and told Sophie she was her daughter. Sophie found her an articulate and delightfully beautiful child and she could see that Triez was very proud of her. For an hour or so all three of them talked and played until it was time to say goodbye. Triez knelt down and stroked Isalia's hair, then kissing her goodbye, she then left her to run back to her friends, Isalia looked back just once.

Neither Sophie nor Triez said a word all the way back to the two rocks. Once outside the city and back in the real world, Triez was ready to talk. A drunken Breeche, for no reason, had shot Isalia two years earlier. Her injuries were extremely serious and threatened her very survival. After Triez had killed the drunken Breeche, she took Isalia away from Kai in the dead Breeche's vessel. She didn't want to see Kai ever again. Isalia had become worse as the vessel passed Par Kallish, so Triez decided to find help. On meeting the inhabitants, Isalia was seconds away from death. The inhabitants could offer only one solution, which was for them to adapt her to live with them in the virtual world. Out of desperation, Triez agreed.

She told Sophie that Isalia had no physical presence and took her over to see the grave where Isalia's body was buried. They sat at the graveside while Triez told her, "The computer will age her accordingly, she'll never go hungry nor be in need of anything her whole life."

Sophie disagreed saying, "She'll always need her mother, even if its only now and then," which brought a smile to Triez's face.

Realising that the inhabitants of Par Kallish were not in any danger, Sophie asked one of the elders if there was anything on the planet that could be of use to the Breeche. The elder informed her that the planet was rich in choronite. Triez explained that with antimatter, it could be a devastating weapon and that she had used it in her suicide device. The elder told Sophie to fly to a landmass in the Southern Hemisphere. That was where the choronite was to be found. Sophie asked for the coordinates. The elder went into the domed classroom and came back with a piece of paper. Turning it over, she could see it was a map. It was now clear to Sophie that the Breeche knew that they would lose a war against the human race and that they lacked any real talent for formulating strategies. She also knew that they could never rule or enslave the human race. Revenge was what they wanted, and only the destruction of Earth could satisfy them.

*

Returning to Triez's ship, Sophie found she had a list of messages on the console. Triez could see Sophie's face drop as she read that the *Crazy Horse* had been destroyed. Sophie felt that the only consolation in all this was the fact that not all of the crew had perished. Looking depressed, Triez felt the need to remind her that they were at total war with an enemy that would never quit and said, "In this situation, there are always heavy casualties, it's something we have to live with. There'll be plenty of time to mourn when it's over." Flexing her hands Sophie stood up and said, "You're right! Let's get on with it."

The next message gave the coordinates of Sally's downed fighter – it was en route to the Southern Hemisphere.

As they reached Sally, Sophie could see her standing upright. She looked a little bruised, with a black eye and a bandaged hand, but she was OK.

Sally updated Sophie on the Breeche vessels' situation. She saw only one Breeche frigate left, and that was the one that got her. She knew that the Kai Captain had brought it down as it followed her down onto the planet. Pointing to a cloud of rising smoke she said, "There it is."

Boarding the ship again, they set off to confront the Breeche and stop them from mining the choronite. Sophie looked through the messages again; there was a list of dead or missing. She saw that many of Dr Phull's staff had died, and Peter Hazelwood was missing. The General told Sophie, "If there's no personal transponder signal, then he's probably perished."

When Triez read that Tom and his clan had survived, she tried to play it down, but a single tear on her cheek told a different story.

With all of the Breeche frigates and four cruisers destroyed, Sophie knew that they still had to deal with sixteen heavily armed cruisers. All she had on her side was an ageing Kai cruiser in orbit, Triez's scout ship, and two of the General's fighters in orbit.

Approaching the target zone, Triez took the ship towards the ground. Ahead of them lay the sixteen Breeche cruisers. Finding a flat piece of ground, Triez landed the ship well away from the cruisers and pushed the front of the vessel into a large pile of thicket; they would be on foot from then on.

Breeche jetpack patrols were passing overhead and, with slow progress, they inched towards the cruisers using whatever cover they could find. They stopped at a high vantage point overlooking the Breeche.

It was like a stone quarry, but with a deadly difference. Sophie told them, "If we detonate any device in the mine it could blow half of the planet out into space; a more subtle tactic is required here."

Triez had a pretty good idea what the Breeche had in mind regarding the choronite and told Sophie, "If it was distributed into Earth's upper atmosphere it would remain in the jet stream; with a single detonation the Breeche could burn off the Earth's atmosphere, killing everything on the planet."

With the sound of a jetpack approaching, Sophie and the others kept their heads down, except for Triez, who had a few ideas of her own. As a single Breeche passed close to the cliff edge, Triez pounced like a cheetah and grabbed a Breeche soldier around the neck. She had learned a lesson from the last time she had tried this in New York. Pushing the steering bar to the right and forward, she took both of them to ground level at the bottom of the cliff. She pulled the soldier out of the rig while holding him round the throat and asked him, "What are the Breeche planning?" Relieving the pressure just enough to get an answer she listened. But as she had expected, he told her to go to hell. In response to that, she grabbed him between the legs. As he tried to scream, she tightened her grip around his throat.

Again relieving the grip around his throat a little, he confirmed her suspicions. With a heavy punch, she knocked him unconscious. Dressed in his tunic, Triez put on the jetpack and carried the unconscious Breeche soldier over the sea and dropped him from a great height.

Watching Triez improvising, Sophie felt fit to do the same and led the rest of them down the cliff face in a more conventional way. There was a more accessible route, a little way back the way that they had approached but, being buzzed by Triez as they struggled on their way down to the bottom, didn't help. On the jetpack, Triez had found an access pad for opening a doorway through the perimeter shielding on all of the Breeche cruisers.

It was a hundred metre sprint over open ground to get to the first cruiser. A sentry had been posted virtually facing the rocks that Sophie's group were hiding behind. Flying over to the sentry, Triez came down behind him, grabbed him around the neck and blasted off over the sea. Again from a great height, she dropped him in.

Entering the first ship unchallenged, it seemed to Sophie that most of the crews were either working in the mine or flying around on jet packs. Locking the door behind them, they made their way towards the bridge of the vessel. Looking through a porthole, Simon could see Triez outside strangling another Breeche sentry. She had her legs around his neck and was swivelling him around at great speed. He thought she looked like a ballerina wearing a jetpack. Simon commented to Sophie on how well Triez had mastered the combined art of strangling and flying at the same time.

The General had gone missing. Unfortunately, they didn't have time to mount a search, so they pressed on. There was a click of a photon rifle to the side of her; Sophie froze. It was a Breeche soldier with the rifle targeted at her head.

With a crack, blood spurted from the side of the soldier's head; it was the General's gunstock. He boasted that stealth was his speciality when he was younger. Sophie was impressed. As they checked cabin by cabin, they could find no more Breeche on board the vessel. Sophie asked Sally if she thought she could fly it alone. She was willing to try and, with a little instruction and translation from Sophie, she had a brief understanding of how to control the vessel.

Sophie gave her the transponder frequency of the *Crazy Horse*. She asked her to pick up the survivors and the ghost's control unit, then rendezvous with the two fighters in orbit. Then Sophie, Simon, and the General left the cruiser. Sally made a rocky lift off, but seemed to be getting the hang of it by the time she had disappeared over the horizon.

Triez was nowhere to be seen; Sophie could only assume that she had entered one of the cruisers. Joining the others, she made her way to the entrance of the mine A conveyor that was carrying the choronite from the mine to one of the cruisers suddenly stopped working. Sophie could hear voices coming from the entrance of the mine that seemed to be getting louder. She realised that the Breeche had mined enough choronite, and were ready to leave. Breeche wearing jetpacks were swarming back to the cruisers. This confirmed her suspicions. Sophie and the others made a run for one of the Breeche cruisers, one stood alone from the others. Once they were aboard, Simon locked the hold door. Looking around the hold, there was no evidence of choronite. Sophie checked that the vessel was functional, and was relieved when the engines started. Waiting for the first of the Breeche vessels to take off, Sophie followed it.

Once orbit had been established, Sophie teleported over to the Breeche cruiser that Sally had taken earlier. Sally had teleported the ghost's control unit to the Kai Captain's vessel for now and had handed control of the vessel to Jamie. It was good to see her crew again. Sophie expressed her sorrow at the loss of his staff to Dr Phull. She found him extremely mellow, with little to say. Big Tom was asking after Triez; Sophie explained to him, "The Breeche have to be stopped at all costs, even if it means destroying the vessel that Triez is on." Tom asked, "Can I teleport onto the Breeche vessels one by one, as I have to find her?" Seeing the concern on his face, Sophie touched his hand and agreed.

Teleporting back to Simon and the General, Sophie had taken Tom, Dr Phull, and enough people to crew the ship. With limited resources, the Doc tried to make Tom look as much like a Breeche as he could. Sophie found a uniform that would fit him and arranged to meet him at the teleport room. At that moment Dieter came over the com and told Sophie and the others to return to Jamie's vessel. When Sophie asked him why he told her that he was not receiving any emissions from their hyperdrive and that the vessel they were travelling on was useless.

Simon checked the readout and confirmed Dieter's suspicions. It made sense to Sophie now why the Breeche were not interested in that vessel, as they had removed the antimatter from the reactor. She knew that if it were mixed with enough choronite, it would make a devastating weapon, possibly enough to destroy a planet.

CHAPTER 10

Sophie met Tom at the teleport, and made it clear to him that she would be using the vessel they were travelling in as a bomb and that once the others had been teleported back to Dieter's ship she would activate the self-destruct amid the Breeche ships in orbit. She told him, "If you haven't found Triez by the time the Breeche depart for Earth, you'll be teleported back to Dieter's ship, along with myself."

Sophie activated the teleport and sent Tom to the first ship. On his arrival, he could hear Breeche voices locally. Knowing that his command of the Breeche language was poor at best, he switched on his translator. As for Breeche mannerisms, he felt he would just have to improvise. He could see that he was standing in the engine room; luckily he had arrived in a corner without raising any suspicion. Stepping onto a catwalk he had a clear view of the engineering section. In his ear was a two-way transmitter. Sophie was listening in on the Breeche conversations but told Tom that there was nothing in their conversation concerning Triez. Making his way towards the bridge, he thought, *I know she's not injured in a sick bay because there are no sick bays on Breeche vessels. If you're sick - they just throw you out of an airlock!*

As Tom entered the bridge he noticed a screen to his left and saw what appeared to be a schematic for a bomb; from what he could make out there were three bombs and all on three separate vessels.

Sophie marked the vessel as a target when it was time to activate the auto destruct. Contacting Tom she activated the teleport again sending him to the next ship. This time he arrived in a cabin with two Breeche males and a female. Tom improvised by picking up a rifle and beating the two males with the stock; the female lunged at him, baring her fangs. She was confused as he held her by the neck and thanked her for the offer, but stated that he had Triez for that sort of thing, and punched her unconscious.

He was moving toward the front of the vessel, when Sophie's voice came over his earpiece to say that Triez was sending out a homing signal. She was on that ship. Sophie warned Tom that the Breeche were breaking orbit and she would have to start the self-destruct sequence.

Tom rushed to the front of the ship but Sophie shouted down his earpiece, "You're going the wrong way! She's in engineering." Turning around, he ran towards the engine room. Sophie activated the ghost's mobile unit and asked it to rig the primary fusion drive to overload next to one of the Breeche vessels that was carrying a bomb. There were five seconds left on the countdown when Sophie teleported and appeared facing Dieter on the pad. "Quick!" she shouted, "Get Tom off that vessel." Dieter said, "Relax, I already have him."

"Three, two, one."

With a massive blast, their ship keeled over to starboard. As Sophie flew off the pad she could see the teleport activating. The ship was now lying on its side with Sophie spread-eagled against the wall, in the confusion she felt heavy weights falling on her, crushing her.

As Jamie levelled the vessel to an upright position again, Sophie saw Tom with Triez clinging to him. Both of them had fallen on top of her. Climbing out from underneath the pair of them, all three looked out through the porthole.

There was twisted metal everywhere. Holly called the teleport room at that moment and made Sophie aware that the wreckage was the equivalent to ten ships being destroyed. Sophie felt that it was too early to celebrate, as there were still three vessels out there, two with the capacity to destroy Earth.

Triez pulled Sophie's arm, dragging her over to the other side of the vessel. Looking out through the porthole, Sophie asked her what they were looking at. There was no reply as Triez just stared incessantly at her watch. A great white flash appeared in the distance, it looked like a supernova. As the shockwave hit their ship, it spun around and caused it to rotate at speed, everyone was stuck to the walls except Jamie who was still in the pilot's chair but unable to move. Sophie knew that without any resistance they would be stuck to the walls indefinitely, or at least until the ship impacted against something.

Triez had a photon pistol in her holster. Sophie spotted it and said, "I've got an idea." She asked Triez if she could reach her pistol. Reaching down, Triez managed to pull it out of the holster. Sophie asked her to set it to the minimum setting and fire it at the thruster levers. Jamie was hanging out of the seat leaving Triez with a clear shot.

As she fired the pistol, the gravity slowed the photon beam down, causing it to hit Jamie in the back. Once the swearing had died down, Triez took another shot; firing wide of Jamie the beam hit two of the levers, sending the ship careering through space. Jamie fell back into his seat and heaved the vessel to.

Sophie asked Triez what the flash and shockwave were about. Triez explained that she had posed as a crewmember on board one of the ships carrying a choronite bomb. Once the bomb had been manufactured, she popped a time-lapse grenade inside the inner casing and then went looking for a way off the ship.

Triez also explained that a large Breeche had grabbed her in the engine room, so she punched him in the face, which would explain why Tom's nose had bled all over Sophie's tunic after the teleportation.

Dieter called in stating that the engine was offline, with slight damage, and would take an hour to restart. Jamie compounded the problem by reporting that there were two Breeche vessels fifteen light years ahead of them. Sophie just hoped that they were suffering the same problems as she was.

It was too far to send the ghost to investigate, so Sophie contacted the Kai Captain. His vessel had been compromised by the blast too, but was still functioning. He offered to give chase to the two remaining vessels. Grateful for his offer of help, Sophie accepted.

Once the Kai ship was in range, Sophie, Triez, and the General teleported aboard.

The Kai Captain made best speed towards the two Breeche vessels, but even in hyperspace, his ship was only running at one-quarter power. Sophie went back to the engine room to see if she could lend a hand.

The General was delighted to see Theras again, and the feeling was mutual. She was aligning the photon cannons and had been hidden away from the General's sight doing mundane tasks. The General offered his assistance; he felt it exhilarating just to spend another moment with her.

Triez sat with the Kai Captain on the bridge, discussing what the new Kai would be like not having to live in the shadow of the Breeche anymore. He said, "With an end to bloodshed and brutality, the next generation would know a very different world to the one that we grew up in."

He welcomed the idea of a close relationship with Earth, even stating that the short time that he had spent in Florida was the happiest time of his life. Triez felt that she and the Kai Captain shared a common commitment to stopping the Breeche from reaching Earth and knew that in order to save the planet the buck would stop with them as there was no one else.

Shouting down the com to the engine room, the Kai Captain asked, "When will full power be restored?" Sophie replied, "In about five minutes." The ghost was in the engine control unit, sending back data to restart the intermix sequence manually.

It accused Sophie of using it as an old spanner. She assured it that it was the most important system on the ship, which seemed to quieten it down a little. When the job was complete she closed the ghost down and put it back in its portable unit. Sophie activated the intermix and with a few whirring noises, the engine started. They had one engine at full power and the other at half power; she knew it would have to do for now.

The Kai Captain had been monitoring the Breeche vessels; they were still heading on a course for Earth but at a reduced speed. One seemed to be leaving the other behind. He was pretty sure that the leading vessel was the one with the bomb on board, and the second was there simply to slow his ship down.

As they approached the slower vessel, Sophie, Triez, and the General armed themselves as well as six of the Kai Captain's men and women. The Kai Captain readied his ship for combat, ordering the gunner to target the forward weapons on the Breeche vessel while their shield was down.

Sophie sent the ghost to the Breeche vessel. It reported back stating that the hold was empty, and was therefore the best place to teleport to.

Immediately, Sophie and the Kais teleported to the hold on the Breeche vessel. The Kai Captain fired on the bridge of the Breeche ship in the hope that the distraction would allow Sophie and the others to make their way forward.

But unfortunately they met heavy resistance around the engine room. Sophie ordered the ghost to interfere with the lighting, which it did. While the lights were flickering Triez crawled along the corridor, as Sophie and four of the Captain's crew laid down suppression fire. Triez had a foothold in the doorway of a cabin; as a grenade came her way she pushed out her rifle butt and hit it back at the Breeche soldiers. The blast took out a bulkhead, allowing Sophie and the others moved forward.

The Kai Captain fired a broadside at the Breeche vessel, collapsing a large section of the hull, narrowly missing Sophie and the others. He now had full engine function on both pods, which allowed his vessel to pass by. Activating the teleport he started pulling his men off the vessel. Sophie and Triez were the last ones to arrive and just in time to hear mines being launched in the path of the Breeche ship.

Triez switched the monitor in the teleport room to reverse angle and zoomed in on the Breeche vessel just in time to see the mines make contact with the bridge. It opened up like a flower, exposing the entire bridge to space. A third and fourth mine hit midships, where the hull had already collapsed, and the whole ship exploded into large pieces.

Dieter had repaired the engines on his vessel and had full power again. Pushing those same engines to the limit Jamie was making good ground, and was not far behind the Kai Captain's ship. Over the com channel, Jamie sounded extremely relieved that it wasn't the Kai Captain's ship that had exploded. Triez explained that in order to destroy the leading Breeche vessel with the bomb on board, they would have to get dangerously close and might not be able to get far enough away to clear the blast zone.

Sophie offered an alternative that seemed more palatable than dying, which was to board the Breeche vessel. The Kai Captain reminded her that their shield was intact. Sophie explained that they had done it before, and that the gunner on Jamie's vessel had an extraordinarily rare talent for disrupting shield harmonics.

Four hours later, Jamie and the Kai Captain's vessel were only one light year behind the Breeche cruiser containing the bomb. Sophie's main concern was that the Breeche vessel was now only one hour from Earth. Sophie signalled Simon to bring herself, Sally and Triez aboard. Once aboard, she told Simon, "Luma had better be on form, or there'll be no Earth to go home to tonight." Dieter had spent a few minutes labelling the knobs and buttons on Luma's console, trying to make it more familiar to her. Luma herself was nervous. Sophie told her, "There's no pressure, just try to relax." Triez whispered in Luma's ear, "You know Big Tom's going to stretch your neck if you cut off his sex supply." On that advice Luma double checked the system.

Sophie had already chosen who would be going with her to the Breeche vessel; it would be Triez, and Sally. She had decided on Sally mainly because she hadn't shown fear in any situation so far and had always risen to any challenge. But, more importantly, Sophie knew she was a crack shot.

All three headed for the teleport room. Dieter was there, ready to operate it. Luma confirmed over the com that she was ready to synchronise with the teleport. As Sophie stepped onto the pad, Luma fired at multiple targets around the rear shield, then targeted the middle and fired a concentrated blast. Like rippling water the shield was disrupted just enough and all three teleported through. In a second the shield was solid again.

They had teleported close to the engine room. Sophie was now more than ever aware of the passage of time, and was starting to worry that they were too late. But was also contemplating how to fight an almost extinct psychotic enemy with nothing to lose.

Triez focused Sophie's mind again by attacking two engineers and a guard. With almost no time left to worry, Sophie and Sally came out shooting like women possessed, while Triez strangled one engineer between her legs and held the other by the neck. It was a female. Sophie asked, "Where's the bomb?" But the female Breeche just scowled and tried to lash out. Punching her Triez threw her over her shoulder and into the intermix.

With a sudden jerk, the ship started to judder. Triez's ferocity took Sally totally by surprise as she passed through the vessel like a tornado. The Breeche ship was now gradually slowing.

At first, Sophie thought that it was due to Triez's additive to the mix that had slowed the ship down but, looking at her watch, she realised that they were nearing Earth. They were too close to the planet for the Kai Captain to destroy the ship, as that action would detonate the bomb and destroy the Earth also.

Triez moved forward and Sophie followed, passing a console. Sophie saw an opportunity, and activated the ghost. "What now? Does a toilet that needs cleaning?" groaned the ghost. Sophie asked it to access the ship's navigation computers, and redirect the Breeche vessel towards the sun. Quickly disappearing into the ship's systems the ghost set about the task. Sophie listened to her com set as the ghost kept her informed of its progress

Not far from the bridge was a large room on the right. Looking through the glass, Triez could see two technicians next to the bomb. She pulled out her pistol but Sophie warned her that her weapon could ignite it. As the technicians moved to the other side of the bomb, Sophie slipped through the door and tried interacting with it. She could see the timer in her mind's eye; it was set to explode in ten minutes.

Triez and Sally entered the room and took the technicians down. Try as she might, Sophie couldn't disarm the bomb and switched tactics. Knowing that the ghost was her last chance, She headed for the bridge followed by Triez and Sally. The ghost was in one of the navigation computers and was having no success at redirecting the vessel. For every move the ghost made, it was counteracted by someone on the bridge, as they kept overriding its instructions. Sally entered the bridge, spraying suppression fire as Triez and Sophie entered behind. Jamming the door shut behind them a huge fire fight started, with only minutes to spare.

Triez tried her luck by shooting at an overhead structure. Sally joined in and brought most of the ceiling down on the Breeche bridge crew. At last, the ghost managed to redirect the vessel towards the sun. Adjusting the speed, it would impact in two minutes. Sophie looked at her watch and realised that they were out of teleport range from the Kai Captain's ship.

Simon came over the com channel and said, "For god's sake get out of there! Everyone's aboard the Kai Captain's ship now." He told Sophie to use the unmanned vessel that Jamie had abandoned, as it was travelling in her direction. He also told her to use it as a halfway house, and to use the teleport on that vessel to reach him.

On Jamie's advice Sophie, Sally and Triez headed for the teleport room. Setting the controls, they teleported to the unmanned Breeche cruiser behind them. They had arrived in the teleport room with only ten seconds to spare. Sophie didn't have time to put in the coordinates of the Kai Captain's vessel and just teleported herself Triez and Sally off the ship, regardless of destination.

Within a second they were all teleporting somewhere. Sophie just hoped that the Kai Captain's vessel was close enough to grab their signal, but nothing! All she could see was a light, a brilliant light with stars showing through it.

It had only been a few seconds that Sophie had been in limbo, and there was no sign of Triez or Sally. Feeling strange, she wondered whether she had entered the afterlife.

After fifteen seconds Sophie could hear Triez calling her name. The stars disappeared and the brilliant light faded to nothing. Standing before her was Triez, intact.

To her left, Sophie could see Sally materialise. Together they found themselves at the bottom of a cliff – it seemed familiar to Sophie. They were standing at the bottom of the cliff where they had observed the Breeche earlier.

Triez said they were on Par Kallish. Climbing back to the top of the cliff, Triez's scout ship confirmed it certainly was Par Kallish. Sophie queried whether they were all dead, with everything around them being the afterlife. Triez replied that if it was the afterlife, she didn't think much of it!

All three climbed aboard the scout ship and Triez laid in the coordinates for the Domed School. Sophie hoped that the elders could shed some light onto what had happened to them and how they had managed to travel light years in seconds.

As they arrived at the equator, Triez picked up a distress signal just below them. She started the descent and activated the scanners. It was a human signature. In the distance, she could see a wrecked fighter.

Standing by the door Sally couldn't believe her eyes, it was Peter! She threw her arms around him in disbelief, shouting, "I thought you were dead!" Peter's flight suit was ripped to pieces and had a great deal of blood smeared over it. Triez told him he was showing his bits and pulled at the suit, exposing him. She said. "Just checking: with all that blood on your suit, I wanted to see if you were complete!" Peter looked at Sophie and told her that all he could remember was being hit by a Breeche photon cannon and crashing into the forest. He added that, with all that damage to his suit and the blood loss, he should've been dead.

Heading off again, all four continued to the Domed School where they were welcomed on their arrival by a female Par Kallish inhabitant who gave Sophie a welcoming embrace. She said, "I'm pleased that you've found Peter." The female told her that they had saved Peter at the crash site and, although his injuries were serious, her people were in time to save him. She apologised for not being able to save those on the *Crazy Horse*, as they were too far gone. The female explained they were far more advanced in medicine, but only the divine spirit could work miracles.

Triez felt drawn to see Isalia once more and walked over to the two illuminated rocks. The female caught her by the arm and told her "You don't have to enter there anymore as Isalia's collecting flowers in the old city grounds."

Triez's stomach felt hollow as an intense feeling spread over her. Sophie took her arm and led her towards the ruins. Stopping at the edge, she allowed Triez to carry on. Kneeling on the ground was a girl of about fourteen of age, It was all too much for Triez to take in as tears streamed down her face. Looking round at Sophie she asked, "Can this be possible? Is it really her?" Sophie took her hand and took her over to where the girl was kneeling. Triez could see the girl's profile. Kneeling down next to her she said, "Isalia, is that you?" The girl's head turned towards Triez and she said, "Mother?" For once in her life, Triez was lost for words. It was Isalia! Triez touched her hair – she was outside and living in the real world. With tears streaming down her face she pulled Isalia close to her and kissed her. Triez had found the one thing in life she needed more than anything: her daughter.

Sophie asked the female how it was possible. The female explained that the best thing that Triez could have done when Isalia was shot, was to leave her with them. A body could always be cloned, but not a mind – that was another matter. She assured Sophie that it really was Isalia and not just a clone; her mind and memories had always been preserved. The elder told Sophie that although they loved Isalia a great deal, her mother's pain was all too much for them to bear and the decision to clone Isalia with a body was taken. The female asked Sophie and the others to stay with them for a while.

*

That evening over a meal, the female explained that from the minute Sophie departed aboard the Breeche cruiser, she was being monitored – every word, every action. The female had placed an implant on the underside of Sophie's arm when she was out of her body at the Temple of Souls. Holding Sophie's arm up, the female placed a silver disc against her skin, and with a single drop of blood, the tracking device dropped onto the table.

The female added that if her people had not intervened, all three of them would have been teleported into open space. Sophie asked how they were delivered to Par Kallish. The female explained that humans see things in four dimensions, time being the fourth, whereas her people saw things in *six* dimensions, and they could also act within them. Sophie and the others had been teleported through a wormhole in the sixth dimension. The woman explained, "My people have travelled beyond the Milky Way to dozens of other galaxies and dimensions. However, we have seldom come across beings as benevolent and caring as you and your friends." She further explained that since the demise of the Breeche, her people were now looking at Kai through fresh eyes!

In the morning Sophie was told by the female that they could not be sent back to Earth using the wormhole as it was far too dangerous for simple commuting.

Triez had a friend with a house of multiple occupancies on Kai and felt sure he would be willing to accommodate everyone. As Kai was the only planet within range of the scout ship, Sophie's options were limited.

It would take four long days to reach Kai with five people on board the tiny vessel, and no one was looking forward to it. The Par Kallish inhabitants loaded the small ship with foods of all varieties. There was a massive turnout to say goodbye. Some were especially sad to see Isalia go, as she had made a great many friends there.

Everyone stood back as the scout ship lifted from the ground and quickly disappeared into the clouds. Passing close to some Breeche cruiser wreckage in orbit, Triez whispered *good riddance* and set a course for Kai.

Two days had passed and, as Sophie took a shower, she looked out of the window of the scout ship. What she saw was a beautiful nebula in the blackness of space; it was something that she had never really appreciated as it couldn't be seen in its true splendour from hyperspace. Sophie had also learned a great deal from Isalia during the journey. Sophie felt she was certainly a gifted child with a great deal of knowledge about populated planets and the peoples that inhabited them. She also felt that being the tortoise instead of the hare had its merits, and was enjoying this time together with her friends.

As they approached Kai, they could see bright red and white patches, even though the areas they were monitoring were under the cover of night. Triez looked worried, stating that she wasn't quite sure how welcome they'd be. Sally called Peter over. She had been listening to radio signals and had worked out that Kai was split between two rival factions vying for power. One faction was a pro-alliance group with Earth and the other an extremely right wing dictator. Triez listened and suspected the dictator of being in it to control and manipulate the split to his own ends.

A state of war had been declared between the factions and all interplanetary arrivals were being turned away. Sophie felt that they might have been better off under the heels of the Breeche. As an alien herself, Sophie would not interfere with internal politics, but would help Triez if she requested it. Triez landed the vessel on a landmass away from the fighting. She had many friends all over the planet and hoped that some of them would be allies.

Triez took Sophie and the others to a house of multiple occupancies; some of the occupants were intellectuals and she hoped that they could shed some light on the situation. Triez knocked on the door of a ground floor apartment. A slim man with a beard answered the door. Triez knew him well: he had been a reporter for a radio station. He told Triez that the armed forces had been bribed and were in the hands of an egotistical hothead called Hylan Varrick, who could see a quick profit in the ignorance of the masses.

Triez had made Varrick's acquaintance once. She remembered him as a self-opinionated, sickening little man with a huge belly and an equally huge amount of wealth. Triez knew that the only way to bring the armed forces to bear, was to kill him and cut off the supply of credit to his supporters. However, she knew that with all that wealth and the armed forces at his side, he'd be a hard target to reach.

Triez and the others slept at the apartment that night. Over breakfast, Sophie enlightened Triez that Earth had had its fair share of fascist dictators in the past, and all the regimes they had cultivated had ended up in disaster.

The man who owned the apartment sat down at the table. He offered to help find some of Triez's old friends, as Triez had lost contact with many of them after the uneasy truce with Breeche. She told Sophie stories of the fearless escapades that she had shared with them four years earlier fighting the Breeche, and felt that they shared the same values as Sophie and herself. Triez spent the day showing Sophie some of the more beautiful parts of Kai. The town that they were staying in was on a canal network and was not unlike Amsterdam. With old buildings and shops, Triez sat Isalia down next to the canal, at a table that was owned by a coffee shop. Sophie sat next to her while Triez went for the drinks. She came back with two very large looking coffee cups and a large orange juice. As usual, the drink was laced with alcohol, but with a very smooth taste. Triez had chosen that exact spot, as it was where she was to meet her old comrades.

Thirty minutes later, six of Triez's friends arrived – four men and two women. They were beside themselves with joy at seeing Triez again. One of the women looked at Isalia; her face dropped as she took hold of Isalia's hands. She asked Triez how it was possible. Triez told her that since she had met the Earth woman many things had become possible, and that she was convinced that a peaceful, prosperous Kai was a possibility too. Triez told them about the destruction of Breeche Prime, and how the remaining Breeche were hunted down and eradicated.

That afternoon, and after many more of the large coffee-type drinks were consumed, the relationship between Triez's friends and Sophie took shape. They trusted her because Triez trusted her, and that was good enough for them. As they were well connected, they promised to spread the word, and try to quieten the misunderstandings that were putting Earth in such a bad light.

It was the first step towards a unified Kai, and a further step towards ending Hylan Varrick's scheming that would certainly send Kai careering into an abyss from which it would never recover.

CHAPTER 11

Back on the Moon, the atmosphere was solemn. Jamie had taken the freighter out three days in succession and found nothing. He had searched every square kilometre of the area and was feeling frustrated at not finding any remains within the range of the teleport system He wanted to believe that his Captain was still alive. A gut feeling told him that the three of them must be out there somewhere. He knew that they had completed the teleport to the half way house ship. He also knew that they were not on that vessel when it plunged into the sun along with the Breeche cruiser. Travelling back to the Moon he had one thought in his mind, *Where the hell are they?*

That night Diel knocked on Jamie's door. Inviting him inside, he asked him to take a seat and poured them both a drink. Diel told him that when a Kai male is in love he forms a particular bond similar to that of a telepathic link that's so strong they can feel their partners presence. He made it clear to Jamie that if Sophie were dead he'd know it.

Early the next morning Jamie went to see Simon and explained to him everything that Diel had told him the night before. Simon told Jamie that he'd call the Kai Captain on Earth to see if he agreed with what Diel had said.

*

The General had set up home with Theras in Portland. Theras shared Triez's liking for Earth and felt settled in the life that she had chosen with the General. They were having breakfast together when the Kai Captain called at the house. He explained to the General that Simon had contacted him and informed him of what Diel had experienced. The General seemed to think that it was all a bit mumbo jumbo until Theras put her hands on his face and held him spellbound. She pushed emotional thoughts into his head about how much she really loved and respected him. His face was hurting a little, so he pulled her hands away.

The General asked her, "Is that really how you feel about me?" She answered, "Yes, of course." And added, "That thing you want to try in bed: it's fine with me!" A little red faced, the General said, "OK, I'm convinced!" The Kai Captain interjected, saying, "A visit to Kai is long overdue." He also told the General that he and his crew would be leaving for Kai the next morning. The General smiled at Theras and offered to join the Captain on the journey to Kai.

The next morning the Kai vessel launched with the General and Theras on board. The General was a rational man but, after the emotional link with Theras, he felt as though his eyes had been opened to a mind full of possibilities.

One hour into the journey, the Kai Captain picked

up a vessel closing in on their position. Sounding battle stations, he armed the rear cannons. Over the com came a familiar sounding voice. It was Simon and the crew of the freighter: they were also heading for Kai. *The search was on!*

On Kai the next morning, a note was pushed underneath the door of the apartment. Triez opened it and gave Sophie a shake until she was half awake. Reading it aloud, Triez made Sophie aware they were to make their way to a base amid the fighting in the Northern Hemisphere, as they were expected to attend a summit meeting. The heads of the pro-alliance would be in Attendance too. Turning the page over, she could see that the coordinates of the meeting were identified. Frowning, Sophie sat up and told Triez, "I hope we can convince them of Earth's good intentions." Triez replied, "You convinced me, didn't you? And stop frowning, or you'll stick like it!"□

Later that morning, Triez kissed Isalia goodbye and, together with Sophie, Sally, and Peter they made their way to the scout ship. It was a frightening forty-minute journey at one hundred feet to the rendezvous. There were groups of Varrick's men and women everywhere. Armed with photon weapons they were shooting at anything above fifty feet. Sophie scanned for incoming fire and advised Triez of necessary course changes to avoid the worst of it. Scanning the ground for a second, she could see that it was littered with the wreckage of pro-alliance vessels. On their arrival, all four left the scout ship. Standing by the door, the sound of photon fire was deafening.

A tall man that Sophie recognised from the coffee shop welcomed Triez. He escorted them to the makeshift control shelter. The builders had taken advantage of a large depression in the ground that also had a large rock formation overhead. Walking down below ground level, the noise lessened. A soldier of high rank handed Sophie a hot beverage; but this time it was without alcohol. He introduced himself, then sat down at a table. His open hand pointed to four chairs on the opposite side of the table; all four sat and listened to what he had to say.

His concern was that if Varrick took control of Kai, he would be no better than the Breeche overlords and that he would need certain assurances that Earth wouldn't do the same. He put it to Sophie that perhaps the anti-alliance was right, and Sophie could be just another version of the Breeche.

She was furious at this. and asserted herself by throwing the table clear of the room. The soldier was alarmed as she approached him, Summoning up her inner strength, she picked the soldier up by the neck. Remembering a few Kai swear words, she directed a torrent of abuse at the soldier.

This behaviour took Triez and the others totally by surprise, as they had never seen this side of Sophie before. Regaining her composure, she dropped the soldier to the ground, lowered her head and asked him to forgive her. Putting one hand on her cheek the soldier said, "I already have."

After a drink and some furniture rearranging, Triez told Sophie she had absolutely gained the soldier's trust and that there was nothing that the Kai loved more than someone showing an outburst of passion about what they truly believed in.

When she'd had a short talk with the soldier, Triez congratulated Sophie at being the supreme commander of the pro-alliance armed forces. Everyone in the room went down on one knee and pledged their allegiance to Sophie. She could only utter one word. "Shit!"

The next day Sophie addressed the air commanders and generals. She told them, "The Fighting between the pro-alliance and anti-alliance forces is a civil war. I have studied Kai history and understand that Kai has never before had to endure a war where brothers take up arms against each other. Here today, we must pledge an oath that once this feud is over it must never be repeated." She suggested that the only reason that the anti-alliance existed was because they were being paid to fight. She told them that what she required were well-trained crack troops to lead an assault on Varrick himself and the source of his wealth.

Sophie had spent the previous evening reading news reports on Hylan Varrick and understood that the main revenue of his empire was coming from a Helium 3 processing plant on Kai's Moon, Phalon. He had made a fortune selling it to the Breeche and now, with the Breeche gone, so was part of his income. Sophie explained to the generals and air commanders that Varrick's plan was to virtually hold Kai to ransom and that taking complete control of the planet was his real goal.

An air commander addressed Sophie, explaining that Phalon had been off limits for years as its defences were impenetrable since it was defended by a state of the art, automated robotic defence system. He added that it was A.I. and capable of adapting to any attacking force's strategies. He also stated that even the Breeche with all their might hadn't been able to penetrate it.

Sophie felt that the ghost could do with stretching his legs a little, and activated it. There was silence in the room, except for a few sharp intakes of breath. It asked Sophie what she wanted it to do now, maybe sing another song or perhaps do a magic trick. She told it that she wanted it to invade Phalon's defence system. The ghost explained to her that the system contained adaptive nanotechnology and that it would be eaten alive. The ghost added that for him it would be like a death sentence. Even though she knew the ghost was just an A.I. machine, Sophie didn't really want to lose it, and considered how she could reduce the risk to it.

That night the fighting ceased, with the pro-alliance retreating to a defensive position. Sophie had designed a defence grid from available components salvaged from crashed vessels. With the help of Triez and some of the others, they crept to a midway point on the battlefield and put the actuators in place. Sophie could see the anti-alliance in the distance. She was wondering why they hadn't attacked and figured that the retreat may have freaked them out a little. Retiring to a safe distance, all four of them watched as the anti-alliance resumed their firing by taking shots at the grid. It was possible to see the photon weapon discharge absorbed by the net; this had the effect of making it stronger, at least in the short-term.

Later that evening Sophie set to work on a system that would save the ghost from being eaten alive by adaptive nano-bots. Her mental enhancement would be stretched to the limit on this one.

Activating the ghost again, she asked it to stand in the middle of the shelter while she did a photon count. If it were to survive and complete its mission, it would need to have the same amount of photons at the end of the mission as it did at the beginning. The portable control unit would not be able to keep the ghost's field open if this was not so. Sophie had a unique idea which involved giving the ghost a ghost of its own, something to keep the nano-bots occupied while it got on with its job.

The next morning Sophie added a sub routine into the portable control unit; it was a non-A.I. copy and completely expendable. The ghost seemed happy with this idea and thanked Sophie for her concern. After the joke that she had played on the bar owner in Greece, it was beginning to think that Sophie didn't really place any value on it.

At eight o'clock that evening Triez's scout ship took off; its destination was Phalon. As they closed in on Kai's Moon, Sophie could see the complex, which made an imposing sight. Checking their watches, it was time to suit up.

As they approached within a hundred miles, a hailstorm of weapons fire came towards the small vessel. Sally and Peter were ready to jump. Waiting for a pause in the weapons fire, Peter counted to three and jumped through the doorway taking Sally with him. Both fired up the suits' thrusters and hastened their pace towards the surface before the firing resumed. Together with the thrusters, they were being drawn down towards the complex by Phalon's weak gravity. Firing the thrusters on their suits, Sally and Peter made a soft landing.

Triez and Sophie were the next to jump. Triez looked behind her and watched as her ship was slowly blown to pieces as the firing resumed. Landing twenty-five metres from Sally and Peter, Sophie promised to find Triez a new and better ship. Making their way to a communications point on the outside wall Sophie activated the ghost once again. It appeared in its Touscal form and told Sophie and the others to be careful. Shrinking in size, it disappeared into the complex's security system. Moving along the outside wall, Triez had spotted a door, she could see that it was guarded by automated weapons and cameras. Using the com link Sophie told the ghost to go for these systems first.

The ghost was shutting down systems everywhere, and it wasn't long before the nano-bots started attacking the ghost's own personal ghost. The none A.I ghost was doing a fine job of fooling the nano-bots and keeping them well away from where it was working. Sophie reminded the ghost that the nano-bots were adaptive and would soon work it out. □

The ghost sensed that the nano-bots had just figured it, out and with just one mad wrecking spree at the security systems. It screamed at Sophie to get it out of the system. Just as it detected a hoard of nano-bots about to pounce, it materialised in front of Sophie. Sally pointed out to the ghost that it seemed to be hyperventilating, to which it replied, "You would too if you'd been in my boots!"

The door seemed to be unlocked and the cameras didn't seem to be working either. Sophie congratulated the ghost on a fine job. The ghost seemed to smile; Triez was sure that it had a smug look on its face.

Carefully, the four of them entered the complex; it was huge. Sophie asked the ghost to float ahead and look out for any guards. Minutes later over her com-set came a report from the ghost, stating that a small group of guards were sitting in a room about two hundred metres ahead of them. As they passed through an electronic barrier, an oxygen-nitrogen atmosphere became present. Unfortunately for them, it had also alerted the guards too. Quickly removing the thruster suits, all four took cover.

Sophie could see six guards crouched over and running along the wall. Triez jumped onto an elevated platform and threw a stun grenade, disabling five of them and, in return, she came under heavy photon fire from the last guard. That was until Peter hit him with a photon pistol charge on stun. Jumping to the next level Triez could see the private apartment of Hylan Varrick. Sophie was pleased that the guards were only stunned, as this was a mission to win hearts and minds and not to alienate and further divide the Kai.

Locking the guards in a storage room Sophie and the others entered an elevator and joined Triez at the higher level. The apartment appeared as a set of double doors. What lay beyond was a mystery. Carefully stepping through one of the doors, Triez marvelled at the pure opulence that this man lived in. The lounge had a sunken floor with huge sofas, beautiful paintings adorned the walls and marble statues stood in the corners. Scanning the area for humanoid life forms, Sophie and the others followed.

With no warning, Sophie noticed a huge animal

charging from the back of the room. It was heading straight for Triez. With a single bound, it pounced. Triez caught the animal by the paws and tried to avoid its salivating jaws. As the creature looked downward, Triez saw her chance and head butted it unconscious. Looking around at Sophie, Triez said, "That was a real dog." Sophie stood over it and kicked it – it was out cold.

Triez had a feeling that someone had unleashed the animal and, with a rush for the door, she could see Varrick running down the huge hallway. Running after him, she was stopped by a sliding steel sheet that dropped from the ceiling. Peter shouted to Triez to stand with her back to the wall, and fired a volley of rounds across the steel sheet. Creasing it in the middle, the sheet folded in half allowing Triez and the others to bound over it.

Varrick had disappeared through one of the doors leading from the hallway. One of the doors was slightly ajar; Sophie took the lead. On the other side of the door was a cavern about forty metres long; it was brightly illuminated by powerful heated lamps and covered in tropical plants of all varieties. Triez thought that it was a good place for Varrick to hide but she was having none of it, and went in after him. In the distance, the heated lamps were disclosing Varrick's whereabouts. Sally could see bushes moving and took a shot. A mass of foliage folded over. Whoever or whatever it was, had been hit.

Moving forward, Triez found Varrick lying unconscious amid the flattened plants. Picking him up, she threw him over her shoulder and carried him back to the lounge. By this time the dog had regained consciousness and was cowering at the sight of Triez manhandling its master. Throwing Varrick on the sofa, Triez poured five glasses of wine and handed a glass to everyone, except for Varrick. She threw the fifth at Varrick's face, thus bringing him round. Sophie congratulated him on his taste in wine and furnishings. Varrick replied that he had struggled and worked hard for everything he owned. Triez reminded him that his humble beginnings had started with him selling arms to the Breeche four years earlier in order to murder the Kai people, and that his hands were soaked in blood from the conflict that was occurring right at that moment. With a smirk on his face, he told Triez that, without him alive, none of them would escape the complex and made her aware that he had sixty troops guarding the space dock.

Triez picked up the wine bottle and smashed it against the fireplace; holding the neck she pointed the razor sharp end of the bottle towards him. Sophie could see that she meant business and placed a hand on Triez's arm, telling her that in a modern democracy everyone had the right to a fair trial.

Sophie told Varrick that due to her enhanced state, together with the other three of them, killing sixty troops would be child's play. Varrick laughed, saying that she couldn't kill Kais, but the ones loyal to him could kill her, and no one would care less. Sophie realised that he had a valid point. She knew that they had to get Varrick back onto Kai soil to stand trial without killing anyone or getting themselves killed in the process.

Sophie knew that without a ship, it was useless returning the way they had entered. Sally called

Sophie over to a monitor; she had been scanning the launch bay at the space dock. She told Sophie, "Varrick's launch is the most accessible vessel at the dock but, as he said, there are about sixty troops fully armed and loyal to him. To get past them without bloodshed is nigh on impossible." Triez marched Varrick to the rear door of the apartment. Sophie and the others followed. They walked along a plush passageway with thick carpet and expensive looking wall coverings. Triez asked Varrick where the passage led to. He told her that it led his office, and he ran his whole empire from there.

Arriving at a large hand-carved door, Triez opened it and, as she did so, another large dog-type thing jumped at her. While Triez was occupied with the animal, Varrick made a run for it. Sally punched the dog with an uppercut to the jaw, spraying Triez's face with saliva. As it fell to the ground Peter put his foot on the dog's head and it was pacified. Triez sarcastically said "Thank you" to Sally as she wiped the saliva from her face.

Letting the dog go, Peter picked up a piece of cord attached to a lamp. Tearing it out of the back of the lamp, he tied it around the dog's collar. Sally told him, "This is no time to take the dog for a walk." He answered, "We should take it with us as it may come in handy." The dog was quite passive towards Peter by now and seemed to regard him as the leader.

Varrick had left the office through a door on the adjacent side of the room. This was Varrick's playroom, which contained four very beautiful women sitting on a sofa. Triez asked one of them, "Where did Varrick go?" Standing up one of the women shrugged her shoulders and walked towards a bar. Triez picked her up in a most undignified way and threw her at the other three. With a crash, the sofa collapsed.

With all three of them sprawled on the floor and screaming, one pointed at the wall. Sophie kicked a section of the wall where the young woman was pointing. Hearing a hollow sound, she opened a small door in the wall. Behind it was a poorly lit tunnel. Peter let the dog go into the tunnel and all four followed it. With the noise of photon rifles firing, they closed in. The tunnel opened up into a dimly lit square room. Two of Varrick's troops were cowering in the corner, with the dog sitting on their rifles. Peter patted the dog on the head and picked up one of the rifles and stunned both of the soldiers. Picking up the dog's leash he led the way. □

About one hundred metres on, the tunnel came to an abrupt end. A large girder bridge lay ahead of them. Five hundred feet below them was the Helium 3 extraction plant. They knew they were underground, but didn't know how far. Sophie took the lead as all four stepped onto the bridge. After walking two hundred feet along the bridge, there was a large explosion behind them. Some of the steelwork was starting to collapse. Sophie could see Varrick on the other side of the bridge; he was standing on a path to the right that lead round a cliff face. He was firing photon shots at the steelwork of the bridge, causing it to collapse. Sophie fired back at Varrick as she and the others started to run along the bridge. □

With another shot from Varrick, the steelwork behind them started to collapse. Sophie ushered Sally and Peter on, but the section Triez was on started to break away. Sophie shouted to her to jump. Hanging by her feet, Sophie hung upside down from a girder. Triez had made the longest jump of her life, as she touched Sophie's fingers. Sophie dropped another few inches. Hanging by one leg, she had Triez's other hand. Pulling Triez back up, they ran for their lives. Turning round at the end, they saw the rest of the bridge collapse.

Triez asked Sophie if it was absolutely necessary to take Varrick in alive. She was furious and wanted his head on a plate. Sophie understood how she felt, but they had to take him in, and in one piece.

On the path, the dog was waiting for Peter. He was sure it was laughing at him as it ran down the path. With an almighty blast, the dog was blown to smithereens. As they approached the blast area they could see that Varrick had left a proximity mine on the cliff face. Triez told Peter that he was right – the dog did have a purpose. With that, she stopped speaking as she could see that he was a little upset at the dog's demise.

With just enough of the path left to squeeze by, all four pressed on. The path was now on a downward incline and the air seemed a little thinner. It was time to hasten the pace, as it occurred to Sophie that Varrick might be venting the air into space.

At the bottom of the incline was a thick metal door fixed to the cliff face. Varrick had locked it behind him. Raising their weapons, all four started shooting at the door in a synchronised manner, but to no avail as the door was firmly locked from the inside. The air was running out fast now and Sophie knew that they had to do something quickly. Triez said that a door was only as strong as its hinges so, with two on each side, and in unison, they charged at it. It was starting to move on its outside edges. With another charge, the door was starting to move inward.☐

Lethargy was setting in as the four of them were feeling the effects of oxygen starvation; with one last charge, the door collapsed inward. Stopping to catch her breath, Sophie could see they were now at the edge of the space dock. As they moved forward, weapons fire opened up, with photon shots hitting the walls all around them. Taking cover, Triez started calling the troops, telling them that Varrick was finished. For a short time, the firing stopped. She told them that there would be no more credit and that they would have to find proper jobs. This seemed to infuriate them, and the weapons fire resumed. Sophie suggested that Triez should leave the diplomacy to her in future.☐

A few moments later the firing stopped again, as the area was quiet, Sophie could hear the troops retreating to a safe distance. With suppression fire aimed towards Varrick's men, a single soldier entered the area. Calling out to Sophie, Triez recognised the voice instantly. It was the soldier from the compound, together with a handful of crack troops.

*

Varrick was hiding on the upper level of the space dock. He knew that if he made a run for his vessel he would be taken down, and he was right. As Triez's ship was now just a pile of mangled wreckage on the surface of Phalon, she watched Varrick's ship with envy. She had the route to the launch bay covered, and nothing would stop her from claiming the vessel as her own.

Varrick shouted at his men to attack. He assured them that Sophie and the others did not dare kill them. With this, Varrick's troops made a frontal attack. Triez and Sally stood their ground along with the soldier and his men. Sophie ran along the top of a wall towards the area where Varrick's voice had come from, while Sally provided cover fire. But Sally's gun was hit by a photon round, leaving Sophie a sitting target. A single round hit Sophie to her side, knocking her off the wall, and she fell twenty-five feet onto concrete. Triez called out to Sophie. She was desperately trying to get to her, but was pinned down by Varrick's men. There were just too many of them.

Varrick took advantage of the situation and made a run for his vessel. Triez could see him running for his vessel and focused her rifle: he was in her sight. Her finger kept flicking the gun's switch from stun to kill and back again. She had seconds to fire. Thinking about what Sophie had said, she set it to stun and fired - Varrick fell to the ground, stunned. Triez shouted, "Varrick's dead!" The firing lessened until it finally stopping altogether, as the troops realised that they were not going to be paid.

Varrick's men laid down their arms, while Triez ran to Sophie's aid. Peter was receiving intel from outside the space dock; it was the freighter. Peter requested Dr Phull's attendance and opened the launch bay doors. Within seconds the Doctor teleported next to Peter. Sophie was in a bad way, with almost no vital signs. The Doctor teleported Sophie and himself directly to the freighter's sick bay.

With Varrick in custody, the troops on Kai laid down their arms. The war was over!

Four hours had passed and Sophie was still on the brink of death. The Doctor couldn't understand it. He'd treated the wound to Sophie's side with his skin cloning technique, and scanned her body and brain: he was at a loss. He was aware that Sophie's implant could be malfunctioning, but didn't have a clue how it worked. It was Touscal technology and was wired into every part of Sophie's brain. As the Doctor stood over her, the ghost entered the operating theatre. The Doctor asked it, "How did you self-activate?" It told him, "I've always had the ability to self-activate, but seldom had the need to, not until now."

Like a genie, the ghost turned into a small white cloud and entered Sophie's mouth. It surrounded the implant and tried to contact Sophie. It quickly diagnosed that the implant was malfunctioning at every level, and would kill her if it totally failed. Carefully, the ghost started to sever the links to Sophie's brain. After it had cut through ten links, her brainwaves started to increase. Encouraged, the ghost carried on severing the connections until her eyes opened. Dr Phull tried to talk to her, but all she could do was blink. He could see that she was able to respond to 'yes' and 'no' questions by blinking her eyes. It was now thirty minutes later and the ghost left Sophie's body. It told the doctor that he could remove the implant as it had been disconnected. Once the Doctor had removed it, Sophie groaned and sat up. She said, "I had the strangest dream about the ghost stomping about inside my head." The Doctor said nothing, and gave her a glass of water.

After breakfast, Sophie tried to summon the ghost, but with little success. She tried to accesses Dr Phull's computer: nothing there either. Pulling the mobile unit from her coat pocket, she tapped it several times, calling, "Come out! I know you're in there! A second later, the ghost appeared. It explained that her ability to interact with computers would no longer be possible, but her brain would still retain its enhanced ability. Sophie didn't really mind that as it made her feel more like everyone else now.

The Kai Captain had taken General Walters with him to meet the Kai senior officers. He had plenty of previous experience of dealing with peace treaties and reconciliation, and they were grateful for his expertise and advice

Later that day Sophie went for a walk through the freighter; chatting to the crew she asked them where they would go next. She felt that with the threat to the Earth over and a few new friends throughout the galaxy, there was little use for a bunch of tired out mercenaries without a cause.

Sophie sat at the communications station and activated the hyperlink to Earth. Calling Holly, she found that she had already found her new vocation in life. She was now the head coordinator of the project that was rebuilding much of the Earth's infrastructure. There would be no more dirty or toxic power stations. With a new supply of Helium 3 and a new customer for the Kai, the Earth would be a much cleaner place to live in, thanks to the new nuclear fusion reactors. The new Kai High Council had given Holly a great deal of technical information concerning new technologies. Sophie promised to send her the blueprints for a linear car powered by hydrogen: it was the car that Sophie had driven on Breeche, and had such a liking for.

CHAPTER 12

Two billion people had died in the conflict on Earth. The Breeche weapons were so destructive that there were very few bodies to be interred or cremated. The human race was picking up the pieces. The cost of winning against the Breeche had been extremely high, but they had survived, and a new better world would emerge from the ashes of the old one.

Luma Tyrol and Jamie McTavish would not be returning to NASA as they would be part of a new directive involved with deep space exploration. It was to be an interplanetary concern involving the Kai and the Mylin but the Touscal had little interest in it. New larger, more powerful vessels were to be constructed, building on what had been learned from the *Crazy Horse*.

Strolling into the engineering department Sophie sat down with Dieter. He was going through the proposed schematics for the new engines that would take the human race far beyond their local stars. He was struggling with the design of the new triple injection system on the up rated reactors. His problem was a lack of efficiency that had shown up on the virtual reality simulation. He had spent most of the morning looking for a solution and was at the end of his tether.

Sophie could see that he was about to explode and set about calming the animal that was starting to rage within him. Handing him her cup of coffee, she told him to take a break. Taking a chair, he sat down and watched Sophie pulling the blueprints round to face her to study them. After ten minutes she found herself becoming irritated by the same problem that had been baffling Dieter. Once he'd finished his coffee he walked back to the table. Sophie scowled at him saying, "Leave me alone," and pushed him away. Quietly he walked back to his seat.

Calming herself for a moment, she reached into the toolbox. Using a hand held scanner she uploaded the sheet onto the computer-aided design system. Converting the chart to 3D she could see the problem and told Dieter that the injectors were of an incorrect rating and should be round, in a concave seating, totally adjustable and connected to a control unit. Walking over to Dieter, Sophie opened her arms towards him and, with a broken smile, said "Sorry." He could see her eyes filling with tears. As he gave her a hug he said, "It's the implant isn't it? Or rather the lack of it." He could feel her head nod against his chest and in a muffled voice she said, "It used to be so easy, but now everything seems so difficult." Wiping a tear from her cheek, Dieter welcomed her back to the real world again. Stroking his face she said, "Thank you... for being you." Sophie realised that without her implant, things were going to be an uphill struggle from then on and consoled herself with the thought, *Well at least the war's over.*

Quietly taking her leave, she made her way to the launch bay. She knew Triez would be there with a certain new acquisition, and thought she might take a look at Varrick's very expensive looking escape vessel. Simon was outside the launch, kicking the struts like the tyres on a second-hand car. He liked it immensely and said, "Triez really has struck gold this time as most of the interior fittings are made of the stuff."

On entering the launch Sophie could smell the quality of the fixtures and fittings. There were gold handles and knobs on every drawer and cabinet. She went into the flight deck and sat next to Triez who was sitting in the Captain's chair; it was draped in the most luxurious leathers and fabrics she'd ever seen. But even more impressive were the flight systems. Accessing the computer, Sophie could see that its range and speed outstripped anything that the *Crazy Horse* was capable of.

Triez had a feeling that it might have been stolen from a planet Varrick had visited and told Sophie, "This vessel is extremely advanced. He didn't get it from anywhere round here." Sophie checked to see whether Varrick had entered an escape route into the flight computer. Sure enough, the information was set up on the system and ready to go – it was a planet well off the normal charts. Triez said, "It's somewhere to go on a rainy day." The smile on her face said it all. Sophie had never seen Triez so happy; she had Tom, Isalia, a position on the Kai High Council, and a diamond encrusted vessel. Who could wish for anything more?

Later that evening Jamie took the freighter down

onto the surface of Kai. He complained, "The sooner they build a bloody spaceport, the better! How the hell am I supposed to land this thing between the trees in the dark?" Luma looked at him grimacing and laughed. Raising his eyebrows he said, "Point taken" and activated the landing thrusters. Once down, they were not far from the State Building. As soon as Sophie walked through the doors, General Walters escorted her into the room and told her he would be returning to Earth on the freighter in the morning. He asked her when she would be returning home. Sophie only remembered home as a depressing existence. She knew now how soldiers felt after a war, and the difficulty that many found trying to settle into everyday life again.

She told the General that she needed some time out, and would be staying on Kai for a while. Simon told Sophie that he'd be on the freighter in the morning and the Prof would be going with him too. His plan was to take a break and join the new directive with Jamie and Luma. He gave Sophie a kiss and said, "I'll always be there for you, you know that?" She responded by saying, "Me too."

Diel approached Sophie. He could see that she was not her usual self. He seemed to know what she needed so, picking up two glasses and a bottle of wine, he took Sophie by the arm and led her into the grounds of the State Building. Stopping at a fountain, he sat Sophie down on a grass slope and sat next to her: pouring two glasses of wine he told her to lie back on the grass.

It was a warm evening on Kai and she could see that it was a full moon. Phalon's light lit up the garden with a pale bluish hue. Diel told Sophie to breathe deeply and look up at Phalon. It seemed to do the trick and had a calming effect on her. They lay there for hours talking and watching the sun rise. Diel asked Sophie how she felt: she said, "Better." He replied, "Good! Now all you need is a job and a place to live." Sophie laughed.

*

Three months had passed since the war against the Breeche and Sophie had settled on Kai. She had a place by the ocean and a job she could manage from home. Although Diel had moved onto pastures new, she felt more content now than she had for a long time. Big Tom had gone back to Earth to complete a building contract in New York and Triez would regularly visit her with Isalia; they would sit on the beach and reminisce about Triez's time in Brooklyn. She would often say how much she missed it, and that she would take Isalia there soon. Sophie felt the pull of Earth too: more frequently by the day. She was now feeling ready to make her mark on the newly rejuvenated Earth.

Arrivals from Earth were a regular occurrence since the war had ended, and the human race was welcomed with open arms at the new spaceport that had only recently been completed. Kai was now prospering as never before as new trade agreements with Earth and the exchange of cultures made it a very bohemian place to live.

A shipment of Helium 3 was made every week to Earth. The freighters would carry ten fare-paying passengers with every shipment; Sophie would be one of the ten that week. With a sad wave to Triez and

Isalia, Sophie boarded the freighter. She gazed out until Kai was just a dot in space and felt a little sad about leaving her second home.

The Helium 3 freighters were not built for speed and would take four long days to reach Earth. It was the second day of the trip when the engine developed a fault and dropped out of hyperspace. Sophie offered to help repair it, but the skipper said that it was all taken care of. An hour later Sophie could see another vessel come alongside through the window. It was an obsolete Kai cruiser; seconds later she heard the freighter cargo doors open.

Still looking out of the window, she could see containers of Helium 3 being pushed across to the old cruiser by three men in thruster suits. Looking over to her left she saw a fourth man leaving the freighter; knowing that the freighter only had a crew of four, she was beginning to feel alarmed.

The old cruiser was now powering up its engine and Sophie knew she was in trouble when the vessel targeted its cannons on the freighter. Running towards the bridge she tried the door; it was locked. With a sense of impending doom, she summoned all her strength and kicked the door out of its frame. The engine read-out said 'nominal'. Now she knew it was a heist, and a heist with no witnesses. Powering up the engine, Sophie swung the ship around at full power.

Two photon shots gouged out two strips of metal from the roof of the bridge. Sophie knew that she couldn't out-run them. She also knew that she couldn't out manoeuvre them and, with no weapons, she was certainly out-gunned. Pulling the freighter around at ninety degrees, Sophie smashed the rear end of the freighter into the engine pods of the old cruiser. Some of the passengers from the freighter were at the door to the bridge panicking. They asked Sophie what was going on. All that she could do at that point was to tell them, "Please return to your seats and trust me, I know what I'm doing." Feeling reassured that there wasn't a problem, they returned to their seats. Sophie had regretted lying to them and also regretted not being able to protect them. Feeling an overwhelming sense of guilt, she felt an urgency to try anything.

The cruiser was damaged, but still manoeuvrable and able to move its cannon turrets. As the weapons locked on to the freighter, two shots from nowhere blew the old cruiser clean in two, and a polished, very expensive looking launch did a victory roll over their heads.

Once docked, Sophie thanked Triez and complimented her on her marksmanship, but Triez could take none of the credit for it and told her, "Isalia's new body is a superior, upgraded version of what's considered normal for a Kai. The inhabitants of Par Kallish had grown extremely fond of her and equipped her to survive under any conditions. Her eyesight alone is up to six times sharper than mine." Triez boasted that her daughter could shoot an insect in a tree from five hundred metres, so a piece of crap like the old cruiser was easy.

The passengers from the freighter were receiving a very unexpected upgrade as Isalia ushered them through the airlock into the launch. Salvaging three containers of Helium 3 and taking the freighter in tow, Triez trained the weapons onto the two halves of the old cruiser and fired. It was a massive explosion, blowing the cruiser into thousands of pieces. Accelerating back into hyperspace, the launch made best speed towards Earth. Sophie asked Triez, "Why are you here anyway?" She answered, "We were going to visit Tom soon, so we just decided to come sooner." She added, "Isalia was missing you and, so was I." Sophie said, "It was lucky that you were passing. I thought I'd have to deal with them myself." Triez pulled a face and said, "Without weapons? Oh yeah!"

Sophie was astounded at the speed of the launch as they reached the Moon by 8.00 pm. The Kai passengers were pointing at the Moon, which drew Sophie's attention to it. Looking out of the window she could see that huge changes had taken place with what looked like a Helium 3 plant and military bases. Triez took the launch in for a closer look. Sophie's base had been extended across the surface, with landing pads and enclosed walkways between the buildings. A warning beacon alerted Triez that she would be fired on if she didn't identify herself. Triez identified herself and added that Sophie was with her.

Simon came over the com, welcoming them home, and said he was looking forward to meeting up with them later. Triez left the freighter in orbit and asked Simon to take care of it. He agreed to, for a cut out of the salvage money, to which Triez agreed.

Sophie noticed that Triez was now speaking without a translator and asked her how she had learned English so quickly. Triez explained that Isalia could learn languages at an accelerated rate, and had been ramming it into her head for months.

Pulling back out of the Moon's orbit, Triez set a heading for Earth. Her vessel had been fitted with a smart transponder that located and laid in a course for Earth's new spaceport. It was Portland, four miles inland, and only half finished. The course took them in over the Portland headlight. It was dusk and the flashing of the lighthouse seemed to enchant Isalia. As Triez brought the launch down to fifteen hundred feet, visitors to the lighthouse watched as it passed overhead. Turning their heads they marvelled at its sheer beauty as it passed over, glistening in the twilight.

With the final approach instructions coming over the com, Triez made a perfect landing at the base. Sophie was surprised by the welcome home she'd received as she had always avoided the limelight in the past. General Walters and his new wife Theras were there to greet them along with Newspaper reporters and photographers. A meal had been arranged for later that evening at one of Portland's finest restaurants. After Sophie had spoken to the media she joined Triez as she watched engineers tow the launch into one of the hangers. Sophie told her to relax as it was in good hands. Looking concerned Triez said, "This is a vessel that I really don't want to lose."

*

The General had made reservations at a large hotel in the bay area. On the way there the General's car stopped at a roadside store. Without saying a word, he entered the store. A few moments later he came out with a large ice cream and presented it to Isalia. She had never tasted anything like it before. The General smiled and told her, "There's plenty more where that came from." Triez told her, "Don't forget to thank Uncle Charlie when you're the size of an elephant!" Isalia asked, "What's an elephant?"☐

Later that evening, over a glass of port, the General gave Sophie and Triez credit and cash cards and told them that several accounts had been opened in their names. He apologised for having to requisition the Moon base but assured them that they, and all their associates, had been generously compensated.

He told Sophie that many of her group had signed up for a new division, which was called the Earth Space Directive. It was aimed at deep space exploration and forming new alliances with other worlds. He was hoping that a conflict with another race like the Breeche could be avoided at all costs.

Sophie was looking at a slip that came with the cards. The amount that had been deposited in her name was staggering. Looking at Triez, she interrupted the General and excitedly told her that she was an extremely wealthy woman. Triez replied with equal enthusiasm that she was too.

The General resumed his conversation and explained that a new fleet of vessels was on the drawing board, and what he really needed was the pair of them to be involved. Sophie said that it was something that she would have to think about, as she wasn't sure what she wanted at the moment. Triez wanted to show Isalia the sights and sounds of New York, and wouldn't be pressured into anything until she had fulfilled her promise. The General understood and ordered more drinks.

Before they left the restaurant, Triez offered the General her launch for reverse engineering but threatened to rip his head off if they didn't put it back together properly. He laughed and promised that he'd do his best.

Once back at the hotel, Sophie asked Triez why she had given the General her launch. Triez told her that if she was going to traipse through the galaxy battling everything she came across, she wanted a decent ship to do it in. Sophie asked her whether she had already accepted the General's offer. Triez replied, "On this money, aren't you?" Sophie paused for a second and told her that she was absolutely right, and ordered some drinks from the bar to celebrate. Finding a picture of an elephant on the web, Isalia shrugged her shoulders and went to bed.

The next morning Triez packed her own and Isalia's bags and arranged to meet Sophie at a certain restaurant on Mulberry Street in Little Italy in two days time. Sophie would be travelling to Montpelier as she felt a family visit was long overdue.

Triez had decided to travel to Brooklyn by car; she had a natural ability for driving but had a heavy right foot and it wasn't long before she had attracted the attention of a Springfield police officer on Interstate 91. Pushing his police car to the limit the officer almost blew the motor trying to pull her over.

Climbing out of his car, the police officer asked, "Have you any idea just how fast you were going?" Triez answered, "I pray you tell me, sir." Isalia leant over and told him, "I'm teaching her Shakespeare. What do you think of her rendition?" Looking confused the officer asked, "About what?" Isalia said

"The Merchant of Venice. Don't you think she's good?" Noticing the faint ridges on their noses he recognised Triez from the media coverage and said "Kai - you're Triez from Kai." Triez smiled at him and pushed her breasts out. Looking a little embarrassed the officer said, "I'd better take a look at your licence all the same." Triez looked at Isalia and asked him "What's a licence?" Answering "Never mind" the officer asked Triez to sign a blank piece of paper, as it was for his daughter. After signing her name in Kai script the officer told her, "Slow down a little and get a licence, as you're not in hyperspace now: you're on Interstate 91." Turning to walk back to his car, he wished them a good day. This whole event confused Triez and Isalia alike, and both felt driven to consult Sophie more about human social customs.

On arriving in Brooklyn Triez parked the car just off Pennsylvania Avenue. As she got out of the car she felt a knife being pressed against her back, along with a male voice demanding her car keys. Triez saw this as playtime for Isalia and asked her to get out of the car. Isalia looked at the man holding the knife at her mother's back and laughed, telling her, "Stop messing about mother!" Giving the man a stout kick in the leg, he lashed out at Isalia. Triez stood and watched to see what her daughter would do next. Isalia kicked the man again causing Triez to laugh out loud. Lunging forward in a single movement, Isalia grabbed the knife and spun herself around behind the man, slitting his chinos from top to bottom on both legs. The man's trousers seem to fall away as he tried to get away from her, but Isalia was having none of it. Like a young lioness, she was playing with her prey, kicking the man's legs from underneath him. He fell to his knees while Isalia straddled him. Trapping his arms behind his back, she asked her mother for her lipstick. Triez told her to do a proper job and handed her some eye shadow too. Isalia was laughing as she smeared the lipstick awkwardly around the man's mouth and blackened both eyes messily with the eye shadow. Letting him go, he picked up his trousers and wrapped them around him like a skirt. Both mother and daughter wolf whistled him as he fled, and gave each other a high five.

Triez had only stopped to buy Isalia an ice cream. But while Isalia had been playing, the store had closed. They both got back into the car and made their way to a Bar Diner where Triez had set up a special reunion. Parking the car outside a bar, Triez took Isalia through to the restaurant and ordered three meals. A loud voice shouted from the end of the room, "You'd better make that six!" It was Tom and his company of three. With a six-way hug, it was like a family reunion.

As with most of the planet, a great deal of rebuilding was taking place in Montpelier. Sophie was relieved to see that her mother's house was still intact. Knocking on the door, her sister answered. It was the first time they had seen each other in two years. It was a tearful reunion as she entered the house. Seeing her mother again left Sophie speechless: it had been so long and so much had happened.☐

For hours Sophie talked about the last two years and how her life had changed, the places that she'd visited, and the new friends she'd made. Sophie stayed for two days at her mother's house but felt drawn to visit some of the old places before she left for New York. She started with Simon's trailer; it seemed strange to know that someone else was living there now. Moving on, she climbed the hill to the entrance of the complex, but the disc wasn't there and the complex was just a hole in the ground. Deciding that the past belonged to the past, she got into her car and headed for New York.

As Sophie walked towards the restaurant on Mulberry Street, she could see Tom and his friends with Triez and Isalia. They were sitting at a table outside eating pasta and drinking beers: she could feel the beginnings of another great night in New York. The General had made Tom and his group quite wealthy people and, with enough money, the only thing left to do was to enjoy themselves. They had already signed up to the space directive and were as keen as ever to serve.

As the evening wore on, Isalia was putting Budweiser's away, one after the other. Sophie asked Triez, "Do you think she'll be OK drinking all that beer?" Triez replied, "Hell! Yes! She's only just started" and added, "Don't worry, Sophie, on this planet she's unbreakable, unlike the ape that hung around that tall building."

It was four thirty in the morning, and Sophie hadn't booked a room anywhere. Triez told her not to worry, as she hadn't either. Nudging Big Tom, Triez asked if they could crash with him, but he said that he and his group were banking on staying with her! The grass on Washington Square made a welcome bed until they were disturbed by a police officer at 9.00 am in the morning. It was time to leave for Portland.

*

It was late afternoon when Sophie and the others arrived at the General's office in Portland. He was over the moon at the prospect of not having to train another crew for the flagship of the proposed fleet.

After a day off to nurse a throbbing head, Sophie joined the engineering team at the directive along with Triez and Isalia. Triez was pleased to see that for every part of her launch that was dismantled, another part was reassembled, thus helping to keep the General's head firmly on his shoulders.

The next day, Isalia was helping Dieter with the upgrades to the already drawn out engines of the prototype. He had noticed what a remarkable eye for detail Isalia had, after pulling him up over access to routine service areas. Grateful for her advise, he had to bite his lip as he felt a little miffed at having a fifteen-year-old telling him.

Supporting the build were some of the technicians from the *Crazy Horse*, and the rest were rookies.

Sophie was spending half her time in the drawing office and the other half being careful about stripping Triez's engines down. She was pleased that it was only the engines, onboard systems, and avionics that needed to be copied. Eventually, the data required was stored within several computers and Triez's launch was reassembled and made functional. This calmed the General and Triez alike.

The same day as the flagship started production, an official from the School Board turned up at the gate asking why Triez had not registered Isalia with the Education Department. After a short silence, both of them burst out laughing. Looking a little bemused, the official asked Sophie why they were laughing. Sophie explained that Isalia had a body buried on Par Kallish, had been cloned back to life, and had been mentally and physically enhanced off the scale. She added that her mind would have made Einstein himself envious. The official said, "All of that doesn't matter, at fifteen she should be in school." After she'd stopped laughing, Isalia offered to give a lecture at any university of the official's choice about sub-nuclear physics and chaos theory.

From the other side of the complex, Dieter called to Isalia asking, "Where did you put the retainers for the antimatter flow control unit?" She shouted back, "I'm on my way, Dieter!" Triez smiled proudly at Isalia, and the official seemed to give in.

After eight months of design and fabrication, the vessel was almost finished. Sophie knew that its place was in orbit and not stuck in a spacecraft hangar. The General had made it clear to her that he was keen to start space trials as soon as possible and that getting a crew together was the only thing slowing things down. He told Sophie, "We have a pilot and weapons officer with Jamie and Luma Tyrol, Triez as the first officer, and Dr Phull's been with us since the beginning." He reminded her that Peter and Sally were now part of his special air ops unit and crucial to Earth's defence. Sophie asked him, "What about Simon? He's proficient in navigation." The General told her, "My hands are tied on that one. Because of what happened to Earth, the Moon base is on constant alert and the efficiency of the base depends on Simon to maintain the high standards required."

Overhearing the pair of them, Isalia offered her services as the navigation officer. Sophie asked her if she would be able to handle it. Isalia made it clear that she had an excellent understanding of their section of the galaxy, including the planet that was on her mother's launch computer. Sophie was a little bowled over by this and asked her to elaborate. Isalia told her, "When I existed in my digital state, information about where the inhabitants of Par Kallish had travelled and the species they had encountered was accessible to me. With a great deal of time on my hands, much of it was spent uploading information about the galaxy into my memory. However I have no knowledge of the result of those encounters." Sophie was impressed and, if it was OK with her mother, then she could see no reason why she should not serve as the navigation officer.

A week later the General gave the launch instructions, which were set for two days' time. The new space directive uniforms were dispatched, and a name had been chosen for the vessel. It was *Hermes*. Sophie was particularly fond of the name, as Hermes was the messenger of the gods, and was allowed into Olympus, Earth, and the Underworld. He was the swiftest of the gods and also the most popular.

Big Tom was pleased with his quarters as it had unbreakable tables and chairs and extra sound-proofing. As Triez inspected her own quarters, she was also quite pleased to see that the table lamps were unbreakable and screwed to the tables. Isalia couldn't understand why it was so Spartan and said, "I don't understand why there's nothing breakable in here." From the doorway came a voice saying, "You will when she starts with Big Tom!" It was Holly. Triez was lost for words and gave her a hug. She introduced Holly to Isalia, telling her, "Ignore everything that she tells you except for the story about the large ape!" Holly said, "I couldn't stay away once I heard that you were going to break new ground." No one was more pleased to see her than Jamie.

Now they had the time to teach Isalia how to pilot and navigate the vessel properly. However, Holly was a little confused at the layout herself, as it was totally different to the *Crazy Horse*, and admitted that she herself would also need a little help.

It was the day of the launch, and the last of the supplies were being loaded into the hold, as well as six fighters and Triez's launch. The *Hermes* had the same coating to its fuselage as the launch and had a sheen to it that glistened in the sun. It was an elegant shape that impressed everyone watching as it was towed from the hanger by two pushback tractors. Once everyone was aboard, Dieter handed control of the engines to Jamie, warning him to look after them, or else! With ease The *Hermes* lifted off the ground using its vertical thrusters. Jamie balanced the vectored outlets and the vessel moved forward, smoothly gaining speed. Once past the Portland headlight, Sophie asked Jamie to head for open space.

Isalia plotted a course but was stopped by Sophie, who asked her to lay in a new course, one that would take them to the destination that was on the launch's navigation computer containing the destination that Hylan Varrick had prepared for his escape.

With the new coordinates entered into the navigation computer, the *Hermes* was at one hundred percent and Sophie was quite confident that it was up to an extended test flight in hyperspace. It felt exciting to her that they were now travelling faster than any human had travelled before: approximately double the speed of the *Crazy Horse*. She asked Triez to join her at her launch in the hold. Once there, Sophie opened the computer files and asked Triez to see if she could find any more information that might help them on their arrival.

Sophie headed back to the bridge and asked Isalia if there was anything that she could add to what she had already told her regarding the visit the inhabitants of Par Kallish had made to the planet. She could tell her nothing except that it was a visit made long ago; she told Sophie that it was at least a hundred years since the Par Kallish had been off-world.

Triez had spent hours looking for information and advised Sophie that she had found nothing on the computer. Feeling the need to stretch her legs, Triez offered to take the night shift on the bridge. At 8.00 am she contacted Jamie over the com link telling him that they had arrived and that she was about to take the ship out of hyperspace. As normal space appeared, the navigation shields automatically doubled in strength. The *Hermes* was approaching a boulder field. At that moment Jamie arrived and took over. Slowing the ship down, he manoeuvred the *Hermes* through the debris. Sophie arrived not long after and analysed the data; she came to the conclusion that what they were looking at was the remains of a moon that had once orbited a planet not too far away.

Enhancing the monitor, Isalia could see a planet

quite clearly in the distance that was orbiting a medium sized star. Taking several preliminary scans of the planet, she realised that it was a strange and lifeless world. Approaching the planet, Sophie scanned its surface. It was destruction on an unparalleled scale, with no communication signals of any kind. Isalia stated that the radiation was at only slightly elevated levels and that whatever had happened down there had happened some time ago.

Sophie selected a landing party, which was to consist of Tom and his group, as well as Triez, Isalia, and Holly. She had picked Holly for her clerical skills, knowing that whatever had happened down there must have been recorded somewhere. Teleporting to the surface, it was clear that some kind of conflict had occurred. Triez's scanner was dating it around a hundred years earlier, judging by the scorch marks on the buildings. Several decomposed bodies were sitting together around the remains of an open fire. Triez scanned the bodies; there were no signs of injuries, just calcium shortages in the bone structures. She told Sophie that it was possibly starvation.

Tom and his Number Three had requested a teleport to the other side of the planet where they had found an old map showing the location of what could only be described as some sort of media centre. Hopefully, this would shine some light on what had happened there. It was night and quite dark.

Tom was the first to reach the building and entered through a pair of glass doors. From what he could tell, it was some kind of news agency with screens and cameras. He could tell that it was a studio that was much more advanced than anything on

Earth but was still recognisable as such. One machine looked like a holographic display projector, which confirmed that they were a highly advanced species. Tom contacted Holly. She was there in minutes and connected a mobile power source to the projector. Stored in its databank was a record of news reports about a battle that was being fought on a worldwide scale. She could see the attacking enemy; although blurry, they seemed familiar. Isalia thought they looked like the Breeche. □

Not long after Sophie and Triez arrived. Sophie asked how was it possible, as the Breeche had only been able to travel in space a hundred years. Isalia, at her mother's request, was asked whether she could translate. Looking at her mother, she said "It's a language you're familiar with: it's Breeche. Sophie looked further back at older records she found: they were written in Breeche and felt that what had happened there was quite confusing. Daylight was breaking by now, making reading a great deal easier.

Going back one hundred and thirty years was a story about the first of the slaves to arrive. They had been sold there by a race called the Par Kallish. In the beginning, they were intelligent, but once their genes had been spliced and cloned several times, they became truculent and even aggressive. They worked in the fields and factories; they were mainly male, but many females were kept to stabilise the cloning technique. Isalia wept, and Sophie knew why. Sophie explained to the rest of the group that the inhabitants of Par Kallish were taking the Kai from their homes, taking them there, and selling them into slavery one hundred and thirty years earlier.

Along with the slaves, they were sold a flawed cloning technique. The result of the flaw in the genes meant that once the Kai's genes had been cloned ten times or more it had the effect of inducing a psychosis; they were affected by a violent insanity and rebelled against their masters who were the original Breeche race. Taking over the cloning facilities for their own ends, the fate of the original Breeche was sealed.

The slaves doubled and trebled their numbers, increasing the psychotic effect ten-fold and waged war on the indigenous inhabitants of the planet. The slaves slaughtered all of them, except the few that managed to escape, only to starve to death later. Sophie could only use conjecture to explain what had happened after that. She said that when the fighting was over, the slaves must have adopted the name from their masters and returned to their home world of Kai in ships from this world, and waged war on the Kai people: their own people.

Occupation changed the language from Kai to Breeche, and technology became available to the Kai, who later fought back several times until an uneasy peace was achieved. Sophie added that when the Breeche invaded the next planet to Kai, now known as Breeche Prime, they might have killed off any civilisation that might have existed prior to that invasion. Breeche Prime may well have been populated by another species. This they would never know. Sophie displayed several still photographs of the original Breeche that had populated the planet they were now standing on. They were a family-orientated humanoid race that had been at peace with themselves until the Par Kallish had introduced greed to their culture. Sophie said, "Two separate races both called Breeche and now both extinct." ☐

There was a solemn moment, while the landing party took it all in and contemplated that the Breeche were the real victims in all of this and that the Par Kallish were the real instigators of this awful crime. ☐

A great deal had been learned from the trip, including the fact that Hylan Varrick didn't get his launch from that planet. The guilt that Sophie had felt since committing genocide against Breeche Prime was now subsiding fast, and being replaced with anger as she thought about the two billion people who had died on Earth because of Par Kallish greed. She could now understand why they had been so benevolent to Isalia, and also understood why they hadn't been off world for over a hundred years. Sophie could now lay the guilt at their door.

Triez shared Sophie's anger, but her anger was more concentrated towards the bloody wars they had fought, only now apparently against her own damaged people. She now understood just how extensive cloning and a life span of only thirty years had made the Breeche develop into the hideous creatures they had become. Isalia said, "It's time to leave this place. It's definitely a warning to anyone contemplating inflicting servitude on another race." Sophie put her arm around Isalia's shoulder and thought, *These are wise words coming from someone so innocent and so young.* ☐

The *Hermes* was steadily cruising through normal space at the request of the Prof, who was studying a small asteroid, not unlike Perness. It had the same blue plume of gas that seemed to be harbouring antimatter. Jamie brought the *Hermes* to a full stop. The Prof had built a small robot that was capable of capturing antimatter and the ability to phase shift where necessary. On completion of its task, the Prof announced the robotic mission as a resounding success that would allow antimatter to be harvested without human intervention.

Resuming their course back towards Earth, Sophie took the night shift. All was quiet on the bridge as the *Hermes* thundered through hyperspace. Sophie passed the time by chatting over the com link with one of Dieter's prodigies whose name was Matthew. Although Sophie was the Captain, she had never seen rank as an obstacle where relationships were involved, and breakfast together was arranged.

At midday, Sophie emerged from her cabin and made her way to the bridge, just in time to see Earth again. It was always a welcome sight. She sat down next to Isalia. She told Sophie, "I'm grateful for my resurrection but I don't really want to return to Par Kallish ever again. She liked Earth and the people who inhabited it and knew that she could be happy there for the rest of her life. □

As the *Hermes* passed over the Portland Headlight, Triez said to Sophie, "I like this ship. I've got a feeling it's going to take us to some wonderful places where we will meet some incredible species." Sophie agreed, and asked her where she was going to live. Looking over Portland she said, "If Isalia's happy to live here, then so am I."

Once on the ground, Sophie received a grilling from General Walters about going absent without official permission with a couple of billion dollars' worth of Uncle Sam's best hardware. Sophie said, "Never mind all that crap. I've got one hell of a story to tell you about the Breeche. I'll tell you all about it over a drink. Get your coat - it's your round!" With a pile of paperwork in front of him, the General was torn between listening to a hell of a yarn or catching up on his work. Isalia pulled at his tunic saying, "Please Uncle Charlie, it's your round." Grabbing his coat he asked, "OK - where are we off to?"

CHAPTER 13

It was autumn in Portland and Triez had purchased a house on Highland Lake where she was living with Isalia. Neither of them had seen anything like it before. They found it beautiful, but in a frightening way. Triez called Sophie and asked her whether the planet had been irradiated, as trees and plants were dying everywhere. Sophie assured her that all was fine as it was a natural process on Earth, which was called autumn. She told her to take Isalia out for a walk and enjoy the good weather while it lasted, and assured her that the trees would be in leaf again by what was termed spring.

Sophie was at the directive base with the General, who asked if it was Triez on the phone. She told him it was, and that she was worried about the trees. Laughing, he asked her why. She told him it was because only a few trees on Kai shed their leaves at this time of the year. With an "Oh!" the General told her that she might like to pop into the tracking station as there was a weak distress signal coming in from deep space: it was on a hyperlink wavelength. □

Sophie was aware that they must have been fairly

advanced, but also knew that it could have taken quite some time to reach Earth. She contacted the S.E.T.I. institute, which was now equipped with a variety of powerful signal pickups. They were also receiving the distress signal and so did the new tracking station on Kai; they had been monitoring it for some time. With the signal being at such a great distance, the only vessel that could make a quick response was the *Hermes*.

Sophie made the calls and within four hours she had a crew. Dr Phull was the first one to arrive; Sophie had teleported him in from the UK where he had been giving a talk at Oxford University about Kai pathogens and bacteria. Sophie apologised for cutting his trip short. He told her, "Don't you worry, as I'm more than happy to be back and not giving lectures on bugs and things." Jamie and Luma were next – they had been sunning themselves in Florida. Then, Dieter teleported in from Hanover, Germany. Holly and Professor Sarah Neilson were on the Moon and it had been arranged for both of them to be picked up en route.

Technicians from the spaceport who were working on the *Hermes* sister ship were called on to work with Dieter in engineering, while Dr Phull called on the services of the local hospital, where there was no shortage of keen volunteers. Triez and Isalia arrived in their new shiny floating car. Sophie spotted it spinning out of control and almost demolishing the sentry box before coming to rest on a pile of gravel. Pulling the sentry out of a bush Triez apologised and popped five dollars into his pocket for not telling the General.

At 10.00 pm the clearing sirens sounded. Once the area was clear the *Hermes* powered up her engines. It had been three months since any of the crew had set foot on her; it was like coming home for most of them, and being reunited with their families.

A last minute teleport request was made from the General for himself and his wife, Theras. They were keen to log a few hours before the end of the year. Once they were aboard, Jamie engaged the thrusters and the *Hermes* launched into the sky leaving a hundred small tornados behind it. Jamie made best speed towards the Moon, passing at one-quarter light speed. Holly and the Prof were ready and teleported aboard. □

Isalia locked onto the beacon and passed the coordinates to Jamie. As the *Hermes* entered into hyperspace, Sophie asked him to find out what the ship was capable of. Dieter crossed his fingers and gave Jamie all the power he needed. With a surge forward, the *Hermes* broke new ground. Even with the dampers on full, Sophie could feel the gravity forces pressing against her chest. Jamie said they were now at full power. Isalia joined Sophie and they watched the navigation shielding deflecting particles and pieces of rock from around the front of the vessel. At that speed it was highly visible and changing into all different colours as it hit the shields.

*

Six hours had now passed and the signal was a little stronger. Holly could now give an estimated time of arrival, and narrowed it down to around six hours fifteen minutes before they would drop out of hyperspace. She reminded Jamie to allow for the extra speed and use the braking thrusters before exiting hyperspace. Triez was in the elevator going from the hold to the medical centre when the braking thrusters engaged. Grabbing a handrail she heard the deafening roar of the engines while the whole ship vibrated as it dropped to normal speed. Looking out of the window, there was a planet to the starboard side. Sophie came over the com asking Triez to prep the launch, as there were particles in the upper atmosphere that made the teleport too risky for teleporting organic matter. Holly, Dr Phull, and Sophie joined Triez in the hold. Once aboard, Triez took the launch out and engaged the shield; the particles glistened against it as they glided towards the surface. Sophie said, "If their shielding had been damaged, it might have been the particles that had affected their vessel on entry."☐

Following the signal, they landed two hundred metres from the beacon. There was a breathable atmosphere, with no serious pathogens. As they approached the beacon, photon shots hit the rocks behind them. Diving for cover, all four drew their weapons. Triez stressed, "They might be pirates, so we shouldn't take any chances." Setting her pistol to kill, she told the others to follow suit.

Triez had knowledge about the violent reputation of the pirates in that sector and hoped that it had been exaggerated. One of them was shouting in an unknown tongue. Sophie switched on her translator. It needed a few words to grab the syntax of their language. She activated the ghost and told it to go over there and make them say something. The ghost replied, "Like what? Twenty questions? Or how big do gorillas grow?" Triez said, "Pretty damn big!" to which Holly burst out laughing.

The ghost drifted off towards the pirate and stopped in front of a large rock. It asked what pirate's favourite food was. The pirate burst out with what sounded like a barrage of abuse; the ghost said, "I haven't come over to be insulted." Holly mumbled to herself, *'Well, where do you normally go?'* The pirate gave out another burst of abuse. In there was a mention of Hylan Varrick and, with that, the translator had grabbed the syntax and was ready.

Sophie knew that she had to be extremely careful about what she said next. Was he really a pirate or one of Varrick's victims? She shouted to him, "We're not here harbouring evil intent," and asked him if he was a pirate. With a loud shriek in his voice, he said, "*Me?* You mean *me?*" He accused Sophie of mass murder and waging war on a peaceful planet with minimum defences. Sophie told him, "I don't have the slightest idea what you're talking about." He called her an outrageous liar, and pointed out that she had arrived on the planet in a stolen launch from the Queen's Royal Fleet. He also said, "Hylan Varrick stole that launch of yours after befriending the Queen. Then he brought in the Breeche to plunder the wealth of our home world. It probably lies in ruins by now." The man's voice had a tearful sound to it. Sophie knew now that she was dealing with a victim and not a pirate.

Sophie asked him if he was alone and how long he had been there, but she knew that trust was something that had to be earned. He told her he was alone. She asked him if he was injured in any way, as they had a doctor with them. This was something that interested him and he asked for the doctor to be sent over to him, unarmed and with no tricks. Sophie gave him her assurances that there would be no tricks. Dr Phull made his way over to the man and asked him if the ghost could come with him. The man could see no harm in that and agreed.

Sophie listened as the ghost gave a minute-by-minute account of what was happening over his mobile unit. The ghost could see three more people further back from the man. Joining the Doctor, both moved towards the other three. As the Doctor approached he could see there were two females and another male. On closer inspection, he could also see that they were in a shocking state, suffering from sores on their faces and malnutrition. He saw that one female had a broken leg and also noticed it had set in the wrong place and needed surgery.

The ghost reported back to Sophie that an identical launch to the one that Triez was using was about fifteen metres behind them with some damage to the landing gear, and photon fire scars across the fuselage.

Dr. Phull walked back to the man with the photon rifle and told him, "Your friends will die soon without immediate treatment." The Doctor urged him, "Release me now and allow the others and myself to be taken to the *Hermes* so that I can treat them properly." The Doctor could see that he was in a similar state to the others. The man told him, "They're not friends: one is the Queen of Temfir with her handmaiden, and the other's a senior member of the planetary government."

Looking him in the face, Dr Phull tried to convince him that they were not pirates and said, "Please will you let me take them?" However, the man was having none of it and told the Doctor that he would have to treat them there. The Doctor protested that it was impossible. The man replied: "Then you make it possible or die." The Doctor gave a list of things he would need to the ghost, who would act as a messenger. The name of the man with the gun was Fernais, and he would allow no one from Triez's launch to assist Dr Phull other than the ghost. He was the personal guard to the Queen and made it very clear that if anything happened to her, it wouldn't bode well for the Doctor.

The planet was a fairly arid place with little water and the sun had a fairly strong presence at their location. As Dr Phull waited for the medical equipment to be brought down from the *Hermes*, Fernais told him that they had been down on the surface for two years. He told the Doctor, "The launch was crammed with supplies when the Queen was whisked away from Temfir for safety, but ran out about six months ago. We've been living on a scarce amount of plants that the planet supplied since then." He told Dr. Phull that the Queen's leg had been broken on landing after the particles in the atmosphere damaged the launch.

Within half an hour the Doctor was sent a field medical canopy along with drugs and medical instruments. One hour later he had stabilised all three patients with the exception of one. He could see that Fernais was badly dehydrated and gave him a water solution that would help. Reluctantly he sipped at it, whilst holding the gun at the Doctor's head. Happy that it was not poison, Fernais allowed him to return to his patients.

Sophie politely asked Fernais if he would allow her to approach him unarmed. Considering her request for a moment, he agreed. Walking slowly, she stopped just short of where Fernais was hiding. Sitting down on a boulder, Sophie told Fernais that the Breeche were dead as a species and that she and her comrades were totally responsible for their demise. Again, he called her a liar. Triez could see that he was getting more agitated by the second. Standing up she shouted, "Sophie take cover." Fernais could see Triez and shouted, "Breeche filth!" Sophie dashed towards a small crevice between him and Triez. Fernais opened fire on the crevice while Sophie pulled herself in as tight as she could. Fernais then fired in an arc causing Triez and Holly to duck as the photon fire came towards them.

Using hand signals, Triez had worked out that Sophie was going to draw his attention. As she pulled herself out of the crevice, Fernais shot at Sophie, narrowly missing her. Triez had taken advantage of the distraction by slipping up to the rock he was hiding behind. Throwing a rock towards Sophie's position, she pounced on him as he was distracted and, with a single punch, he was out for the count. It was two hours before he came round properly, even though she'd used restraint. Triez was concerned that she may have given him brain damage and feeling more than a little concerned, gave him a good shaking. Fernais became fully conscious at that point and asked her to stop shaking him as he was becoming nauseous.

He quickly realised, as he lay on the launch bay floor that he'd been disarmed and asked Triez, "Why haven't you killed me?" To which she answered, "Although you stink something awful, I can't see any reason to." Confused, he asked where the Queen had been taken. Triez told him that she was in surgery and that he could see her when the Doctor had finished. She felt that he'd been through enough that day, and spent the next hour explaining about who the Breeche were, and how they had been manipulated by Hylan Varrick to do his bidding. Fernais asked, "And what of Varrick?" She told him that he was serving life in a Kai prison, and it was the launch that he had stolen from the Queen that they were presently using. She further explained that although technically Varrick was a Kai, she didn't really believe it and explained, "I know my people, and he just doesn't fit the bill." She then handed Fernais half of a tuna sandwich she was eating, and felt that he was warming towards her just a little.▢

Out of surgery and looking a great deal healthier, the Queen asked Dr Phull if she could see the Captain. Using the correct protocol, Sophie arrived and introduced herself. The Queen thanked her and congratulated her on a fine vessel and crew. She told Sophie that the Doctor had filled her in on the situation and added, "He's quite forceful and, unlike most people, doesn't seem to give a damn about me being royalty." Sophie replied, "In the Doctor's surgery you're just a lump of meat and he's the royalty." The Queen laughed and said, "I haven't done that for a while." Sophie said, "Don't laugh. I mean every word of it!" □

Triez was waiting outside the launch bay shower with clean clothes, while Fernais washed and scraped off two years of dirt from himself. Leaving the shower, he was surprised to see her standing there, and rushed to pull a towel around himself. She just laughed and pulled the towel from his waist. Holding one corner she used it to chase him around the launch bay whilst flicking it at his backside. She saw it as an exercise in diplomacy until they were both dizzy, and then stopped. Handing him the towel she said, "Sorry about the punch. Are we friends?" Trying the clothes on he answered warily, "OK – friends." Fernais looked very smart wearing a designer suit that had been stolen by Triez in New York, and when he visited the Queen she seemed a little surprised to see him like that after having worn rags for two years.

Jamie and Holly had worked out the most direct route to Temfir, which was a little larger than Earth, with a gravity difference that was negligible, and an oxygen-nitrogen atmosphere. With the *Hermes* cruising at a moderate speed, it would take a day or so before reaching the Queen's home planet. Sophie took the opportunity of giving her a tour of the *Hermes* in a wheelchair, hoping it would give them both a chance to get to know each other and the crew a little better. The Queen was surprised to see her launch being repaired and refitted by some of Dieter's team and a couple of rookies. Sophie offered to give her Triez's launch back, but she told her that they could keep it, as it was the least she could do. Sophie was relieved, as Triez would never have forgiven her.

As they arrived at Temfir, the planet was

surrounded by robots and people in space suits repairing satellites and badly damaged space stations. Sophie could see that it had once been a formidable planet before the Breeche had attacked. Fernais asked Jamie to head for a large space station not far from their current position. As they came upon it, they found it to be a huge leviathan, as big as a shopping mall. A request came over the com channel asking them to release control of their vessel. As Jamie released the controls they felt a tractor beam take hold of the ship and, with precise accuracy, they were drawn into a landing bay and lowered onto the pad. The Queen asked Sophie if she would stay a while and sample the sights and tastes of a world that she was so proud of; Sophie agreed.

*

Sophie had barely seen the General since they had left Portland. Banging on the door to his quarters, he opened it, looking totally wrecked. She asked him if he was aware of what had been going on. He grabbed his dressing gown and asked her, "Who are we at war with now?" She told him that he should don his VIP head, as they were the guests of the Queen of Temfir. The door slammed shut as Theras dragged him back to bed!

A ceremony was to be arranged for the next day when the Queen would make an entrance back onto Temfir soil from the door of her launch. Her advisors saw this as a great morale booster for the planet. Again, over two billion people had died there too, and the infrastructure of the planet was only just starting to function again after being partially destroyed. It was 8.00 am and the occasion called for full dress uniform; the General arrived to do the inspection line-up. Triez whispered in Sophie's ear, "Is he wearing makeup?" Sophie could see it around his eyes; it looked like he was covering up dark circles. In a half-hearted way, the General was happy with the inspection and passed it off. Pulling the General to one side, Sophie told him, "You need to go and see the Doctor for a stimulant and leave the hanky panky alone for five minutes." He told her that Theras was very demanding: fun, but extremely demanding. □

An hour later and full of drugs, the General was looking almost normal. Sophie then introduced him to the Queen, who wondered why she hadn't seen him before. His excuse was that he had been tied into a project that couldn't be ignored, and he would have to get back to it as soon as he could.

Dieter was in the hold as the Queen entered. She remarked on what a beautiful job his team had made of the launch and told him that it held a certain sentimentality for her as it had been her home for the last two years. The fittings glistened and she could see that it was finished to the highest standard.

Fernais took the pilot's chair and directed the launch towards one of the larger landmasses and after a few minutes landed it in the grounds of a battle-damaged palace. There was a massive turnout for the Queen's return. Most of the crew from the *Hermes* had teleported to the surface and there was a great deal of cheering as she made the effort to walk from the launch, supported by the senior member of the government and her handmaiden. For many of the crowd, it brought a sense of closure to a war that had cost them so much.

Part of the palace had been made habitable for the Queen, in the hope that she would one day return. Sophie felt that their part in this was now finished, and it was time to move on. The next day the Queen called for Sophie to visit the palace. On arrival, Fernais met her. He had been instructed to reward Sophie with a gift of great value for her part in the Queen's rescue. Sophie's gift was in the palace grounds. Fernais escorted her there and asked her what she thought of it, but she could see nothing at all and told Fernais so. He said, "Is it not marvellous?" □

Sophie said again, "I can see nothing!" Fernais told her that there were tonnes of building materials right in front of her; now she was beginning to understand that it was some sort of cloaking device. With the flick of a switch on a handset, the building materials appeared. Fernais explained that they had only just discovered it when the Breeche struck. If it had been two weeks later, it would have been installed on their military vessels, and they would have been able to fight them off. He told Sophie that the Queen had seen only good in her, and felt that they would be great friends with the human race. It had seemed only logical to her to share this technology with a friend that she would never fear. As requested, Fernais took Sophie to see the Queen, who was pleased that Sophie saw the value in such a defensive weapon. After sitting with her and talking for an hour about the future, over a traditional herbal drink, Sophie bid the Queen farewell for now and teleported to the *Hermes*.

The next day Dieter and Sophie started work on installing the camouflage system components that Fernais had given them. Their next destination would be Kai and Sophie was hoping that the *Hermes* could creep up on the planet unnoticed. Jamie had left Holly at the helm while he plotted a course with Isalia that would take them to Kai, Par Kallish, Touscal, and back home in time for Christmas. Sophie was interested in a theory that Triez had about Hylan Varrick. Her theory was that he was not Kai at all. In the launch bay, she explained to Sophie that a Kai would never obsess over wealth and power the way he did, as they were a humble people. Having said that, she told Sophie, "We need to find out who he really is." Climbing aboard her launch she powered up the engines: it was time to test the camouflage system that Dieter's team had just finished installing. □

With all of the projection units in place on the *Hermes*, the ship was ready. Flying out of the launch bay Triez swung the launch around just in time to see the *Hermes* disappear from sight. Squinting her eyes, she peered through the window but could see nothing. Checking her instruments she could see there was nothing on the scanner either. Holly took the *Hermes* closer to the launch. Triez could only see empty space, nothing more. With a press of a button from Sophie, the *Hermes* dwarfed the launch, with only a couple of metres between them. Triez reeled back in her seat and nervously called it a resounding success, but wasn't sure if she needed to change her underwear or not!

As Kai came into range, Holly activated the camouflage system. Sophie ordered radio silence, and the *Hermes* quietly slipped through Kai's defence scanners. Heading for the new spaceport Sophie announced her arrival and de-camouflaged. The air traffic controllers were panic stricken as they picked up the *Hermes* steadily cruising towards the spaceport. Quickly allotting a new slot for the vessel, they brought it under their control and guided it into the spaceport. Sophie felt that the cloak was a wonderful asset and could see the true value in what the Queen had given her. Isalia was glad to see Kai again; she was now sixteen and had only spent seven of those years living there. Her mother put her hand on Isalia's shoulder and suggested that they visit some friends and have some fun.

Sophie had travelled to the government building with Dr Phull and made a request for a meeting with the prison governor. On meeting a government official she asked that Hylan Varrick's DNA be tested. When the government official asked why, she said that according to Triez he might not be Kai at all. The government official stated that he would allow the test, just as long as it was done on the prison premises, to which Sophie agreed. Visiting the secure unit, Sophie found Varrick was not very cooperative about the DNA test. He told her, "I'm quite happy living on Kai as a Kai." Sophie replied, "That's just the point. You're not Kai at all, are you? Or you'd take the test." He told her, "I like this place, so leave me alone." Sophie replied, "It's only because you're working on an escape plan. What I have in mind is a prison that's a great deal more secure." Varrick was confused; he thought that he was in the most secure prison on Kai. Sophie hinted that some old friends of his would like to be reacquainted with him. At Sophie's request, a Kai prison guard restrained Varrick while Dr Phull did the test. After a two-minute wait, the scanner indicated that he was *not* Kai.

Returning to the government building, Sophie had a hunch where Varrick was really from, and the best way to secure him would be back at that place. The government official trusted Sophie and told her, "If you think that Kai would be better off with him off the planet, then that's OK with me." He thanked her and said, "This is going to be a huge saving on the prison budget." ☐

Varrick was delivered with the papers to the *Hermes* two days later and imprisoned in the ship's brig. With everyone back on board, Jamie set a heading for Par Kallish. Sophie went to the brig that night and saw Varrick, who wanted to know where he was being taken. Sophie told him to wait and see. She scanned him with a medical scanner and detected scar tissue around his ears, eyes and nose. She told him that where he was going he'd be free to go anywhere and do anything, within certain boundaries. ☐

On their arrival, Jamie put the *Hermes* into orbit around Par Kallish. Sophie, Triez and Isalia accompanied Varrick to the surface. There to meet them was the woman that Sophie had met when they had collected Isalia. The woman asked Isalia how she liked the outside world. Isalia told her that she was having a wonderful time; the woman seemed pleased. She looked at Varrick and calling him by his real name which was Maroc. She said, "Well, well Maroc I wondered when you would return." Sophie knew that Triez's hunch was right. The woman asked Sophie and the others to accompany her and Maroc into the digital world. Sophie called Jamie, instructing him to lay waste to the entire area if she was not in touch within twenty minutes. A male appeared from the two rocks and confirmed that a vessel in orbit had targeted the entire complex. The woman congratulated Sophie on being very astute and told her, "You're learning, Sophie."

Once they had passed the two lights on the rocks, Maroc was free to do whatever he wanted to do for the rest of his life.

The woman seemed well aware of what Maroc had been up to and asked Sophie and the others to follow her back outside. As they followed the woman to the old city, she clapped her hands and the ground separated, revealing a staircase leading to an underground area where thousands of bodies were suspended in what seemed to be a stasis field. The woman walked for about twenty metres, then stopped and turned around; she pulled a photon pistol out from the inside of her robe.

The woman raised her arms at the sight of Triez holding her pistol – it was pointed between the woman's eyes. Triez kept the pistol trained on her as she disabled a single field containing one adult. As the body fell to the ground, Sophie could see that it was Maroc's body. Turning the setting on the pistol to maximum, the woman fired on the body. After the blast, there was barely any ash left. The woman put the pistol back into her robe and pulled out a scanner. She aimed it at the ash residue. With a reading that displayed no DNA present, the woman asked Sophie if she was satisfied that Maroc could never be cloned again and would spend the rest of his days in the virtual world. Sophie said, "I'm satisfied."

As they climbed the stairs back into the ruins of the old city, Sophie signalled Jamie to stand down. The woman admitted that in the past she, and her people, had committed the most appalling atrocities. She said that her people were trying to make amends for their past, but kept falling down. She admitted to bribing the Breeche with choronite to gain neutrality, even in the knowledge that it would be used against Earth. The woman asked Sophie to forgive her and her people, as they were creatures of habit. She told Sophie that if she was ever in need of help, she should visit them on Par Kallish, and they would do their best to assist her. She also told Sophie how envious her people were of human compassion for others. She said they were trying to change, but their evolution was a slow process with constant slip-ups and old habits creeping in.

Sophie asked the woman who the original inhabitants of Breeche Prime were. She told Sophie that the original planet and its two moons were inhabited by beings at the Iron Age stage of their evolution. The Breeche arrived, enslaved the inhabitants and finally destroyed the two moons and their people for the metal at the two moon's cores. Wishing Sophie a safe trip, the woman asked her for a little understanding. Sophie told her to try a little harder, and headed for the teleport point. Back on the *Hermes*, the first person Sophie saw at the teleport room was the General. She asked him whether he had fallen out with Theras. He replied that he hadn't and apologized for his behavior. She told him to forget it; she had been there with Diel and knew how strong the draw was between human and Kai pheromones. She thought it was nature's gift to both races and should be seen for what it was. With that, she offered to buy the General a drink and a chili dog!

CHAPTER 14

On Sophie's orders, Jamie laid in a course for Touscal. She was feeling a little concerned about how much trouble Ruman might get into over helping them to defeat the Breeche. She felt that if she could speak up for him it might change the mood of the Touscal a little.

Strolling down to the lounge Sophie joined the General as he sat at the bar. She asked him how the fleet would be deployed once the other two vessels were completed. Defence was his main concern. He was now aware that there was a great deal of intelligent life out there and not all of it was amiable. His general opinion about how they had been perceived so far was fairly positive. Taking a sip from a glass of Jack Daniels he asked Sophie, "How could anyone possibly hate us as we're the pussycats of the galaxy?" Sophie answered, "Not everyone likes cats and if we're perceived as cats by somebody out there, they might see us as quite large ones and I for one don't relish the thought that someone out there may want to hang my head on the wall as a trophy." The General asked what she meant, Sophie told him, "I have a strange feeling about the Touscal, Ruman seems OK but I'm not so sure about the rest of them." The General asked her about the Omicron order, she answered, "From what I've gathered they don't exactly see eye to eye with the Touscal as they sabotaged my enhancement. If they hadn't the Earth would be in the hands of the Breeche or something worse by now." The General said, "You know Sophie, I think they're people we can do business with, they seem to be more like the Mylin than the Touscal." Putting her hand on her chin she wondered who Ruman was siding with.

Later that afternoon Sophie bumped into Triez outside the chapel. She was curious about human religion; she knew a little about Christianity, Islam, and Buddhism but didn't know where Sophie's faith lay. Sophie asked, "Do you have a religion?" She told her, "My religion is drinking, sex, and being a general arsehole when I'm hung over." Sophie said, "That's amazing born two hundred light years apart and we both share the same religion!" Triez asked her, "Do you feel like praying?" Sophie said, "OK it's your round!"

An hour later Sophie heard the braking thrusters fire. She told Triez that a higher power was calling her and left the bar. Arriving at the bridge she could see that Jamie seemed a little confused. He told her, "Captain my instruments tell me that the *Hermes* is less than eight hundred kilometres from Touscal." Sophie zoomed in on the scanner but could see nothing. Jamie ran a diagnostic on the vessel's navigation systems. The system report came back stating that they were working at one hundred percent efficiency. Contacting the Mylin home world, Sophie asked if there had been any contact with Touscal within the last twenty-four hours. The Mylin control centre made her aware that all contact had been lost with Touscal for over thirty-six hours and they were about to launch a rescue mission. Sophie told them, "There's no need to dispatch a vessel as we're in the vicinity at the moment and are investigating the situation."

Holly did a sweep of the area that Touscal had previously occupied and said, "Captain there's no evidence of spatial distortion caused by the planet's displacement of space, therefore it isn't cloaked." Sophie uploaded old data from a previous visit to Touscal and checked for spatial distortion. Sure enough, the planet was there, but there was no displacement of space. She could only come to one conclusion and felt that they had experienced an illusion on their previous visit. Holly asked her, "How did the sensors manage to record the image of Touscal?" She answered, "It must have been a projection of some kind, whether the planet had ever really existed in any physical sense, I don't know." She was even starting to wonder if Ruman himself had ever been real. Looking at the evidence. She told Holly, "We shouldn't feel too foolish about it though, the Mylin have been under the illusion of the Touscal's existence for hundreds of years." One question remained that kept going through Sophie's mind. *Who exactly are the Touscal.*

Holly detected what looked like debris floating in space. Zooming in on the scanner, she could see that it was the tablet in its whole form. Sophie scanned it for radiation traces but found it to be clean. Placing her hand below her chin she shared a hunch with Holly, that the only thing that was real about Touscal was probably the tablet itself. She had a theory that the tablet may be a portal to another dimension, and that the Touscal may have been using it for hundreds of years to visit this dimension masquerading as a benevolent society. Holly agreed and said, "Well it is one possibility." Sophie answered, "One of many!"☐

Teleporting the tablet aboard, it seemed to Sophie that the Touscal were probably real but existed somewhere else in time and thought *maybe they're from the future*. Joining Triez, Isalia, and the general at the teleport room she asked them to give her some help to lift it off the pad. As they grabbed the tablet with both hands, it turned into a brilliant, blinding white light. They tried to pull themselves away from it, but their hands were as if they had become a part of it. As the light receded, Sophie could see that they were no longer aboard the *Hermes*. As the light faded to nothing so did the tablet. With apparently no way back to the Hermes Sophie felt the need to just except the fact that she was in another unpredictable situation. She could see that they were in the remains of a modern city street and could hear photonic weapon fire not far away.

Looking around at the buildings and the goods in broken shop windows told Sophie that they were on a fairly advanced planet, and was starting to think that it may even be as advanced as Earth or Kai. It was dark, wet, and a little chilly. The general gave Isalia his jacket and asked Sophie if she had any idea who was responsible for this. Sophie asked him whether he meant for the war or the bastards that had dropped them in the middle of it; he said the latter. All that she could tell him was, "I've got a feeling it's something to do with the Touscal." □

Triez thought it might be a good idea to find some warm clothes. Picking up what looked like a news stand, she threw it through the department store window, while Isalia and the others used the door. The clothing department was on a higher level; as the elevator wasn't working, they used the staircase. Isalia told her mother that she could read the signs on the wall. It was a place that the Par Kallish had visited some time ago. A great deal of information that Isalia had in her head had been put there by direct transfer, which meant that the information was without time, date, or place. Triez told her, "We'll have to fill in the gaps as move along."

Having found suitable attire, and now being at an elevated level, Sophie looked out of the window. She could see a battle raging about three blocks away that was taking place at street level. Calling the General over, who looked very warm in an incredibly versatile jacket, hat and gloves, Sophie asked him what he made of it. He told her, "It looks like guerrilla warfare, that's something I know a great deal about. From here on I'd better take the lead." Leaving the store he lead the way, moving stealthily at speed from one street corner to the next. Sophie thought that the General was extremely agile for a man of his size, and assumed that it was due to endless hours of satisfying a sex-addicted Kai wife that had kept him so fit.

Triez was at the back of the group and had noticed a male figure sitting alone, about thirty metres away on a side street, that seemed to be eating something. She was pretty sure that he hadn't seen them. Tapping Isalia on the shoulder they separated from the other two, they were like a pair of leopards closing in for the kill. Isalia distracted the man with cat-like noises, while Triez slipped behind him and grabbed him around the neck. With Isalia carrying the man by his feet and Triez at the other end, they delivered the man to Sophie. Isalia told him that if he kept quiet they wouldn't harm him; they just wanted a few answers. He could see that they were not of the same appearance as himself and asked, "Who are you people?" Isalia told him that they had just been dropped there. They didn't know why or by whom, only that they must be there for a reason. She asked him what the war was about and how long it had been going on. As he spoke Isalia translated. □

He told them that thirty years earlier, people of a similar appearance to them arrived on the planet. It was a time not long after the invention of the internal combustion engine. With them they brought about great changes to their way of life, giving them information and showing them how to build things, from orbital space vessels to floating vehicles, and buildings of immense proportions. However, there was a cost for this information. They had paid the visitors in gold. Once they had received enough gold they took to their ships and left the planet five years ago. With a broken voice, he told them that the visitors had left them with a parting gift. Sophie asked what the gift was. He said that it was a system of destruction aimed at the population of the planet. He added that two-thirds of the population were already dead. Sophie asked what was killing them. He replied robotic machines heavily armed and self-reproducing. He stated, "It's like living in a nightmare as the more machines we destroy the more the machine shops produce." She asked him where the machine shops were that made the replacements. He told her that there were six dotted around the globe and that they were impregnable; thousands had died trying to destroy them.

Sophie had the ghost in her pocket and activated it. The man moved backwards as the ghost grew to full size. Sophie asked it to take on the image of a Par Kallish inhabitant. As it changed, the man started to recognise the image; he identified the ghost's image as the visitors. He said that he was tired of the war, and asked them if they were there to help. Sophie said that it looked as if that choice had been made for them already. Sophie thanked him, and all four went looking for somewhere to shelter for the night.

Finding an apartment that was empty on the second floor of a building was a stroke of luck. It had no form of heat but would have to do. Settling down for the night, Sophie asked the ghost who had sent them there. The ghost looked a little sheepish and clammed up. She was in no mood for this type of behaviour and ordered it to tell her immediately or she would smash the mobile unit. It had a self-preservation subroutine, or so it seemed to her as the ghost capitulated very quickly. It told her, "The Touscal are you! They're humans from the far future and are extremely advanced. They've almost reached a god-like state. The Touscal illusion had been put in place many years ago and had been put there to protect human evolution from renegade time tourists who are humans from your near future. The renegade time tourists caused the Breech attack on Earth the greys and everything else concerned with unwelcome paradoxes. "You're being tested."

Sophie asked it "For what? and what are grey's?"

It said, "Never mind about the greys, thanks to you they had never existed, that's what kind of power you wield. The Touscal are wary of you, wary of the huge amount of power that has been entrusted to a miniscule being."

She questioned, "Do you mean me?"

The ghost said, "Yes, but don't get upset as they think the same about every being. But for some reason, they thought you were different." She asked it, "In what way?" The ghost told her "Your incorruptible and capable of bringing out the best in anyone or any situation. But you've really angered them. Its your enhancement, Its not what they had in mind. They wanted to kill you after the Par Kallish affair, but the Omicron order stopped them!" The ghost gave it to her straight and said: "The Touscal can only be destroyed by temporal meddling, meaning that they can only be destroyed by someone in their own past and they're frightened that, that someone could be you." It told her, "This is like a test for you; the first being the Breeche, and the second was Hylan Varrick, you take it all in your stride. You're showing them up for what they really are They're going to kill you in this place . If you can't defend yourself it will be the finish of you, and you will go down in history as one of their mistakes." Sophie asked, "How are they going to kill me ? what am I expected to do?"

Even the ghost couldn't answer that one!

After a night's sleep, Sophie felt more prepared for what lay ahead. It was another mess left by the inhabitants of Par Kallish, designed to get rid of the evidence about their interference of a lesser culture. Sophie told the General that they would have to split up. Triez and Isalia would have to find food, while she and the General would find out just what they were up against.

Triez and Isalia headed towards where the photon fire fight had taken place the previous night. On the way there they searched through stores that appeared as if they might contain food inside , but they had already been ransacked of anything edible. As they turned the corner, they could see a group of young people sitting around a fire, eating something. Triez told Isalia to stay put, while she approached them. Triez walked steadily in their direction. One of them alerted the others. Picking up their weapons they took cover. Trying not to look hostile she asked Isalia to translate. Triez told them, "I won't harm you, I only want to talk." Isalia shouted from the corner with the translated version. They seemed agitated and started to panic. She asked Isalia what she had told them, she said: "Exactly what you said, but I heard one of them say that there was a great big killing machine coming this way." The word "shit" didn't seem to need translation as the young men and women took flight! Isalia joined her mother and followed them.

Triez pulled Isalia down behind a burned out vehicle. Approaching was a robot that looked quite menacing, with two legs capable of swivelling at ninety degrees, a built-in photon cannon, and a flamethrower. Triez looked for a vulnerable point on its structure but found it looked fairly well constructed. Isalia reminded her mother that this was no Brooklyn mugger; it was a well-established killing machine with all mod cons, bells and whistles, but she knew that trying to keep control of her mother was like asking a eunuch to scratch his balls! As Triez crept up behind it, the robot took her totally by surprise as it swivelled around to face her. Now understanding what Isalia meant she found herself completely dumbstruck. Jumping up she wrapped her legs around the robot's head and pulled out her knife. Finding a slight gap on the machines head she started to prise off the steel faceplate with the knife. □

Isalia ducked down as the machine fired off round after round of photon fire. If that wasn't bad enough she found herself having to keep changing location due to it setting fire to everything around her with its flamethrower. Triez could feel her backside heating up and stamped on the flamethrower. On the third stamp, it sheared off leaving a stump spraying what smelled like gasoline everywhere. Squeezing the knife through a gap in the faceplate, she plunged it into the head and was blown clear of the inferno by a massive electric shock. Lying on her side she could see the robot spinning round, completely blind and being consumed by fire. A minute later it slumped over and cease to function. Isalia helped her mother up as the robot burned. Further down the street the young men and women emerged and approached Isalia. In their own language, she told them, "This idiot's my mother, and I'm very proud of her!" It was time to find Sophie. Heading back with a few new friends, Triez was given some food. Isalia told her, "Its a thank you gift from the youngsters. They're extremely impressed and feel a sense of belonging towards you."

Sophie and the General had been watching two of the robots that seemed to be working in tandem and corralling people into a corner that was surrounded by a wall. The General picked up a large piece of concrete. Climbing onto the back of a derelict commercial vehicle, he could see over the wall and balanced the piece of concrete on the top. As the robots closed in for the kill, the General pushed the piece of concrete from the wall. With a crash, it smashed into one of the machines and knocked the other one over. Sophie quickly ushered the people from the enclosed area. It seemed to her that the reason that their casualties were so high was down to a lack of knowledge about how to deal with the robots.

Surprised at the Generals behaviour they stood there watching him as he approached the machines. One was trying to stand up until he kicked its leg from beneath it. With gasoline leaking from the other robot, he picked up a stone and slashed it across the machines steel bodywork. Sophie watched as the sparks ignited a pool of gasoline that was surrounding the two machines. In a ball of fire, both were consumed.

Triez and her group entered the arena of fire and told the General, "I'm impressed at your two for one mentality!" She could see that apart from herself he had earned some food for them, as the would-be victims bestowed the gifts upon him.

Sophie smiled at the General and told him, "You wouldn't have benefited from a physical upgrade as your a psychotic bastard already!" He seemed to take this as a compliment and smiled back at her. With the ranks swelling, there were twenty-four people in the group now. Sitting around a fire that evening with Isalia translating, the General laid down his plan. He told them that the goal was to destroy the robot killing machines and restore some sort of civilisation on the planet. He added that it was a waste of time killing the machines as they could be reproduced at the same rate. They would, therefore, have to formulate a plan to destroy the workshops that made them.☐

After a long night talking to the locals, Sophie was told that there was an abandoned spaceport sixty kilometres to the west. She knew that if it was possible to get into orbit, she might be able to find a way of attacking the automated workshops. The next morning she and Triez set off for the spaceport. The General and Isalia would head south with their new friends to the nearest of the six workshops, forty-five kilometres away. Avoiding the robots, Sophie and Triez made good ground on the first day, covering over fifty kilometres. Sophie activated the ghost and asked it to monitor any fusion reaction in the local area. It told her that there was a small amount of fusion reaction taking place fourteen kilometres to the west. ☐

The next morning, just as the ghost had predicted, there in the distance stood the spaceport. It was in a derelict state, but it did have one redeeming quality, it had a vessel on the tarmac; it was a shuttle. Checking for robot activity, Triez gave the all clear and both women approached the vessel and entered through the cargo hold. The wind had ravaged most of the interior as it had been left open to the elements for the past five years which had taken their toll on the small vessel.☐

Triez accessed the engine compartment; she could see a control panel just behind the door and sighed with relief as it said 'nominal'. Calling to Sophie, she asked her to prime the engine.

Once the engine was primed, Sophie engaged the fusion reactor and closed the loading bay door. Triez joined her in the cockpit amid the dust and grime and they both blasted off into the unknown. Triez thought that it was a pile of junk but Sophie was content in the knowledge that there were no holes in the floor and they could probably land it somewhere other than a lake.

As they entered orbit Sophie could see a large space station that lay before them with an internal docking area. Pulling into the bay she could see that the station had faired well and was still in good condition since it was deserted five years earlier. On one of the consoles was what looked like a teleport for small items, next to it was a communication device and a couple of photon pistols. When they were on the same side of the planet as the General she would try to send them to him. An hour later Triez had located him on what seemed to be a spy satellite system. Zooming in on the General and Isalia, she gave Sophie their coordinates. Seconds after she had activated the teleport the items materialised a couple of metres ahead of the him, and it wasn't long before he was communicating with Sophie.

They were now only five kilometres from the first workshop. They had avoided all but one of the robots. It had been pursuing them for almost an hour and the General was pretty sure that it would have called for reinforcements. Triez made him aware that there were two more robots ahead of him that had been recently dispatched from the workshop and they were heading right towards him. □

Further Investigating the space station, Triez had located an escape pod, she had worked out that it was possible to guide and land the pod from a console that lay in front of her. Launching it, she carefully guiding it towards the General's position. Disabling the braking thrusters and powering up the engine the pod careered towards the ground. As the General looked on, he could see the two robots in the distance heading towards him. Suddenly a great fiery mass appeared out of the clouds doing at least Mach two. With an incredible explosion, it ploughed directly into the middle of the workshop, knocking him and the others off their feet. The two advancing machines and the one behind seemed to have stopped in their tracks. Picking himself up, the General approached the workshop. He congratulated Triez on a perfect shot with the escape pod. It had hit the central processing area at the heart of the workshop and had completely demolished the building. As the Generals group closed in on the plant they could see robot components scattered all over the place. □

Wandering through the remains of the robot factory, the General asked one of the inhabitants why it had been built in the first place. With Isalia translating. He said they were designed to do manual labour, but shortly before the Par Kallish had left, the computers were reprogrammed to fit weapons to the end of the arms instead of tools, and their main directive was to destroy all humanoid life on sight.

The General was extremely angry and raged that the Par Kallish had interfered with the natural development of the planet for the sake of gold, and then tried to kill the inhabitants off to make it look as if they had done it to themselves. Isalia told him, "Forget it, the Par Kallish can't help themselves, but at least with the Earth now space bound, we can keep an eye on them." Turning round, they headed back the way they had travelled.

Sophie had found a few small fusion reactors in a locker. They were used for the electric power and life support on the station. She figured that on overload they would give them enough explosive energy to finish the job. Triez had found a few timers and detonators and wired them up to the storage capacitors on each of the devices. There were five workshops left to destroy. Climbing back into the shuttle with the explosive devices Triez closed the loading bay door and left the space dock, as they closed in on the upper atmosphere Sophie set the first timer. Triez had logged all of the locations required, using the spy satellite, and fed the coordinates into the shuttles computer.

As they entered the atmosphere it became clear that the first destination was a desert location close to the ocean. Approaching it, they experienced photon weapon fire. It was from the inhabitants but soon died down as they neared the workshop. Triez took the shuttle down to two hundred feet and hovered. Sophie threw out the first reactor on overload with the timer set at eight seconds. She held on for dear life as Triez accelerated away from the area. The blast was huge and much larger than the escape pod explosion at the first robot factory. Sophie felt confident that it was a job well done as she watched a large white plume appear in the sky. The next two were easy targets, leaving numbers five and six.□

Number five was the most dangerous target; as the shuttle had to hover close to a cliff edge with an overhang, they only had a hundred foot drop height and with the timer set at only four seconds they both knew of the impending danger that they were facing. As Triez powered up the engine, the blast blew them into the cliff face. Breaking off part of the wing edge and damaging the fuselage, smoke billowed out of the engine compartment, Sophie attempted to vent the smoke through the open loading bay door. With five hundred and fifty kilometres to the last target in a rural location, Triez struggled to keep the shuttle's nose up. As they approached the workshop she hoped that the vessel could maintain enough height to clear the building. Sophie set the timer for two seconds and crossed her fingers. Triez swooped over the building, taking part of an antenna with them. □

Sophie dropped the bomb right on target. The blast blew off the loading bay door and thrust Sophie up towards the cockpit. The shuttle was now completely out of control and flying only a few metres above the ground. Sophie climbed into the co-pilot's chair and strapped herself in while Triez fired what thrusters they had left. The shuttle skimmed across a field until the broken wing dug into the soft ground, acting like a plough it spun the vessel round and stopped.

The safety harness on Sophie's seat had snapped throwing her into the control panel. Triez pushed her back into her seat and asked, "Are you all right?" Holding her leg Sophie replied, "Yes I think so, where are we?" On exiting the smoking, crumpled wreck, neither of them had a clue where they were. It was time to summon up the ghost.

When it appeared, the ghost asked, "What have you done now?" Bruised and bleeding, Sophie was tired of trying to save an ungrateful galaxy and told the ghost so. For a second the ghost's face went into a state of flux. Triez had noticed it and said, "What's going on with the ghost?" Looking at It square in the face Sophie said, "Hello." Standing back she watched as it started to change. Looking at the ground she could see a pair of feet starting to grow. Throbbing in and out for a second, the ghost settled into a human form. It was a face she had seen before, It was Ruman.

Walking towards her he gave Sophie a hug. She hadn't seen him since the war with the Breeche. Giving Triez a hug, Ruman backed off quickly after she grabbed his ass. He told her "I'm seen as a god in certain circles and should be respected." She laughed and said, "If you're a God then listen to my prayer and get us out of this shit hole!" This seemed to raise a smile on his face. He told Sophie, "You've done everything that's been asked of you and more. I've always fought in your corner right from the beginning. If they knew I was here now I'd be in serious trouble. Your strength and mental agility frightens my people as they now realised that they can't take back those strengths without killing you." He could see that she was tired out, and had little fight left in her.

Ruman opened a window out of thin air. Through it, they could see the Queen of Temfir. She was visiting a stonemason. It was a rough shape but Sophie could tell that it was a female. The vision zoomed in on the nameplate, which read 'Captain S Schultz'. Sophie was astonished. Ruman told her, "If you hadn't answered the distress call, the Queen would be dead by now." By returning home she gave the planet the lift that was needed to recover from the Breeche. The window flickered and Kai came onto the screen. Triez was astounded this time – it was Kai ten years into the future, then the Earth, and then it switched to Mylin: a group of prosperous planets that shared technology, the arts, music, and defence. Ruman said, "This is the influence that you will project onto these worlds" The next picture was Kai in ruins under the heel of the Breech. Mylin and the Earth were just boulder fields. Sophie asked, "What are we looking at now?" He told her that it was the galaxy without her.

The screen switched again; this time it was the learning dome on Par Kallish. The children were learning about their ancestry and the mistakes and greed that blighted them as a people; each generation would be a better one than the one before and that was now law on Par Kallish.

Ruman told them that it was nearly time for him to go back to his own dimension and vacate the ghost's matrix. He told her that he was a human from the far future, much further than the temporal tourists she had met on the Moon . He told them that his people were very old and regularly travelled back in time, to a more agreeable age, when there were stars to be seen in the sky. He added his people lived in a separate dimension from the Mylin to prevent temporal incursions and only ever interfaced with other races when they posed as the Touscal. He had seen the future, the past and present and told Sophie that once he was human, but now just energy, and summoned up a body when he needed one. He told her that she would have to destroy the tablet. If she didn't, his people would use it to kill her. She asked him, "How will we find it?" He pointed in the direction of where they had travelled and told her "It's three hundred and fifty kilometres in that direction until you reach a narrow sea. Cross the sea and you will find Isalia, the General, and the tablet: you must destroy it" And with that, the ghost became itself again.

Sophie had learned a few new swear words in Kai, mainly from listening to Triez and directed them towards him as he slowly disappeared. Triez said, "You should have called the asshole that when he was here." Sophie complained that Ruman was as much use as a chocolate teapot and felt that he could have done more to help her. Starting the long walk back the two women struggled through the miles while they nursed their injuries. Five miles on, an elderly gent told them to get off the road as the killer machines would get them. As they didn't speak the language they hadn't got a clue what he was saying. What they did see was the robot that he was pointing at. Sophie sat down and rubbed her badly bruised legs, while Triez walked calmly over to the robot. By this time the old man was frantic as he watched her tip it over and drag it back towards Sophie. Triez used a very basic form of sign language in order to get some tools from the old man. Understanding her to some degree he beckoned her to follow him into a large outbuilding. In there was the most ridiculous looking piece of transport that she had inflicted on Sophie so far. Feeling a little ambivalent about walking or riding, she chose the contraption. It had an engine, three wheels, and handlebars, but still seemed a better option than going on foot. Taking some tools from a box she returned to the robot.

As she started to dismantle it Sophie was beginning to take an interest in what Triez was planning.

Once the breastplate had been removed it was possible to see the flamethrower's gasoline tank opposite the main fusion power supply. It seemed to be made of plastic. Slipping off the retainers Triez removed the tank and asked Sophie to hold it in an upright position. Disappearing into the outbuilding, she came back with the contraption. With an extremely wonky set of wheels, a set of bent handlebars, and no seat, Triez held out an open hand saying, "This is the way home." Sophie answered, "If home is a cemetery five kilometres in that direction, then you might be right." The old man mumbled something, Triez said: "I haven't a clue what he just said."

Sophie said, "He's asking if we have any life insurance?"

Triez took the tank from Sophie and poured the fuel into the tank of the contraption. The old man laid a piece of foam across the frame, and Triez was ready to go. Sophie sat on the machine and Triez pushed. Letting go of the clutch, the engine burst into life and the old man cheered. With a wave, Triez jumped on board and they were on their way. A few metres on Triez asked Sophie to stop and jumped off the machine. Chasing what looked like a turkey-sized chicken. She returned to the old man with the bird under her arm and presented it to him. He seemed grateful, though confused. Sophie said, "It's probably his pet as neither of us has actually seen anyone eat any meat since we've been here."

*

The contraption had held up well, as the ghost clocked up their two hundredth-kilometre, but they were almost out of fuel. A robot standing facing a wall seemed the best way to fill the tank. Triez hopped off the contraption and pulled the robot over onto its back; within five minutes the tank was full again and they were ready to go. Sophie had wandered over to the other side of the wall. To her horror, she saw a mother and child who were dehydrated and bordering on starvation. Triez joined her and felt equally disturbed by their condition. Pulling out what food they had between them, they gave it to the young mother while Triez emptied what water they had left into a bowl and gave it to her. Sophie rigged a cover to shade the pair from the sun and stayed with them both until the next morning. The young mothers condition seemed to have improved a little by the morning as Sophie saw that she was starting to feed the baby again, and just wondered how many more people were out there suffering like this . She told Triez that once the tablet was destroyed they would have to try and make a difference there because no one else would: Triez agreed.

Waving the young mother goodbye, they set off again. In a cloud of smoke, the pair of them disappeared from sight. By evening they had reached the narrow sea. Triez found a man with a ferry who would be leaving at 9.00 am the following morning. The price for their passage was the contraption itself along with whatever gas was left in the tank; the ferryman seemed OK with the deal though why he was so fascinated with it was a mystery to Sophie.

Early the next morning the boat set sail, it was a one-hour crossing through calm waters. As they approached the other side there were a group of people standing on the beach. Sitting alone two hundred metres from them were Isalia and the General. Word had got out that the killing machines had been destroyed and it was all thanks to some newcomers that had done it for them. Sophie was having second thoughts about what an ungrateful galaxy it was as she watched the ferryman's body language as he spoke to his first mate. They seemed full of praise for the newcomers, it was as if they felt an overwhelming need to thank them personally for improving their lives. leaning over the balustrade Sophie and Triez watched the celebrations taking place at the far end of the beach. Triez told Sophie "I think we're probably the most loved people on the planet right now," Sophie smiled to herself and said, "You know I think we are." On landing at a quay, the General took Sophie to one side and showed her the tablet. He told her that it had just appeared in the night from nowhere. Sophie told him that she had met Ruman the day before who had informed her that it had to be smashed at all costs. At that moment the tablet started to glow; Sophie knew it was too late to stop it.

CHAPTER 15

Erecting itself upright, the tablet allowed one after the other of Ruman's people through, until six of them stood before Sophie armed with plasma rifles. Sophie wasn't listening to what they were telling her as she already knew that it was a firing squad sent there to kill her for being an unknown quantity. However, the General was listening, and with a heavy punch to the back of the head, he relieved one of the men of their rifles. Sophie was shocked to see him standing there with no sign of him backing down even though the other five were pointing their rifles at him.

Instantly, all five rifles flew out of the hands of the assassins and hung in the air just out of reach. Isalia's talents had never ceased to amaze her mother, it was now telekinesis. With the six of them trying to get back to the tablet Isalia lifted that into the air too. A few seconds later Isalia let the rifles drop to the ground.

Sophie picked up two and so did Triez, firing them at the tablet they could hear "No!" amplified six times.

Isalia picked up the last rifle and joined in. By now

the tablet was glowing bright red and starting to crack. Sophie told the General, "My rifles are fading fast, I'm nearly out of power." In response the General aimed and fired a continuous volley of shots with his rifle. There was now a tremendous amount of heat being generated within the tablet and with a loud crack it separated down the middle. As it hit to the ground it shattered into a thousand pieces.

One of the six young men stood forward and asked: "Why the hell did you destroy the portal that was our only way home, we're trapped here now and so are you!" Sophie told them, "Trapped, now that's a strange word to hear from a bunch of *go anywhere eternal beings."* Poking him in the stomach with the gun barrel she said, "One hundred and fifty kilometres from here is a mother and child starving to death, they're the ones that are really trapped, not some god-like pretentious morons like you." With that, she wished them, "Good luck, you'll need it." One of the bolder young men shouted, "You'd have been killed a long time ago if it hadn't been for the Omicron order." Sophie realised that for the first time she was starting to see the Omicron order more as an ally than a threat and wondered *who are they and what do they want from me?*

Re-boarding the ferry all four made their way back across the narrow sea. During the crossing, Sophie re-purchased the contraption from the boatman using food. It was a currency they had plenty of as it had been bestowed on the General in heaps since the demise of the robots.

*

The contraption ran a little slower on the return

journey as it had four people riding on it. Luckily it didn't need to stop as there was enough fuel to reach the young mother and her child that were some distance further on.

As Sophie approached the home made canopy she could see that they were still there and still alive. For two days everyone helped the mother and child back to health; assisting them with gentle exercise and decent food. It was a slow process but by the end of the second day, they were starting to look a great deal healthier.

The General had been collecting gasoline from disabled robots after finding an old car that had been abandoned in a lock up garage. Using some tools that were lying in the trunk he gave the vehicle a basic service. Once the tank was full, he sat in the car, then pushed the gear lever into second and was totally surprised as it started from a short roll down a hill.

As the General pulled up with his arm hanging out of the window, Sophie and the others were overjoyed to see what the General had found and realised another one of his remarkable talents; he was a great forager too.

Isalia had discovered that the young mother's name was Shiral, her partner was dead and she was all alone in the world with just a young child to care for. Listening to her plight Sophie decided that Shiral and her child would stand a better chance of survival if they left her with the old man further down the road.

The next morning the General readied the old car for the journey and took the contraption in tow. The automobile had been a great deal kinder to their backsides than their earlier form of transport and quicker too, as it wasn't long before they arrived at the old man's house. He seemed pleased to see Sophie and Triez again with his old contraption tied behind the car and seemed to take a shine to Shiral and her child straight away.

Isalia spoke to him and explained that all of the killer robots had been destroyed and now people would have to work together to survive, it was her opening spiel to get him to accept Shiral and her child as non-paying tenants. Another one of Isalia's talents was seeing empathy in others; she knew that she didn't really need to ask him as his kindness was clearly apparent.

The next morning Sophie and the others left almost all of their food and water with the old man as a token of their appreciation and drove the vehicle towards the coast.

The old man had spoken of an abandoned spaceport near to the eastern sea. It was a first step in finding out exactly where about in the galaxy they were.

By evening they had found what they believed to be the spaceport; it was in total darkness, finding some comfortable chairs in a reception area, they settled down for the night.

The next morning was a hot one, and after a short swim in the sea, it was time to explore the spaceport. Inside one of the hangers was a short range scout ship, and next to it was a type of passenger shuttle.

Both seemed to be powered by fusion reactor technology, and both seemed to be working to some degree. In one of the offices, Sophie analysed the star charts, recognising some of the constellations she found it was possible to triangulate their exact position. After thirty minutes it was apparent that they were twenty light years away from where *Hermes* was last positioned.

It was clear to Sophie now that the only way to contact the *Hermes* was through a hyperlinked message, but with such primitive equipment, they would need to be in space to send it. As it was the only option, the four of them prepared the scout ship for space travel.

Two days later, and they were ready. With Sophie and the General on board, the vessel lifted from the pad; switching from thrusters to the main engine the vessel thundered through the upper atmosphere.

With no inertial dampers, they found themselves floating about the cabin, the General seemed to enjoy it immensely and gambolled through the ship relentlessly. Once orbit had been achieved, Sophie activated the makeshift transmitter; it was creating a hyperlink carrier wave with a basic message attached to it, she just hoped that the *Hermes* was still out there and ready to receive it. Feeling a little bored Sophie and the General went exploring. There was all sorts of space junk but one piece particularly interested Sophie, it looked like something that the Par Kallish had left behind. It was in a high orbit, and its size became apparent as they closed in on it. Sophie could see what looked like a universal docking ring and tried the scout ship for size. Once an airtight seal was formed, she activated the door mechanism.

On entering the bridge the General was completely

lost for words, he understood the controls of *Hermes* but this was totally alien to him. Sophie realised that the Par Kallish had travelled not only further than any other known species, they had also travelled between dimensions. The more she delved into the computer the more fantastic it became. With food construct systems and an oxygen refurbishment system to die for, this was a vessel that she really had to have. Activating the ghost she asked it to record anything on the main computer that it considered to be of importance to their mission.

She now realised just how secretive the Par Kallish had been about their earlier space voyages and wondered how much more damage they were responsible for in the Galaxy.

The ghost had recorded a great deal of information, including a flight manual, a weapons system file and a life support introduction manual. The ghost then projected it onto the view and screen Sophie started to absorb the information like a sponge absorbing water.

Once she had enough information she released the scout ship from the docking ring and powered up the engine. Though the vessel was built for a crew of at least five, she figured that with the General's help they could make a safe landing on the planet below. She then proceeded in bringing him up to speed on how the vessels systems worked.

An hour later Sophie started the descent, while the General monitored the heat shield and calibrated the braking thrusters to the angle of descent. From the ground, Triez and Isalia watched as the vessel headed towards them. Triez worried that it may have been a weapon until she saw the undercarriage activate. Isalia loved the colour, it was red flake, and she liked the sound of it too; it was as if she had seen it before, all of it felt strangely familiar to her.

With a cloud of dust surrounding it, the vessel safely touched down, now all four knew that they had found a way home.

As Isalia stepped through the hatch, she made straight for the galley and came out a couple of minutes later with four glasses and handed them round, Sophie tasted it, it was as smooth as silk, with a wonderful taste and said, "This is a vessel that just keeps giving, I just love it."

Isalia told Sophie that her familiarity with the vessel was probably just some more of the junk left in her head after her cloning; and said: "For some reason, I seem to know every system on the vessel like the back of my hand, how can that be?" Sophie answered, "I'm just grateful that you do, we should never look a gift horse in the mouth!"

*

The next day was another hot one, Sophie told the other three, "As no contact with *Hermes* has been established, I think we should travel back home in the Par Kallish vessel." Sophie was feeling quite confident, that with Isalia's help they could find their way back. Considering the six assassins, she felt it necessary to remove them from the planet and leave them in their own dimension en route, where they could do no harm.

Isalia had boarded the Par Kallish vessel that afternoon and been printing building plans, motor schematics, and farming techniques on paper. Her mother asked who were they for. She told her, "They are parting gift for the people of this world," her link to the Par Kallish had given her a feeling of immense guilt about what had happened to them. Triez stroked her hair and told her, "You're my child, and could only ever do good things," and added, "you don't have a bad bone in that cloned body of yours." Reacting to her mother's praise she asked her "Will you help me make up food parcels from the food construct dispenser." Her mother told her that she'd be happy to.

Sophie and the General had been visiting the robot workshop sites in the passenger shuttle. As the gasoline tanks were separate to the workshops, they were still intact and full of fuel. They had been adapting the gasoline dispensers for the robot flamethrowers so that they could be used to fill gasoline-powered vehicles. As the last one was finished a grateful crowd approached them, shaking their hands, arms, and shoulders. It seemed to Sophie that shaking anyone anywhere was a sign of gratitude on that planet.

The General suggested that it was time to pick up the six assassins before they had a chance to cause any more trouble. With the General at the controls, Sophie looked out of the windows to see if they were in the vicinity, but all she could see was the odd traveller and what looked like wild goats. Travelling all the way back to the beach next to the narrow sea, the General landed the shuttle. Still sitting where Sophie had left them were the six assassins. Leaving the shuttle she walked up to them, knelt down and bowed her head saying, "I'm not worthy, I'm not worthy." Standing up she said, "I suppose those bodies you're occupying are hungry by now aren't they, didn't it ever occur to you to look for food?" Sophie had noticed that one of them seemed a little bolder than the others who said: "Scavenging for food is what animals do." Sophie threw a vegetable amongst them and watched as the once god-like immortals fought each other over something as bland as a potato. Walking amongst them she grabbed the bolder one by the scruff of his neck and told him to get himself and the others aboard the shuttle. He asked, "Where are we being taken, are you going to eat us or something?" She said, "Jesus Christ what century do you think I'm from?"

It seemed to Sophie, after a short conversation on the shuttle, that there didn't seem to be a great deal of intelligence between all six of them as they seemed to be totally dependent on technology.

Once they reached the spaceport, Isalia stood amongst a pile of parcels. On each one in their own language was a plan for living, with schematics and information about what the inhabitants needed to know in order to rebuild their planet. Sophie put her hand on Isalia's cheek and told her "It's a wonderful thing that you've done, I'm sure they'll appreciate your efforts." They were kind words from Sophie that seemed to cause Isalia's guilt to subside a little.

Keeping the assassins handy, Sophie asked them, "Load the parcels onto the shuttle and I'll give you some food; the bold one restated that he was god-like within certain circles. Sophie told him, "I've heard just about enough from you, so just shut your mouth and start loading, or I might change my mind about eating you!"

Once airborne, the General flew the shuttle at a fairly low altitude in order to spot any groups of people on the ground. If it looked as though there was a collection of people he would hover the shuttle and ask the assassins to throw the parcels out. How many parcels depended on how many people were assembled there. With one parcel left the General made his way to the old man's house. There, sitting outside in the afternoon sunshine were the old man, Shiral, and her child. Sophie handed over the parcel personally. Shiral held her forearms and gently shook them. With Isalia translating she called Sophie and her friends 'her new family'. Sophie told her, "I'll be calling in on the planet from time to time to visit my new family," and wished her well.

With a wave goodbye, the shuttle headed back towards the spaceport. After an uneventful journey, Sophie stepped down from the shuttle and felt a sudden sharp stabbing pain in her back, with her arms, splayed out she fell to her knee's. The head assassin had thrust a shard of glass into Sophie's back and laughed as she fell forward onto the tarmac. Motionless she lay there face-down with blood pouring from the open wound.☐

Triez knelt down and looked at the wound, she could see that it was deep. Turning round she ran at the assassin. Picking him up above her head she threw him across the tarmac causing him to crash down on top of a luggage trolley, agony overwhelmed him as he felt the bones in his leg break. Running towards him again, she barged into him, knocking him another five metres sideways into a pile of old engines. Isalia ran after her mother trying to calm her. Hanging on to Triez's waist she begged her to stop. But she was heaving with anger. Isalia stroked her mother's hair as she had done to her so many times in the past; this seemed to do the trick as Triez seemed to calm down a little and refrained herself from killing the assassin.

Dragging him behind her she returned to the Par Kallish vessel and ordered the other five into the brig; they did so without hesitation after witnessing their colleague's terrible injuries. Once inside the brig, the General activated the force field. Picking Sophie up Triez carried her aboard the vessel and placed her on her side on an operating table located in the medical centre. Isalia dressed the wound and activated a stasis field around Sophie in the hope that it would stem the flow of blood and have the effect of stabilising her for a while.

Triez stayed at Sophie's side, as Isalia laid in a course for Touscal's last known position. She seemed to know every bell and whistle on the vessel and hurled it through hyperspace like an Indy car champion on his last lap.

The General could see a look on Triez's face. It was something he had seen many times in the past as soldiers had lost close friends to the enemy. He could sense that Triez was burning up inside with anger and knew that if Sophie died she'd tear each one of the assassins to pieces with her bare hands.

Isalia picked up a faint trace where the tablet had existed before it teleported them to the planet and slipped into the dimension that matched the trace.

After a few minutes, the vessel arrived at a blue planet, not unlike Earth. In the distance she detected vessels closing in on their position. Isalia engaged the shields and asked the General to bring one of the assassins to the bridge. On doing so, Isalia grabbed him by the throat. Baring her fangs she asked him to point out the government building. Shaking like a leaf, he pointed it out on the tactical display. Pacing the vessel with the planets rotational speed she armed the weapons and locked them on the building along with five other targets, one being the main power grid. She knew from that position she could neutralise the planet completely.

Over the com came a threat to stand down. However, Isalia wasn't in a bargaining mood and blasted one of the power grid's reserve banks. Staying calm she watched the lighting start to dim over a third of the planet.

Isalia demanded a Doctor and Ruman be sent to her ship immediately, or the next shot would destroy the infrastructure of the whole planet. She was pretty sure that this action would render anyone in an energy state to be paralysed. She knew that her instincts were built on solid ground when a teleport request was made for two individuals: Isalia accepted the request. The General stood in the teleport room with a photon rifle set to kill and covered the pads as the two individuals started to materialise.

Seconds later Ruman and a female medic appeared, Isalia joined the General and used the ghost to confirm that they were genuine people and not more assassins. Without delay, the medic set about her work while Triez kept one hand on her pistol.

Removing the stasis field, the medic removed the shard of glass and repaired the internal damage with a probe. Pulling an instrument from her bag Triez raised her weapon and asked, "What's that?" she replied, "It's for closing the wound" and called it a 'dermal knit,' Triez watched as the machine fused the skin from both sides of the wound and could see that it was a seamless repair. Triez replaced her gun in her holster and said: "You might like to take a look at one of the assassins." The medic was appalled at the condition of Triez's adversary and asked: "Did a wild animal do this?" Isalia laughed and said, "You could say that!"

He had a broken leg, some internal injuries, a fractured skull, and deep lacerations all over his body.

On seeing Sophie awake Ruman strolled into the medical centre and apologised to her, she was still feeling a little sore but accepted his apology. He turned to the assassin and told him, "You got what you deserved, you were so convinced that Sophie was the real threat that you completely overlooked Triez. Her ferocity is legendary didn't your trainers tell you that?" Holding Sophie's hand he laughed and told her "Isalia had created havoc on the planet's surface as my people have never faced a threat of such ferocity they were completely terrified." Sophie said, "I think she takes after her mother, God forbid!" He told her that her would-be assassin was feeling a great deal of pain at that moment. It was something that his people hadn't experienced for a very long time. It was pain that he would have to tolerate until he was back on the planet's surface where he could revert to an energy state. And added "The problem with my people is they think of themselves as being impregnable by hiding away in a separate dimension. The war with the Breeche opened my eyes to reality and that's why I've always stood by you. I'm pretty sure they'll leave you alone now." Sophie told him, "That planet where we last met needs help in a big way and I fear for their very survival." He told her, "After today my people will help them. The fear of paradoxes rendering them as non-existent has terrified them into obscurity and dominated their existence for so long that they've forgotten what life's about. But they have started to realise that existence is nothing without experience, and now understand that It's time to reconnect with the rest of humanity." ☐

Ruman kissed Sophie's hand saying, "Look after yourself Sophie, it wouldn't be the same out there without you." Once Ruman and the medic had teleported off the ship, Isalia took the vessel back towards their own dimension. As soon as they were there the General hailed the *Hermes* and was over the moon at the sound of Jamie's voice. The *Hermes* had searched everywhere but had only just received their signal. As they closed in on each other, Jamie asked what they were travelling in, the General told him that it was a remarkable piece of equipment to add to the fleet.

Travelling back to Earth with the Par Kallish vessel in tow, Sophie asked Triez how she would like to spend the Christmas holidays. She answered, "With Isalia, Simon, Tom and hopefully you." She didn't really know much about Christmas, other than it was a religious festival. Sophie told her that most people saw it as a time to get together with friends and family and be generally nice to each other. And added that part of it included the exchange of gifts.

*

It was December 23rd and Isalia was focused on the view screen, it was a sight of home that she never tired of, but this time it seemed special as the approach to the Portland headlight looked even more beautiful than ever. She watched the snow-covered trees in the distance leading to the Portland base. Once there Jamie lowered the *Hermes* down to thirty feet and hovered over the base while Triez teleported to the Par Kallish vessel and activated the undercarriage. Carefully Jamie lowered both vessels onto the tarmac.

Jamie and Luma made their way to the teleport room for the two of them, it was Scotland for two weeks for Hogmanay. Dieter activated the teleport for them and asked Holly if she would send him to a particular restaurant in Hanover Germany. Setting the teleport up for her he said, "Just press that button once I'm on the pad." As Dieter disappeared on the pad, Holly herself was desperate to see the big apple again and had a hankering for some New York cheesecake but with the teleport room empty and little knowledge about how to operate it, she went looking for someone to send her. Spotting Dr Phull at the end of the corridor she called out his name, responding to her call he walked towards her. With both of them standing at the teleport console Holly asked him to send her to 42nd street as she was meeting friends there. After an attempt to set the coordinates she told the doctor that all he had to do was touch the two buttons in unison to send her there. Placing his hand on the console he didn't realise that he had touched and activated the emergency protocol panel. It was a built-in failsafe that was designed to send a person to a randomly chosen location on failure of the system. Touching the buttons in unison he watched her disappear, but was horrified when he received a message on the screen; it read Front Street, Nome, Alaska. □

Calling Sophie, he asked her to come to the teleport room as he feared that Holly may be in danger from a polar bear or something worse. Confused she made her way there. Taking a look at the log she tried to contact Holly on her com-set but with no answer, she had to assume that she didn't have it with her. Contacting Triez Sophie asked her to meet her in the teleport room with three sets of arctic clothing. Triez asked, "Why?" Sophie told her, "Holly's gone to the far end of Alaska in a short skirt, camisole top, and high heels." The line went extremely quiet, Curiously Sophie squeezed the earpiece tight against her head and could hear Triez laughing hysterically in the background. Finally arriving at the teleport room she turned up with the clothing and once they were dressed both women stood on the pads while Matthew from engineering operated the teleport.□

Arriving on Front Street wearing arctic clothing both women started the search along Nome's snow covered streets. Following the search protocol Sophie asked a passing stranger where the most popular place in town was, he answered: "The Fur Trading Saloon gets pretty busy at this time of the day." Thanking him for his time they followed his directions. Triez had spotted a trail of deep pointed holes in the snow and started to follow them, calling Sophie over both of them followed the trail right up to the front door of the saloon. Once inside it didn't take long to find Holly as she was the only person there who was dressed for a summer garden fete. ☐☐

Sophie approached her from behind and asked: "You're not going to kill the doctor if I send you back are you?" Looking pleased to see them both Holly said: "Who wants to go back, just take a look at this place it's great." Looking around the room which had live music and dancing Triez could only agree and took off her hat and gloves. With the words "See ya", she walked onto the dance floor while Sophie and Holly ordered the drinks. At 2.00 am all three women found themselves lying on a snow bank watching the aurora borealis. They were totally pissed, totally broke and totally satisfied that it had been the best night of their lives. ☐

Arriving back on the *Hermes* at 9.00 am the next morning Sophie, Holly, and Triez made for their cabins for some long overdue sleep.

Later that afternoon Sophie teleported Holly to New York and took a truck from the base. Travelling to a garden centre she purchased a seven-foot Christmas tree, lights, tinsel, and glass bulbs. The next stop was a department store, where she purchased clothes for everyone she knew, along with Christmas cards and labels. She had written a list in Kai script and given it to Triez and Isalia asking them to get a turkey, stuffing, vegetables, and a large Christmas pudding.

Arriving at Triez's house, Sophie asked Isalia to help her with the tree. Isalia was a little confused when Sophie took the tree inside the house and set it upright in the corner of the lounge. Sophie asked her to help by hanging the glass bulbs and tinsel on the tree, while She turned on the lights.

Triez came in from the kitchen and was spellbound by the tree in all of its splendour. She told Sophie, "I'm beginning to understand it now, I can feel a special atmosphere growing," and added, "I want everyone to join us for Christmas." She called Doctor Phull and the Prof and asked them over to stay with her over the Christmas period. Simon and Tom arrived later that evening and were welcomed at the door by a very excited Triez holding a tray full of glasses filled with Bourbon. Sophie smiled at Isalia and said, "I think she's getting into the spirit of things."□

Christmas morning was completed with the arrival of the General and Theras bearing gifts.

Triez opened her gift from Sophie – it was a beautiful dress with matching shoes and accessories. She put it on immediately; she loved it, and so did Tom. He had never seen her in such a feminine state and found it hard to avert his eyes.

In the kitchen, Sophie did her best to tutor Isalia, the Prof and the Doctor in cooking the perfect Christmas lunch and together they had done a fairly good job. The proof came after lunch when most of the guests collapsed into the armchairs, full to the brim. Sophie could see the satisfaction on Triez's face as she cleared the plates away and poured herself another drink. As everyone was all together Theras thought it to be a good time to make an announcement and tapped a glass with a spoon, having gained everyone's attention. She said, "I'm expecting a baby, what do you think about that?" Triez asked, "Who's the father?" to which she answered, "Tom of course!" The expression on the General's face had them reeling with laughter.

Triez put her hand on Theras's stomach and told her that it would be a special baby, the first of its kind. She raised her glass and said, "To Theras's baby, and may it be as beautiful as her mother." The General just sat there trying to take it all in. He had imbibed a great deal of bourbon since he had arrived and was now regretting it. Theras knelt down in front of him and asked whether he was unhappy. He leant forward, kissed her on the forehead and told her that she had made him the happiest man on the planet and that he had never loved her as much as he did at that moment.

Later that afternoon there was a knock at the door. As Triez opened it she screamed at the top of her voice. It was the Kai Captain. Throwing her arms around him she dragged him inside, Triez's Christmas was complete.

*

It was December the 27th, and it had been a wonderful boozy Christmas. Sophie told Triez that she was a natural host and that everyone had enjoyed her hospitality. With the Kai Captain almost sober, he told Triez, "I want to show you something of great beauty." She was intrigued. Together with Sophie and the General, they left for the spaceport. As they entered the gate, Sophie noticed the extra guards on the door to the *Hermes*' hanger. As the doors opened they revealed a beautiful light blue vessel next to *Hermes*, it was almost the same size. Triez asked

"What is it exactly," the Kai Captain said. "It's the result of a collaboration between NASA and the Kai space directive, most of it was constructed on Kai." Sophie said, "It looks like its curves have been designed to deflect incoming fire from an enemy." The Kai Captain said, "You're absolutely correct." Sophie called it a fine vessel which brought a broad smile to his face. She could see how happy he was and didn't want to rain on his parade so she refrained from telling him that the *Hermes* had a camouflage device.

The Kai Captain said that the crew would be back the next day and he would appreciate it if they would attend further space trials en route to Kai; Sophie and the others agreed.

The next day at 8.00 am Sophie, Triez, and the General arrived at the base. As they entered the vessel through the main entrance Sophie could see the extreme quality that had been engineered into the vessel. She felt that it was plush enough to entertain ambassadors or royalty and sat down on one of the most comfortable chairs she had ever tried in her life. Once all of the checks were made the vessel powered up its engines and ascended very smoothly towards the upper atmosphere where it seamlessly glided into space as if it was perfectly created to be there. Sophie was extremely impressed by this time and took the elevator down to the engine room. Entering through double sliding doors she could see that it was a clean polished and a purely functional area. Next to the engine room was the hanger deck, with one launch and two fighters.

On exiting the elevator at the bridge level Sophie

was thrown against the wall and with a heavy crash, the whole vessel lunged forward at tremendous speed. Sophie could see that they were caught in a powerful tractor beam. Trying the manual override the Kai Captain realised that he had no control over the vessel whatsoever as it hurtled through hyperspace at incredible speed.

He told Sophie, "The ships starting to exceed the design specifications and if it travels any faster we're going to start breaking apart." Sophie sat at the weapons console and channelled the entire weapons system energy into the beam; Triez joined her by directing the total amount of engine power into the mix too and directed it along the beam. Crossing their fingers Sophie and Triez overloaded every system on the vessel and directed it at the source of the extremely powerful beam.

Firing everything at once had blown out almost every system on the vessel and sparks rained down everywhere. The Kai Captain could see that the bow of the vessel had lost some of its integrity as the emergency shields came into play.

Suddenly without warning the beam stopped and Sophie knew that their actions had worked as they were now out of its influence. In the distance was a massive explosion, it was on a planetary scale. The Kai Captain was trying to triangulate their position in respect to the nearest planet. On the tactical display appeared a chart that suggested that Par Kallish was initially where the beam had originated. Sophie looked at the view screen and feared that the round ball of fire it displayed was all that was left of Par Kallish.

The repair crews struggled to get control of the

vessel as it drifted towards the huge fireball at great speed. Triez could see that it truly was Par Kallish and felt that they had dabbled in other people's affairs once too often.

Sophie could only offer one explanation and told the Kai Captain, "It was as if they didn't recognise the configuration of the vessel, and slipped into their old ways again." This time Sophie could feel no guilt as she knew that the Par Kallish themselves were aware of what might happen if they picked a fight with someone who could fight back. Triez told her, "They were warned to change their ways or suffer the consequences." The General agreed to say, "It was the large amounts of highly explosive choronite below the planet's surface that had been their undoing."

Managing to slow the vessel down, the Kai Captains crew did an analysis of the damage to the vessel and came to the conclusion that it was seriously impaired. The Kai Captain had no choice other than to travel onwards to the dockyards on Kai for immediate repairs.

It was a short journey to Kai on the broken ship as the tractor beam had dragged them most of the way to Kai in a matter of seconds. Once they were at the Kai dockyards Sophie was curious about how Kai was fairing after the civil war. Triez took her to the waterfront area with the General, where she knew they would be surprised at the changes. Sophie really was surprised to see well-known stores and burger bars from Earth that had sprung up from nowhere. Triez said, "There are quite a few Kai food outlets now thriving in New York also. They spent the afternoon drinking coffee while they waited for a transport to take them back to Earth. On returning to the dockyards for their lift home, Sophie stopped to look at the damage that had been inflicted on the Kai Captain's vessel. The General pointed out that the whole underside of the ship's shell had been torn away – she realised that if the emergency shields hadn't activated when they did, they would all have been exposed to space and would most certainly have died.

Sophie told Triez and the General the vessel would be out of commission for at least two months. Triez agreed, saying that even then they would need to address the strength of the vessels hull structure before it could be deemed worthy to join the *Hermes* on the proposed exploration missions. She added, "It's a very pretty vessel, but it's not the *Hermes*."

With the help of one of her contacts, Triez had managed to cadge a lift on a brand new Kai frigate that was travelling to Earth. The skipper claimed that it was a fairly quick vessel and could make Earth in less than fifteen hours. Sophie felt that Earth was becoming much closer to Kai by the day with every new piece of technology that was being developed between the two worlds.

Back at her home next to the lake, Triez was happy to see that Isalia had cleaned up the house after Christmas and taken the decorations down. As a 'thank you', Triez took her to Portland where they spent the day shopping and visited the Headlight. Isalia had only ever seen it from the air, but now standing next to it seemed to give her a special affinity towards it, as if it was an integral part of every mission they'd ever been on.

On the way back they stopped off at Sophie's apartment. Standing at the doorstep they could hear music playing quite loud. Having rung the bell with no answer, Triez tried the door and found it to be open.

She could see Sophie lying on the sofa with her eyes closed. Listening to the music they felt themselves being mesmerised by its dulcet tones. It sounded beautiful to their ears and left them in a trance-like state, lying on the floor they absorbed every note. Nothing stirred for five minutes until the track stopped. Sophie was quite surprised to see the pair of them lying on her lounge floor, she smiled and asked them if they were OK. Isalia said, "Fine, but what was that beautiful music?" Sophie told her, "It written by a Russian called Alexander Borodin It's from an opera called Prince Igor; the Polovtsian dances to be exact." Triez wanted more. Sophie realised that there was still so much more for her to see on the Earth for herself. So she understood exactly how the pair of them felt, experiencing Earth's culture for the first time.

Sophie asked Triez, "Being that the Kai Captain's vessel's in a dock for two months, how would feel about travelling around the globe for that time with Isalia and myself?"

They were beyond excitement, especially when Sophie suggested doing it the old fashioned way with backpacks, hopping from one country to the next on aeroplanes and motor vehicles.

Early the next morning the General picked all three of them up from Triez's house and dropped them at the airport, he said: "I can only envy what your doing, have fun and send me a postcard." With a kiss to the Generals cheek, all three of them left for the plane.

CHAPTER 16

Once on board the Boeing 747, Isalia started to panic. She was used to vessels with a heavily built fuselage and shielding. As the plane took off, she watched the wings move with the air currents. An hour into the flight and Isalia asked Sophie how the engine worked. She told her that air was dragged into the front of the engine by thin, curved blades; a series of compressors compressed the air and threw it out of the back of the engine as thrust. □

Isalia asked her if they had ever had failures, to which Sophie answered that they did sometimes. Sophie noticed that some of the newspapers, handbags, and cups of coffee were starting to float above the heads of the other passengers. She asked Isalia, "Is that you're doing?" She told Sophie, "It's beyond my control as I'm feeling stressed at the sight of that wing flapping about like a piece of paper. I can't control my telekinetic powers as they're trying to keep the plane in the air automatically!" Her mother leant over and told her, "If you don't pack it in you'll end up plunging all of us into the sea." With a crash of coffee cups and a few shrieks, Isalia tried to relax.

As the plane came into Heathrow airport, there was heavy rain and thick cloud, with a fair amount of turbulence. The plane seemed to bump with every air pocket they hit. ☐

The flight attendants were alarmed by a number of things floating in the cabin again and were starting to think that the plane was haunted.☐

Triez understood how Isalia felt, as she too thought the plane was extremely fragile compared to the *Hermes,* which was such a heavy and powerful vessel with multiple failsafe procedures at hand. She didn't admit it to Isalia but was alarmed herself at the fact that all that was keeping them from dying was a thin manganese-aluminium alloy tube and four weak engines.

London had a fascination about it for all of them. Once they had found a hotel and checked into the room, they were straight out again and onto the streets. It reminded Triez of home a little, with old buildings that were perfectly preserved.

As they watched Tower Bridge rise to let a boat pass down the Thames, Triez asked, "Why didn't they just make the bridge higher." Sophie told her, "It's London, many things here don't make much sense and it's all part of the city's charm." After seeing the congestion on streets that were too narrow, Triez started to understand.

After two days in the city, they checked out of the hotel. Sophie had hired a car and arranged to meet up with Jamie and Luma in Scotland for Hogmanay. With no hotel rooms booked Sophie thought that they might just crash with them in Edinburgh.

On their arrival in Edinburgh, they found the city to be extremely lively, this was a place that Isalia loved; freezing cold, but with an atmosphere that was a living entity in itself. Leaving the car outside Jamie's place, Sophie knocked at the door and Luma answered, she was so happy to see them that she shrieked out loud and ushered them in.

Jamie had arranged a meal at a restaurant for later that evening that was supposed to be haunted. This human fascination with ghosts seemed to excite Isalia and her mother alike as they looked forward to their first paranormal experience. Sophie just thought that it was a load of old baloney, but went along with it all the same.

The meal was a sumptuous affair with what seemed like a gallon of wine between them. Later in the evening, Isalia headed for the ladies' powder room. As she left the room she was sure that a voice whispered something in her ear. Turning round quickly, she was quite sure that just for a second she had seen a shadow against the wall. This stirred her inner feelings, but it was what felt like a hand on her shoulder that really freaked her out; running downstairs back into the restaurant, Sophie noticed the lamp shades in the room had started swinging to and fro. She asked Isalia if it was her again, she told Sophie that this time it was nothing to do with her and was pretty sure she had seen something in the powder room that defied description. Patting Isalia on the back, Sophie congratulated her on seeing her first ghost. Triez said that it was more to do with the strength of the wine as she was expecting a visit from the black dog later that evening herself.

Sophie activated a ghost of her own but kept it to about two inches tall. She asked it if there were any abnormalities in the building, straight away it picked up a disturbance in one of the upstairs rooms. Sophie said, "All of you come with me." The two inch ghost sat on its mobile unit as Sophie held it close to her chest and followed its directions.

Climbing the stairs it asked Sophie to stop and turn into a room on the right and told her to keep the lights off for the best effect. All five of them stood against the back wall next to the door and kept completely silent. The ghost said, "It seems to be a hotspot for temporal fissures, they're cracks in the fabric of time itself." It also reminded Sophie that the fissures were a two-way street and if they could see images from the past then the characters from the past could see them too. As they watched, the ghost said: "A fissure's opening right there, in the right-hand corner of the room." All five watched, as what looked like a maid appeared. She seemed to be making a bed. Though a little blurry they could make out the outline of the maid herself. After a few seconds, the vision disappeared. Triez felt a touch to her cheek and so did the other four, the ghost explained that the touch was the fissure closing as it passed over them.

Back in the restaurant, Sophie closed the ghost's mobile unit and said, "I've seen enough ghosts for one night," and asked the waiter for the bill.

The royal mile was buzzing with people out to celebrate the new year. After several visits to some traditional pubs, it was time to head for the fireworks. Isalia marvelled at them, she had never seen so many in one place. Watching everyone enjoying themselves made Sophie feel quite proud that she'd brought them to the best place in the world for New Year's Eve.

The next day Sophie took the hire car in and purchased an ageing Jaguar for the next part of their journey. Bidding Jamie and Luma farewell, the three of them made their way towards France. Triez liked the Jag; it was a fairly old XJ6. Sophie bought it cheap and thought *If it gets wrecked, who cares.* Sophie asked Isalia if she could move anything as large as a car, she answered that she could lift anything if she was frightened enough. Sophie said, "Good your the new hood ornament when we reach Russia." Having travelled the entire length of the United Kingdom they caught the Dover ferry and on reaching Calais they made their way towards Paris.

Despite the damage to many of the capital's beautiful buildings, Paris was still stunning. After a visit to the Eiffel Tower, the Louvre and the Petit Palais they were ready for dinner. Paris had left all three of them in a romantic mood. Triez wasn't wearing a small prosthesis that Doctor Phull had modelled for them both. As aliens, he felt that they may attract some unsavoury people. But in Paris, it was just the opposite, with the owner of the restaurant serving a special meal in her honour. She was well known there from media coverage and was also the first Kai that he had actually met. She found him extremely charming and asked him to join them for a drink. In ignorance, he accepted and paid the price as Triez caroused French wines and only called it a day when the restaurant owner fell off his chair.

*

Making an early start the next morning, Sophie had

arranged to meet Dieter in Grindelwald, Switzerland as he had promised them a lesson in climbing on their arrival. Triez was stretched out on the back seat of the Jaguar swearing that she would never drink that much again. Isalia told her to spare a thought for the restaurant owner as he was probably in a worse state.☐

Grindelwald, with its snow-covered mountains and beautiful scenery, pulled Triez out of her hung-over state, but as soon as they arrived at the hotel, Triez made for the bar. Isalia couldn't believe her mother and was sure that she was an alcoholic. Calling her a drunken old sot, Isalia felt a little guilty as she watched her mother drink a litre of water in less than ten seconds, and head for the ladies' room.

Sophie asked if Dieter had arrived at the hotel, the receptionist told her, "Yes, he arrived yesterday, he's gone climbing with some of the other climbers who are presently staying at the hotel. They're expected to return around 5.00 pm."

With an empty stomach, Triez offered to buy lunch. Having their meal served outside all three were spellbound by the sight of the mountains in all of their glory. There was something that seemed correct about sitting outside in Switzerland and eating lunch in the cold that Isalia couldn't quite put her finger on until she looked at the beauty of the scenery. She observed the gullies, gorges, the sheer faces and snow-covered upper levels, it was as if they demanded her admiration.

As 5.00 pm approached, there was no sign of Dieter or the others, the receptionist told Sophie that a weather front was closing in, and if they didn't show up by 6.00 pm, it would be the concern of the rescue services. At that point, Sophie was beginning to regret that Dieter had not received the physical enhancement. She asked, "Has climbing equipment been reserved in his name?" The receptionist replied that it had. Sophie asked, "Then we'd like to have it," and asked for extra supplies, tents and blankets. The receptionist warned her that it would be impossible to do anything before morning. Triez looked out at the weather front closing in and demanded the extra equipment there and then. Reluctantly, the receptionist agreed.

Sophie was aware that none of them knew the first thing about climbing, but was confident that their special abilities would greatly compensate for the lack of experience. Fully dressed in mountaineering attire, with ropes and crampons they set out for the Eiger.☐

Catching the train to the mountain, all three jumped off early. Following the Eiger trail, they made a heading for the west face whilst averaging a speed of thirty kilometres per hour. Triez was the first to start the climb and with a single bound the others followed. It was snowing quite heavily by now with a gale blowing. Bounding from one rock to another all three resembled snow leopards on amphetamines. Triez had mastered a technique of grabbing rock holds and throwing herself up the mountain, but with Isalia's superior eyesight she could see the next hold sooner than her mother and overtook her, while Sophie just followed, using the same holds as the other two. At ten thousand feet all three stopped and listened for voices, but the wind was now howling and drowning out any voices other than their own.

Climbing at a slower rate Isalia could hear voices

ahead; it was at a higher level. As they moved around a large rock formation, they could see Dieter and the other climbers. Sophie could see one man hanging upside down from a snapped rope that had snagged itself on a sheer face, he appeared to be injured. Sophie knew Dieter and knew that he would never leave a man behind, even if it meant losing his own life.

Making their way up the rock face Dieter spotted them as they climbed onto the ledge. Walking over to him Sophie could see that he was a little lost for words. She grabbed his hands and started rubbing them. Laughing he said, "Why is it that you three never fail to amaze me?" She told him, "Maybe it's because I'm an amazing person." □

Catching Dieters' eye was the sight of Triez climbing across the west face with the adhesion of a gecko. Stretching out she grabbed the end of the trapped rope. Freeing it she pulled the climber up and made her way back to the others with the climber hanging below her. Isalia hung over the edge and pulled him up onto the ledge, he seemed greatly relieved and thanked her. By now the other climbers knew that this was no ordinary rescue team. Sophie and Isalia pulled out tents and extra blankets for the climbers and set up camp on the ledge.

The snow and wind were now calming down a little as darkness covered the mountain. Dieter watched as Sophie treated the injured climber's ankle with a bandage and dosed him with Jack Daniels and soup. Walking to the rim of the ledge Dieter asked Triez, "Where did you learn to use a climbing rope with such skill?" She told him, "We didn't use a rope, just gloves and an energy drink." Dieter laughed, then realising that she wasn't kidding he said, "Really? with a nod from her, she answered, "Really!"☐

Using a camping stove, Isalia heated up tinned soup and handed it round. One of the younger climbers asked her who she was; as she lowered her scarf he could see that she was Kai and a very beautiful one at that. They spent most of the night talking and laughing, as the wind howled at the tent opening. At 7.00 am everyone was out of the tents and ready to make the descent. Spotting Isalia climbing out of one of the tents, Triez called her a dirty stop out. She told her mother, "I'm not, and besides, it's too cold for that sort of thing."

As Dieter and the climbers made their way down the mountain, the three women continued to the summit and sat there in the sun and silence for over an hour whilst taking in the scenery.

Ready to descend the mountain, Triez led the way down at quite a pace. All three found that with their upper body strength and superior balance, they could descend the mountain at great speed and caught up with Dieter's group before they reached ground level.

Arriving back at the hotel, Dieter was done with climbing for that year and asked, "Where are you three off to next?" Sophie answered, "Russia and you've got to come with us." He agreed but was a little dismayed when he saw their means of transport; Sophie told him it was a classic. Dieter answered, "OK whatever!" ☐

Travelling through Austria and Hungary, they entered the Ukraine. The Jaguar was going really well, with Isalia in the passenger seat. Her telekinetic strength was being put to the test as she'd pushed two beer crates and a gas bottle out of the path of the car without causing any harm.

Three days after leaving Switzerland, they arrived in Moscow at 8.00 pm. After checking into a hotel, they all went looking for a restaurant. Moscow wasn't at all what Sophie expected, it was a modern metropolis with shops, bars, and restaurants of all descriptions. She found the architecture, particularly the old buildings had a quality about them that was unique to Russian The others seemed impressed too.

The next day they all rose fairly late. Sophie had promised them something special for that evening. Leaving the Hotel at 10.00 am, they spent most of the day sightseeing. Dieter explained communism to Triez as they walked through Red Square. He told her, "Russia hasn't always been the place it is today, with the freedom that its people enjoy." Triez was starting to feel that the Russians had suffered too, and had a lot in common with her own people.

Back at the Hotel, it was 6.00 pm Sophie told them to get dressed up and get ready for the surprise. Stopping for a light meal on the way, she told them to finish up or they would be late. Isalia was pinching Sophie's waist, trying to persuade her to tell her where they were going. Sophie just laughed; not much further on Sophie stopped outside the Bolshoi Theatre. By this time Dieter was laughing as Triez and Isalia were both pinching Sophie's waist, trying to get an answer to where they were going. She told them, "We're here." Looking around them they could see a grand imposing palatial building with a statue of horses above a set of huge pillars. As they entered the building Sophie handed over the tickets.

Isalia was spellbound as they stepped onto the grand staircase; it seemed to impress the others too. The foyer was adorned by a gold and red colour scheme and plaster mouldings on a grand scale. As they entered the box, the true majesty of the place bestowed itself upon them. Sitting down on the gold and red plush chairs, Sophie told them that as they seemed to like the music that she had played in her apartment so much, she thought they might like this. Triez could hardly contain herself when Sophie told her that it was the opera, Prince Igor.

As the curtain rose there was complete silence from Triez and Isalia until the interval. Sophie had never seen either of them so well behaved; with the second half seeming even quieter she realised it was as if they didn't want to miss a single second of it.

Leaving the theatre at the end of the performance, Dieter asked Isalia if she had enjoyed it. She told him, "The choreography of the dance sequences and everything about it was perfection, I loved it."

*

The next morning, the General called Sophie concerning a vessel that was travelling in Earth's direction at extreme speed. It had signalled the Earth directive, and Simon had confirmed that it had a Temfir signature. Sophie asked, "So what's your problem?" He told her, "I haven't had any experience of dealing with a planetary leader before and in particular a Queen." She replied, "Don't fart in her presence, and definitely don't feed her chilli dogs." He was desperate and told her, "It's not joking matter

I've already dispatched the freighter to pick all of you up from Red Square, so be ready to meet it in thirty minutes." She reluctantly agreed but thought, *it might be nice to get to know the Queen a little better, as she seems to be an important player in the way that things are starting to shape up in our part of the Galaxy.*

There was quite a gathering of people at Red Square that evening and the police were holding them back at a safe distance as the freighter descended into the middle of the square. Two young Russian airmen approached and saluted Sophie; they told her that the General had invited them to serve with the Earth directive over a one-year period, and asked if she was ready to receive their password. Sophie called Isalia over and whispered in her ear, asking her if they would do. Isalia felt one's arm muscles and danced around him. Looking totally bemused, he took his hat off as the freighter touched down, and wondered what he had let himself in for.

They were called Vasily and Alexei, and according to a text message from the General on Sophie's phone, were two of Russia's finest young officers. As Sophie loaded her beloved old Jaguar she watched Isalia eying up the young Russians, like a hawk eying up a tasty pigeon.

Dieter on the other hand was pleased to be heading for Portland as he missed being off-world. He offered to dump Sophie's old Jaguar on the moon if she liked. Securing the car down she told him that it would last longer than him if he didn't get himself enhanced. She told him that the mountain was a warning and without her help, he would have perished with the others, on the west face of the Eiger. □

He told Sophie, "The idea of having my muscles torn apart has never really appealed to me." However, he felt that he might need it in an unknown and sometimes unfriendly galaxy.

CHAPTER 17

As the freighter headed out over the Atlantic with a rookie pilot at the helm, Triez asked Sophie if she thought Isalia was OK with the two Russian officers. She said, "She will be if she can stop them from being so wary of her," and added, "she's like her mother, our first meeting ended with a hell of a fight in the hold of the *Crazy Horse*." Sophie told her, "Relax they're Russia's finest, and history's always recorded them as a pretty brave race, they'll soon get used to her ways."

Isalia sat down with her mother in the mess and asked if the humans thought she was a freak. Triez laughed, saying that she was at an awkward age. She told her that she was still finding her feet, and probably found it a little more difficult than most, having been dead and resurrected as a superior being. Isalia said, "Thanks, Mother if I didn't feel like a freak before; I do now!" Triez put both hands on her daughter's head and told Isalia, "Everyone at the directive loves you, along with every human, Kai, and any other species that we've met. Relax, be yourself, and the young Russians will warm to you." □

As the freighter approached Portland, Isalia took her place next to Jamie facing the forward screen as they passed over the Portland headlight. Alexei was curious about what she found so fascinating. With an arm around her shoulder, he joined her and said, "What a welcoming sight the headlight seems to be." Isalia knew that in the end, she could always trust her mother's word.

Once on the ground, the General was anxious that the human race made a good impression. Sophie asked, "How far out are they?" He told her, "They'll be here within the hour." □

To calm the General down Sophie called the base on the Moon and asked Simon to launch two fighters as an official escort for the Queen's vessel. She also contacted Holly and gave her the job of arranging a meeting of the planet's leaders in two days' time. Calling a contact on the press council, Sophie arranged for a press extravaganza that was set to commence within thirty minutes of the Queens arrival.□

With a stamp of her foot, she asked: "What are you all waiting for? I want full dress uniform from everyone and that means from the rookies to you General." She asked Triez, Isalia, and the two Russians to get the best food they could possibly find and start cooking it at Triez's home as soon as possible. She knew that she would have to stall the Queen as long as she could with introductions to the personnel at the base.□

With the base's surrounding area full of press and spectators alike, the Queen's vessel made its final approach. Sophie watched as the vessel, complete with royal insignia, touched down at the base. Sophie shoved the General forward as the Queen appeared at the vessel's doorway; with a smile, he took her hand and guided her towards an inspection of the base personnel.

Fernais, the Queen's personal confidant and bodyguard, was at her side. Sophie asked him, "Would the Queen care to say a few word for the press, as there's a great deal of interest and fascination about her? The last aliens that many of them saw were the Breeche carrying weapons, It's time to allay their fears and show them that not all aliens are a potential threat."

She was happy to do this and using a translation device she thanked the people of Earth for receiving her with such a warm welcome and hoped that it would lead to a great friendship between their two peoples.

Climbing into the official car, the Queen, Fernais, Sophie, and the General headed for Triez's home by the lake. With the front door wide open Triez welcomed the Queen to her home. She was as pleased to see Triez as she was Sophie, though Fernais held back a little.

Sophie told Triez that beans on toast wouldn't cut it with this bunch; Triez assured her that she was in full control of the situation. Sophie warned her, "If we poison the Queen we'll all be in the shit!"

With the Queen seated, Isalia and Triez entered with the courses. Sophie was surprised as it was extremely good. Sneaking into the kitchen, she found the two Russians throwing food to each other with precise accuracy. Isalia asked her what she thought of their cooking so far. She gave it five stars and asked what the main course was. Isalia told her it was Forel po-armyanski. Sophie asked her what it was, she replied, "Rainbow Trout with artichoke hearts and capers."

Sophie peered over Vasily's shoulder and observed what he was cooking. Patting him on the shoulder she told him, "You're heading for a promotion young man, keep it up!"

With the Queen impressed at her treatment so far, they all retired to the lounge. She asked Sophie and the others to call her by her name, as she would feel more comfortable – it was Alorolia.

The next day Sophie took Triez's boat out on the lake. She told Alorolia that in about a month's time the *Hermes* would be leaving with a research vessel for deep space exploration. She asked her if she would care to find a volunteer from her crew to join them. She asked Fernais, "What about you? would like to go along with them? I'll miss you but you're the only person I know that I can trust with maintaining this friendship between the humans and myself." He was in agreement as long as she could manage without him, she said that she could and asked him to bring some images back with him.

Alorolia wanted to see the Earth as a normal person would see it, without all of the pomp and ceremony. Sophie promised after the next day's meeting with the world's leaders she would show her New York warts and all.

*□

The Queen met with the leaders at 10.00 am the

next morning; she had been flown in with Sophie by helicopter to the United Nations building. After her meeting with many of the world leaders, she had made an excellent impression and commented to Sophie, "It's remarkable how well they all seemed to get along with each other." Sophie told her, "It hasn't always been like that as it had taken a direct threat of the end of the world to bring them together in unison." □

After a lunch in the Queens honour, Sophie told her, "Time to go." It was now 4.00 pm and Sophie had made plans. The Queen became Alorolia and both of them made their excuses and left. Outside the building was Triez, sitting on the fender of Sophie's old Jaguar, wearing her party clothes. As Alorolia climbed into the back seat of the car, Isalia handed her some of her mother's party clothes. Jamie was at the wheel and averted his eyes as she changed into a party animal. As Jamie wheel-spinned the car away from the United Nations, Triez sat astride Alorolia and pinned her head back against the headrest. Isalia applied face cream and wiped off the official makeup, and replaced it with her mother's wild stuff. □

The night started with an Irish saloon for drinks then onto two dance clubs. The last one had Alorolia dancing with a man in a very provocative way, until Triez joined in and made it more like a soft porn movie. Which in turn led to their expulsion at 3.00 am. Sophie had made reservations at a Hotel near to Fifth Avenue and with Jamie driving they managed to get there in one piece as he was the only one that hadn't tried to drink the entire bar stocks dry that evening.

Surprisingly Alorolia was the only one that didn't seem to have a hangover in the morning, and what was more surprising was the fact that she had imbibed more than anyone else. She was due to depart for Temfir at 10.00 pm Triez told her not to worry about it by telling her, "If they haven't got the cargo they're not going anywhere."

After breakfast, Sophie showed Alorolia some of New York's main points of interest before heading out towards Portland, and thanks to Triez, she believed that a great ape had spent many a fine hour languishing in the Empire State Building sipping martinis. Sophie had considered showing Triez the King Kong movie but felt that it was more fun not to do so.

Back at Triez's house, Alorolia changed back into the Queen of Temfir. She thanked them all for making her visit so enjoyable.

Fernais asked Sophie if she had been looking after the Queen in his absence. She assured him that the Queen's needs had been met in full, and looked forward to meeting him on Temfir in a month's time. Triez told Sophie, "You know, I think there's more going on in that relationship than we assume!" Sophie put her hand on her chin and said: "Hmm, we'll have to see!"

*

It was now mid-February and the *Hermes* was due to rendezvous with the Kai Captain's vessel. Sophie arrived at the base and apologised to the General that she would probably not be back in time for the birth of Theras's baby; the General understood and told her to take care out there. Simon, Sally, and Peter were there to see them off. Sophie told Simon that he was now responsible for the whole planet's security. She asked Sally if she would be returning to the police; she told Sophie, "I never really left, I just changed location." Looking at Peter, she asked him to support Simon while they were away. He told her that he always had, and always would.

Feeling that Earth was in good hands Sophie entered the hold before they departed to check that all of the *Hermes* supply requirements had been met. And after a quick check, she was satisfied that they had been – with the exception of one piece of extra cargo. It was Sophie's old Jaguar. Dieter stood behind her and said, "I've really grown to like it as it feels like a good luck charm and who knows, out there we might just need it." As the hold doors closed, Jamie lifted the *Hermes* off the pad and made best speed towards Temfir.☐

*

The Kai Captain was well on the way to Temfir when the *Hermes* caught up with them. Triez called him over the hyperlink and asked him, "When are you going to give that girly ship of yours a name?" He told her, "She's had a few enhancements since you last saw her and you'll see them in action if we get into trouble out there."

Two hours later both vessels entered orbit around Temfir. Sophie and the two Russians teleported down to the surface. Alorolia was in the palace gardens with Fernais. Vasily and Alexei strode around in circles trying to take it all in. They knew they were the first Russians to stand on another planet and excitedly took in the atmosphere and sites of this new exciting world. As Fernais led Sophie into the garden she could see the statue that Ruman had first shown her in its unfinished condition. As she got closer she could see a definite likeness. It felt strange as if she were dead, and someone had erected a memorial to her.

She told Alorolia "I feel extremely honoured." Alorolia told her that it was a guide for her people to follow, about morals and doing what's right. She hoped that it would help unite her people always and make them do the right thing at the right time. Sophie told her, "It's an awful lot to expect from a statue!" Alorolia told her, "It's more than just a statue it's an idea, your directive, it interests me, we'll have to talk more about it on your return." Sophie asked her where the Statue would be placed, the Queen answered: "In a prominent position on the palace grounds where it can be seen as an inspiration to thousands of people."

Sophie told her that she would arrange another wild night out again on her return. Smiling, Alorolia said, "I'll look forward to that." Sophie made the call to the *Hermes* and said to Alorolia, "Be happy" and in a haze of bright light Fernais, Sophie and two Russians were teleported aboard. As the Hermes orbited Temfir, Sophie made her way to her quarters. Standing in the centre of the room she could see the ghost, she could see that it had self-activated and was starting to grow a pair of legs again. Anticipating a visit from Ruman she pulled out a chair and sat down, once he had completed the transformation Sophie said, "It's you, isn't it? The Omicron order, it was you all along."

Ruman answered, "History's a strange concept as it once recorded an event where a young mild-mannered woman had taken a group of people away from Earth in an Ark where they settled on several planets that damaged their DNA and caused many mutations. They couldn't return to Earth as all that remained of it was a boulder field left behind by the Breeche. But thanks to the Omicron order and a little meddling with a mental enhancer we have you in an alternative future. A fearless warrior with a perfect sense of right and wrong. What I told you before about the Touscal standing outside time was not entirely true, as only the Omicron order can do that and I am indeed the Omicron order."

Sophie asked, "Then you're not from Touscal?"

He answered, "No I'm just living there at present, I'm one of nature's mutations and find pleasure in re-adjusting history. Personally, I think this version is a far better than what the Touscal and Mylin had planned for Earth. You have a mission Sophie Schultz, you've read the engraved tablet, now go out there and do it, be the saviours of the universe and make it a place worth living in." After watching Ruman change back into the ghost, Sophie walked back to the bridge. Calling the Kai Captain she told him, "We're departing in five minutes." Answering her with the word "Affirmative." Sophie said, "Jamie take us out." Leaving orbit, the Kai Captain showed off the speed of his vessel and passed the *Hermes*, but what into? That was the exciting part.

THE END